THE GIRL WITHOUT MAGIC

THE CHRONICLES OF MAGGIE TRENT, BOOK ONE

MEGAN O'RUSSELL

Ink Worlds Press

DEDICATION

To the Mantis Shrimp of Witches

THE GIRL WITHOUT MAGIC

CHAPTER 1

*D*eath wasn't all that bad. Living had been harder. Dying hadn't even been painful. Every pain from the battle had stopped as soon as the world had gone black. Now there was nothing left but darkness and quiet.

The screams of her friends echoed in her mind with nothing in the silence to block out the unending wails. Were they lying in the dark, too? Free from pain and fear? Were they still fighting, alive and in danger?

Maybe they'd won. Maybe there was someone left to know she had died.

Did they leave her in the woods? Had there been a funeral? A hearse and a casket? Flowers with bright blooms? Did it matter?

She knew only darkness. Unrelenting black.

It did seem a little unfair that death should be so boring. If this was how it was going to be, perhaps existing wasn't worth it. Being alone with nothing but her own thoughts forever? Maggie had never expected much from death, but oblivion would have been better than knowledgeable nothingness.

Days passed in the darkness, or perhaps it was centuries.

There was no way to know without anything to measure the passing of time.

The blackness was maddening. It wasn't until Maggie clenched her fist in frustration at the absolute endlessness of it all that she realized she had a hand. Two hands actually. And a back, which was pressed into a hard floor.

Slowly unclenching her hands, Maggie ran her fingers across the ground. It was cool. How had she not noticed how cold the floor was? Carefully, Maggie rolled onto her stomach, feeling the darkness in all directions, stretching her toes out to see if the ground encased her or if she was lying on the precipice of a deeper blackness.

But there were no walls to run into or holes to tumble through. Pushing herself onto her knees, Maggie crawled a little ways forward, expecting to find something to tell her the size of her dark prison.

But still, there was nothing. Only endless darkness she could crawl around.

"Why?" Maggie asked the darkness, finding her voice as she pushed herself to her feet. "Why should I be able to move if there is nothing to see!" She had expected an echo, but her voice drifted away as though her cage were endless.

Recklessness surged through her. She was already dead— what was the worst that could happen?

Maggie took off at a run. Sprinting through the darkness. After a few minutes, her legs burned, and her breathing came in quick gasps.

"Couldn't get a nice breeze for the running dead girl, huh?" Maggie shouted.

Before the words had fully left her lips, a breeze whispered past her, cooling the back of her neck, kissing her face, and pushing her to run faster. The air even had a scent, like the ocean right before a rainstorm. The tang of salt filled her lungs. She could be running on a beach, an endless beach, but the floor was hard and maddeningly flat. And there was no sound of crashing waves.

"I wish I could see," Maggie whispered.

With a scream, she dropped to her knees, covering her face with her hands. Her heart racing in her chest, Maggie slowly opened her eyes, blinking at the dazzling light that surrounded her.

It was as bright as the sun but didn't come from a fixed point in the sky. Rather, it was like the air itself contained light.

The ground wasn't the hard stone Maggie had imagined. The floor shone a bright, pale color, like it was made of pure platinum.

"It's better than darkness," Maggie muttered.

Now that there was light to see by, the idea that this place went on forever seemed absurd. The floor had to lead somewhere. There had to be an end to it.

"Right." Maggie ran her hands through her hair. It was gritty with dirt and ashes and caked with blood at her temple. "Gross." Maggie moved to wipe her hands on her jeans, but they too were covered with dirt and blood. "I couldn't have clean clothes for eternity? All I want is a hot bath."

As though the air had heard her words, the light around her began to shimmer, twisting and folding into a hundred different colors. Coming closer, and growing solid, until, as quickly as it began, the air stopped moving.

Maggie swallowed the bile that had risen into her throat as the world twisted, blinking to adjust her eyes to the dim light of the tent. Her arms tingled like she had just tried to do a very long spell. Maggie gripped her hands together, willing the feeling to stop as she looked around the tent. And she *was* standing in a tent. It was small, only large enough for the little cot that stood at one end and the tub at the other.

The tent was made of deep blue fabric, which colored the light that streamed in from outside.

"Spiced Ale for sale!" a voice bellowed right outside Maggie's tent. She covered her mouth to keep from screaming. Slowly, she crept toward the flap of the tent.

Voices answered the ale seller's call. Bargaining and shouting came from off in the distance, too.

She pulled back the flap of the tent just far enough to be able to peer outside with one eye.

In the bright sunlight outside her tent, a street teemed with people. And not just wizards. There was a centaur at the end of the road, laughing with a group of witches. A troll sat not fifteen feet away, drinking from a mug the size of Maggie's head.

Maggie took a breath. Centaurs and trolls existed—she had known that for years. If she were dead, then why shouldn't she be with other members of Magickind? She gripped the tent flap, willing herself to walk onto the street and ask someone what was going on. How had death shifted from eternal darkness to a crowded street?

But everyone on the street looked whole and healthy, happy even. She was covered in blood and dirt. She glanced back at the tub in the corner. Thin wisps of steam rose from the water. If she was going to spend the rest of eternity here, she shouldn't scare the locals looking like she had just come from a blood bath.

The dried blood on her shirt crackled as she fumbled the mud-caked plastic buttons. The water burned as she slipped into the tub.

"At least a dead girl can still get a bath." Maggie sighed, leaning back into the water, running her fingers through her hair.

Her blood was in her hair—that much she knew for sure—and coating her sleeve, along with the blood of one of the wizard boys she had been fighting with. If he had died, maybe he would be here, too. But there was more blood.

She tried to think back through the fight, to remember what had happened before she had fallen into darkness. But the more she thought, the more disgusted she became. There could be dozens of people's blood on her.

"I wish I had some soap." No sooner had she said it than a bar of soap was floating in the tub, right next to her hand. A tingle in her chest made her pause as she reached for the soap. It felt like she had done magic. Like a little bit of her power had drained away.

That part was normal, but the tiny little space the magic had left behind wasn't refilling itself. It was just...empty.

Maggie scrubbed her hair and under her nails, washing her arms so hard they were bright red by the time she finally felt clean.

A soft towel waited for her next to the tub. It smelled of flowers and fresh air. Maggie breathed in the scent. Her clothes wouldn't smell like that. They would never be clean again.

"I wish," Maggie began, looking around the tent to see if anyone was even there to listen, "I wish for a clean set of clothes." Her stomach rumbled. "And some food."

Instantly, clothes appeared at the foot of the cot, and a platter of food sat on the table, filling the tent with the scent of roasted meat.

A sharp tingling shot through Maggie's fingers for the briefest moment. If she hadn't been thinking about it, she might not have noticed the tiny drain on the magic inside her. Her magic had always felt like a bottomless well before. She could feel it leaving when she did a spell, could feel her body channeling the energy, but it never seemed as though she might run out—as though there were a finite amount of magic she could access.

The scent of the food was enough to lure her from the warmth of the bath. Maggie took a shuddering breath and stood, wobbling on her shaking legs for a moment before stepping out of the tub. Maybe she wasn't using up her magic. Maybe she was just hungry.

Dripping on the grass that was the floor of the tent, Maggie sat in the spindly chair at the wooden table to eat.

She had always assumed, wrongly it seemed, that once you died you didn't have to bother with things like feeling like you hadn't eaten in a month. She had died only a little while ago. Or maybe it had been a hundred years. She wasn't sure it mattered.

A fresh loaf of bread sat on the carved wooden tray along with a hunk of roasted meat and a bowl of fruit. There was fruit that looked like an apple-sized blueberry that had grown spikes, bright orange berries, and a lavender thing the size of her fist that had a peel like an orange.

Maggie tore off a hunk of bread and stared at the bowl of fruit. Those weren't normal. They weren't real. But then maybe she wasn't real anymore either. Her head started to spin. Not knowing what was happening was beginning to feel worse than being trapped in the darkness. Her stomach turned, and she pushed the tray of food away.

"A trip toward the sea." A woman spoke outside the tent.

With a squeak, Maggie tipped out of her chair and fell to the ground.

"I'm tired of the streets," the woman continued, sounding so close Maggie could have reached out and touched her if the canvas hadn't been in the way.

"It's too crowded. I want to see the Endless Sea!"

Another woman giggled something Maggie couldn't understand, and then the two voices faded into the clatter.

Maggie lay on the ground, staring up at the blue fabric above her.

"Maggie Trent, you cannot lay here for the rest of your afterlife." She dug the heels of her hands into her eyes so hard spots danced in front of them. "You are going to go out there and ask someone what's going on." She let her arms fall to her sides. "Because talking to a troll isn't nearly as bad as lying naked in a tent talking to yourself. At least the grass is soft." Maggie laughed.

It started as a chuckle then turned quickly into a tearful laugh as panic crept into her.

She had charged into the woods knowing she might die. She had fought and killed. And then her life had ended. But being in a tent where food magically appeared was somehow more terrifying than fighting.

Maggie lifted her right hand, looking at the bracelet that wrapped around her wrist. It was only a bit of leather cord attached to a silver pendant. A crescent moon and three stars, the crest of the Virginia Clan. The last thing that tied her to her family. Funny it should follow her into death.

Reaching up onto the cot, she pulled down the new clothes. A loose-fitting pale top, dark pants, and a wide, sapphire-colored belt were all she had been given. Maggie pulled the clothes on, feeling a little like she was playing dress up. Not that she really remembered playing dress up. That had stopped when she was five.

Twelve years before I died.

Maggie ran her fingers through her short hair and, squaring her shoulders, pulled back the flap of the tent.

CHAPTER 2

*T*he light outside the tent was brighter than Maggie had expected it to be. The sun beat down on her, and she swayed as a centaur brushed past her. This wasn't Earth—it definitely wasn't. There was a wizard juggling balls of bright blue flames and a woman selling pastries shaped like dragon claws. There was nowhere like this on Earth.

Maggie took a deep, shuddering breath. The air smelled like spices, carried on a wind chased by a storm. She scanned the crowd, searching for a person she could talk to. Someone who might be willing to tell her why it felt like her magic was disappearing.

The troll was still sitting on her own at a table in front of a large red tent. Her table was laden with food, and she ate with abandon. Everyone else on the street seemed busy, either meandering to someplace or talking to the people around them.

Pushing her shoulders back, Maggie headed toward the troll. The red tent behind the troll seemed to be a restaurant of some sort. Empty tables sat in the shade inside the tent. There was only one man lurking deep in the shadows—a large man who looked angry as he held a cloth over his nose.

Three feet away from the troll, Maggie opened her mouth to speak, but before she could say, "Excuse me, ma'am," a foul stench filled her nose and flooded her mouth. Gagging, Maggie turned away, hoping the troll hadn't noticed her.

"Watch yourself," a man said when Maggie nearly backed into him.

"I'm sorry," Maggie said. "Actually, could you—"

The man walked away without listening to Maggie's question.

"Excuse me." Maggie stepped in front of a passing woman.

The woman was one of the most beautiful people Maggie had ever seen. She had silvery blond hair that hung down to her waist, lips the color of raspberries, and bright green eyes.

The woman looked at Maggie, her gaze drifting from Maggie's short brown hair to her plain boots. A coy smile floated across the woman's face before she spoke. "Whatever you are looking for, little girl, you aren't ready for me." She turned to walk away, but Maggie caught the woman's arm.

"Please," Maggie said, "I just need some answers. I don't even know where I am."

The woman laughed a slow, deep laugh.

"And I am not a little girl." Maggie let go of the woman's arm, fighting the urge to ball her hands into fists. "I'm seventeen. Or I was before I died. And it doesn't matter what I'm ready for. I'm here."

"You died?" the woman said with a fresh peal of laughter. "Poor child. Bertrand," the woman called over Maggie's shoulder.

Maggie spun to see who the beautiful woman might be calling. The street was full of people, none of whom seemed to be responding.

"Please just help me." Maggie turned back toward the woman.

The woman stood staring at her for a long moment before a man appeared over her shoulder.

"Did I interrupt something, Bertrand?" the woman asked, not bothering to look at the man.

"You are never an interruption, Lena." Bertrand gave a bow Lena didn't turn to see.

"This one *died*," Lena said.

"It's really not funny," Maggie said, wishing she had stayed back in her tent. "I was in a battle, and I got killed. I was fighting for the good guys when I died, so you could be a little nicer about it."

"Fighting for the good guys?" Lena laughed. "She thinks there are good guys. Oh, Bertrand, I just had to call for you."

"I can see why." Bertrand eyed Maggie as though examining a moderately interesting rock. "I shall do my best to help her."

Lena nodded and disappeared into the crowd.

Maggie warred with herself, not sure if she should shout a thank you after Lena or a string of curses.

"May I introduce myself?" Bertrand asked, the wrinkle of his brow showing his awareness that Maggie was considering saying no.

There was something about the man. He didn't seem to be much older than herself, probably only a little over twenty. But something in his eyes made Maggie wonder if he was two-hundred instead.

His long, dark hair was pulled back in a ponytail, and instead of the light clothing most of the others on the street wore, he sported a finely-made coat and vest, which matched his deep blue knickers, long white socks, and silver buckled shoes. Maggie had only ever seen clothing like that in old paintings. But she was dead, and if he had died a long time before she had ever been born, maybe those clothes were normal to him.

"Please do." Maggie's words came out a little angrier than she had meant them to.

"Very well." Bertrand smiled. "I am Bertrand Wayland."

"Wayland?" Maggie asked, her hands balling instinctively into fists.

"Yes. Wayland." Bertrand bowed. "Have you heard of my family?"

"I knew a Wayland." Maggie nodded. "Before I...well, you know...died."

"In battle?" Bertrand asked.

Maggie nodded.

Bertrand tented his fingers under his chin. "How very interesting, Miss?"

"Maggie Trent." Manners told her to reach out and shake his hand. Experience told her not to.

"Well, Miss Trent," Bertrand said, "I have the happy pleasure of telling you you are not, in fact, dead."

"What?" Relief flooded Maggie for only a moment before confusion washed it away.

"You are very much alive," Bertrand said, "but judging from your firm belief in your demise, I now have the unhappy duty of telling you that you are far from home. Very far from home, Miss Trent, and you are in a place I doubt you've ever heard of."

"So where are we?"

"The Siren's Realm." Bertrand spread his arms wide. "Welcome. It's not often we have arrivals who haven't meant to end up here, so I suppose you'll be more confused than most."

"Do people arrive here often?"

"I'm not really sure. If you'll follow me." Bertrand bowed before turning and striding down the street. "You see, time here is a bit funny. A day can feel like an hour or a year. It is all done by the will of the Siren."

"And you're the welcoming committee?" Maggie asked, having to run a few steps to catch up to Bertrand. The sights around her were enough to make her forget to wonder where he was leading her. A centaur smoking a pipe that puffed purple haze stood beside a woman selling jewels of every color Maggie had ever imagined.

"Oh no." Bertrand laughed. "I have simply been here for a

while without losing my love for the outside and those who dwell there."

"So who is the Siren?" Maggie asked. "And what do you mean *outside?*"

They had turned off the street where the red tent was and onto a tiny lane. The tents here were short like the one she had bathed in. There were no food vendors here or nearly as many people. A woman sipping wine sat outside the flap of her tent.

"Afternoon." The woman smiled.

Bertrand nodded to the woman as they passed, whispering to Maggie as soon as they were out of earshot, "Never trust that one. She'll cheat you every time."

"Cheat you at what?" Maggie asked. "Look, can you help me get out of here? If I'm not dead, then I might still be able to get"— Maggie stumbled on the word *home*—"back to where I belong. My friends could still be fighting. They might need me."

"Ah." Bertrand stopped so quickly Maggie ran into him. He took her by both shoulders to steady her. "Leaving the Siren's Realm is possible."

"Then how—"

"But getting back to the battle you left...I am afraid, Miss Trent, that might well be impossible." He strode down the lane, once again leaving Maggie running to catch up.

He led her onto a street so wide, centaurs walked down it four across. A line of people waited outside a vivid green tent trimmed with purple silk and embroidered with golden patterns. It was so beautiful Maggie wanted to stop and take a closer look, but Bertrand was still moving, and she didn't want to risk being left behind.

"Why couldn't I get back to the battle?" Maggie asked when she finally managed to get next to Bertrand. "How did I even get here? Why was I stuck in the dark?"

"All from the beginning." Bertrand turned left into a large square packed with people. "It's the best way forward."

He weaved through the crowd toward a fountain at the center of the square. A woman formed of the same shining metal the bright floor had been made of stood at the center of the fountain, her body draped in thin fabric. Her face was beautiful, but in a terrible way that made Maggie's chest tighten just looking at her. In one hand the woman held a goblet, which rained down bright, golden liquid. The other hand was encrusted with jewels of every color and reached toward the bright sky.

The golden liquid from the goblet filled a pool at the woman's feet, and people swam in the bright water.

"Here you are, Miss Trent." Bertrand bowed, gesturing toward the fountain.

"This is the beginning?" Maggie asked.

"The Siren is the beginning and the end. Knowing her rules is vital to living in her realm." He gestured to the fountain again, and this time Maggie found what he was showing her.

Inscribed in the side of the fountain was a verse.

In the Siren's Realm a wish need only be made.
Her desire to please shall never be swayed.
But should those around you wish you ill,
the Siren's love shall protect you still.
No two blessings shall contradict,
so be sure your requests are carefully picked.
Wish for joyful pleasure to be shared by all
of the good and the brave who have risked the fall.
But a warning to you once the wish is made,
the Siren's price must always be paid.

Maggie read through the verse three times without stopping. "What is that?" she asked when her eyes moved up to read a fourth time. "Some kind of demented nursery rhyme?"

"It is the Siren's Decree," Bertrand said, his tone giving a gentle reprimand for Maggie's remark. "It is the most basic rule we live under within her realm. Whether you meant to or not, Maggie Trent, you have become one of the brave who chanced the fall. You have arrived in the Siren's Realm where her greatest wish is for us all to live lives of pleasure and joy. You have, in short, arrived in paradise."

CHAPTER 3

*M*aggie blinked for a moment. "But you said I'm not dead."

"You aren't. Though as you fell into the Siren's Realm without meaning to, I can understand the confusion."

"So who is the Siren?" Maggie asked. "Can I talk to her, ask to get sent home?"

"Miss Trent, I am afraid that is not possible," Bertrand said. "It would be like allowing you to fly a broom before you've learned to levitate. There would be no hope for success."

"But I need—"

"A witch of your caliber should be able to navigate the Siren's Realm quickly enough, and then you will be able to request whatever you like."

"I'm not a witch," Maggie lied, the words falling from her mouth before she knew she had meant to say them. "I'm not a witch. I'm human."

"Yet you know a Wayland and fought in a wizard's battle?" Bertrand's eyebrows knit together as he examined Maggie.

"I have friends who do magic," Maggie said, hoping her excuse would be good enough.

"Then your path to an audience with the Siren will be long indeed." For the first time, Bertrand sounded as though he might actually feel sorry for Not Dead Maggie.

"Why should it be long?" Maggie asked, her temper flaring at the sympathy on Bertrand's face. "I just got here. Why can't I go back?"

"The Siren gives us a land of peace and beauty." Bertrand spread his arms wide. "She gives us the light from above, wonderful food, and loving companionship. But all things must come with a price."

"What price?"

"To be transported back from the Siren's Realm to a particular place requires a lot of magic—"

"But then how did I get here?"

"—and you will need to pay a significant amount of magic if you want to be placed back at the right time and place. And even with all the magic in the Siren's Realm, it still might not be possible. The Siren's ways are as indiscernible as a figure shrouded in mist."

"How"—Maggie cut across Bertrand as he opened his mouth to continue—"did I get here? If I'm not dead, then what happened to me?"

"The Siren's Realm is a world between worlds. It is above and below, hidden in the cracks, just out of sight. Her realm is stitched to ours and a hundred others, holding them fast together. But where those stitches are, there are holes between places. If you did not come here intentionally, then my truest guess would be that you stumbled through one of those stitches."

"Then if I find where the connection is here, I can go home." Maggie searched over the heads of the crowd, looking for anything that might lead her away.

"I'm afraid that might not be as easy as you would like, Miss Trent."

Maggie clenched her teeth, biting back the words the pity in his tone made her long to scream.

"I'm afraid the only way to get back where you want to go is with the blessing and aid of the Siren. And to get that, you'll need magic, quite a bit of it. But please don't despair, Miss Trent. Magic may be the currency in the Siren's Realm, but even a human can make do. The Siren's price must be paid, but it can be done through honest labor. If you are willing to serve wizards who trade in magic, you might eventually be able to find a way home. Not that I would ever recommend abandoning the Siren, but if it remains your will when the possibility arises…"

"People pay in magic here?" The very thought of it turned Maggie's stomach. Her magic was a part of her, as much a part of who she was as her face or her soul. To trade that for what? Food? The bath?

Suddenly, Maggie was very grateful for her lie. She didn't want this man to know she had any magic to trade or have stolen. She wouldn't trade a part of herself to him or anyone else.

"Yes, well, thank you for your help." Maggie backed away from Bertrand. "I think I understand enough to be getting on with now."

"But Miss Trent, you haven't seen the glorious sights the Siren's Realm has to offer."

"I really think I'm fine." Maggie kept walking backward. She stepped on someone's foot and heard them grunt. "Sorry," she said without turning back. "But I really think," she spoke to Bertrand again, "that I'll be fine."

"But a human thrown into a world so magical?" Bertrand bowed. "Miss Trent, it is lucky I was summoned to help you so quickly. Perhaps the golden threads of fate sought to bring us together."

"I really don't think so." Maggie bowed back. "And I have to go."

Without another word, Maggie spun around and sprinted

down the nearest street, not stopping until she was thoroughly lost.

She wasn't really sure how far she had run, but somehow she had ended up on a street unlike any she had ever seen. The ground here gleamed like the metal of the fountain with bright, shimmering jewels of every color set into the ornate engravings.

Maggie stared down at the ground. Her Academy-issued boots, given to her as a student of the magical school, were filthy and worn. She glanced around, waiting for someone to yell at her and tell her she shouldn't be standing on such a precious work of art. But the others around her just strolled past, seemingly unconcerned with Maggie's shoes. There weren't many people out on this street, and all those in view wore finely made clothes, fitting in perfectly with their lavish surroundings.

The tents here were made of the same bright fabric as her blue one, but these were coated in jewels to match their colors. The sun had begun to set, and the bright rays made the tents sparkle brilliantly. Maggie walked closer to the tents, pressing away the terrible feeling she wasn't meant to be there.

A bright, white tent, laden with diamonds, stood at the very center of the street. It was taller than a two-story house and wider than a barn. The flaps at the front had been tied open, letting in the evening breeze.

Someone moved inside, their shadow gliding past the opening. Maggie stepped forward, reaching her hand out toward the tent. Inside, she would find peace. A place to rest, comfortable, and safe.

The shadow stopped when Maggie's hand was inches from the gap in front of her. The shadow waited unmoving, willing Maggie forward.

"No!" Maggie shouted. The heads of the passersby turned toward her as she ran back up the street, searching for the path that had brought her to the street of jewels.

The price of peace was too high. How much magic would the shadow want from her?

All of it.

Maggie ran faster, pushing back the tears that threatened to spill over. It would be dark soon. She needed to find the blue tent with the bed and the food.

Perhaps the endless darkness had been better.

"Watch it!" a voice shouted an instant before Maggie screamed and fell to the ground.

She had run smack into an old man pushing a wooden cart. The man smelled like sweat and seaweed. The cart smelled like roasted meat.

"I'm sorry," Maggie said as she pushed herself off the ground. Her wrists ached, and her skinned palms stung.

"You better watch where yer runnin'," the man grumbled, checking his cart for signs of damage. "I'm a nice feller, but not all around here would be so kind about bein' run over. What if you had trampled a dwarf?"

"Sorry," Maggie said again. "I'm just…"

"Lost?" the man said. "Jumped into the Siren's Realm and now you don't know what to do?"

"Apparently I fell in accidentally." Maggie's heart suddenly felt hollow. She had fallen away from the battle where everyone left in the world she cared about could have been killed. And now she was worried about running into the guy with the meat cart.

"You did?" the man said, suddenly seeming much more interested in Maggie. He examined her for a moment, looking from her skinned and bloody palms to her old boots. "Somethin' terrible was happening and then all of a sudden you end up in the dark, eh?"

Maggie nodded.

"And yer not magic at all?"

Maggie shook her head, clinging to the lie though she didn't know why.

"Poor thing. I remember fallin' into this place. I was in a ship-wreck, you see. It was awful confusin'. I mean to say, me endin' up here with a bunch of wizards and talking damn half-horses?" The man laughed. "You'll be all right, girl. Find yerself an honest trade, and they'll pay you for it with magic. You can't use it fer spells, but neither can they. Then you'll have a bit of that energy folk here trade like gold, and you'll be able to survive just fine."

"Just find a trade?"

"Aye," the man said. "At least it doesn't get cold here. The storms may be fierce, but they only come up once in a while." He paused, apparently waiting for Maggie to speak, but she couldn't think of anything to say. "I'm Gabriel." He held out a hand.

Maggie took it, feeling his rough callouses on her skinned palm. "Maggie."

"You got a place to rest for the night?" Gabriel asked. "Some folk round here do some strange things come dark. Wouldn't be right for a girl to be out alone."

"I was in a tent, but I got lost," Maggie said, feeling like a child alone in a shopping mall.

"The Siren has a way of givin' what's needed to point you in the right direction. Try and find yer tent, and you should get there." Gabriel smiled kindly, showing a few missing teeth. "And if you need help, look for me. There aren't many of us folk with no natural magic find our way to the Siren's Realm, and we've got to stick together, those of us that do."

"Thank you, Gabriel."

Gabriel nodded, pushed his cart away, and was soon swallowed by the crowd.

Maggie stood still. Part of her wanted to call after Gabriel and admit that she'd lied, that she was a witch. But what did it matter? There was no part of her that was a witch anymore. No tiny shred of her being that wanted anything to do with magic. Maybe the witch part of her had died in the battle even if she hadn't. She wished Gabriel were still with her, if for no other reason than to have a person to talk to.

Standing in the middle of the street, Maggie closed her eyes, letting the crowd move around her, picturing the blue tent with the tiny cot and the loaf of bread. A place to sleep safely for the night. She waited for a flash of insight or a map to appear in her hands, but nothing happened.

Sighing, Maggie began walking down the street.

My tent. My tent. All I want is to find my tent. My tent.

She repeated the words in her head as she moved down tight alleys of dingy, worn tents and broad streets lined with stalls displaying shining wares.

My tent. My tent.

The sun had dipped low when she came to the fountain square.

Bertrand Wayland stood in the fountain, shirtless and surrounded by giggling women.

Maggie ducked, walking faster to avoid Bertrand's notice. She didn't need pity or patronizing worry. What she needed was her tent.

My tent. My tent!

The stale smell of troll greeted her as she turned onto a street with a ruby red tent whose tables were filled with people drinking and singing along as a centaur played a strange song on a violin.

And at the end of the street was a blue tent. Small and dark in the night.

Maggie ran forward and leapt through the tent flap, grateful to be alone in the darkness.

CHAPTER 4

*T*he sea was bright that morning. It had been every morning since Maggie had arrived in the Siren's Realm. The bright sun rose, sparkling on the water, and the breeze carried in fresh, salty air.

Maggie sat in the opening of her tent, her legs spread out on the rock in front of her. Sea birds stared at her as she ate her breakfast. "Get your own bread," she grumbled. But really she was glad for the birds' company. They woke her every morning with their cawing. It was the closest thing to a *good morning* she got.

"Fine." Maggie tossed the last few crumbs to them, smiling as they cawed appreciatively. They probably hadn't meant to end up in the Siren's Realm either. But there they were, at the edge of the Endless Sea, surviving.

She tucked her food for lunch safely away in the tent, tying the flap shut against the birds and breezes. Hers was the only tent on the rock outcropping that jutted out over the sea. She had carried it there herself after that first awful night. Moved everything but the bathtub. She may only have a cot, table and chair, but it was hers. The rock where she lived was hers, and the sea would give her what she needed to survive.

Hoisting her net onto her shoulder, Maggie scrambled barefoot down the ledge, landing in the water with a splash. The sea was cool and wonderful. Maggie smiled as the waves lapped at her waist.

Catch the fish, bring them to the market square for trade, buy what she needed, and come home. It was simple enough. The magic she would be given for the fish was enough for her to survive on. Not since that first night had she touched the stores that lived deep within her. The magic she traded didn't penetrate her as her own did. It floated on the surface. Feeling like a glove as merchants added to it or took away from it with a handshake.

It was barely noon when Maggie dragged her net of fish to the market square. People milled about, buying silk gowns dripping with jewels or perfumes that smelled like faraway lands Maggie had never seen. No one noticed the girl with the fish as she passed by.

There was something in the air that morning. A tone to the chatter that sounded different than Maggie was used to. But gossip had nothing to do with the fish in her net, so she kept moving, only catching bits of conversation as she passed.

"Hoarding," a woman wearing a brilliantly green silk dress spat. "Don't they understand the trade of a finite supply?"

A young-looking man who had the countenance of someone much older stood close to a centaur, muttering, "It's happening again. I can feel it coming on the wind."

Maggie took a deep breath, smelling only fish and perfume on the breeze.

"Find more for me, girl?" Mathilda bustled to the front of her stall. She, like many of the occupants of the Siren's Realm, wore clothes that made her appear to have fallen out of time. Mathilda wore a long, heavy skirt, billowing blouse, and mob cap. "Fish!" Mathilda shouted in Maggie's ear. "Did you bring fish?"

"Yep." Maggie lowered the net onto the ground, letting Mathilda examine her catch.

"You always bring a good catch." Mathilda weighed the fish in her hands. "It's nice to see a new one taking to work so quickly. You know, when I first got here, I lived a life of pleasure. Swimming in the fountains, running about in a scandalous way.

"Ah if the people back home could have seen it! Then one morning I decided not to get out of bed. Didn't seem worth it if all I was going to do was lie around all day anyway. That's when I decided to take up a trade again. Gives the fun meaning if you've worked hard for it."

Mathilda hoisted the net and led Maggie behind the counter to the preparing table. "You'd be amazed what people turn to when they run out of magic. Good to see a pretty thing like you working hard, rather than…" Mathilda gave a disapproving *tsk* as she lopped off the head of a fish.

Maggie nodded silently.

Mathilda decapitated another fish before looking at Maggie. "But then I suppose someone with no natural magic was always going to have to work for the Siren in order to survive. You should be glad she lets fish into her sea."

"There's a whale, too," Maggie said. "I've seen him offshore. I think he might be alone though."

"A whale?" Mathilda asked, one eyebrow climbing high on her forehead. "Wonder how he slipped in through one of the stitches? Funny, the Siren wanting a whale, but perhaps someone missed seeing them in the distance. What a desire to have!"

Maggie rocked on her toes, her most pressing desire to be paid and on her way.

"A whale, I ask you," Mathilda said again before looking back at Maggie. "Time for paying, is it?"

"Please, ma'am."

"When you've been here long enough, you won't be in such a hurry," Mathilda said. "Here we have endless days of sun. You'll never find sickness or hunger. The Siren has given us a land of pleasure. It's a pity to go wasting it by trying so hard to rush through it all." Mathilda reached out and shook Maggie's hand with her own fish-covered one.

Maggie was practiced enough by now she didn't flinch at either the slime coating Mathilda's palm or the tingle that flew in through her hand and up her arm, leaving her skin buzzing.

"Thank you, ma'am," Maggie said politely, turning toward the street.

"See you tomorrow, girl?" Mathilda asked.

"If there are fish in the Endless Sea!" Maggie called back as she walked down the street.

She was used to the streets of the Siren's Realm by now, at least the ones she traveled every day. The streets that led her to the market from the rocks by the sea where she had made her home. Then through the square with the fountain to see Gabriel. There were other familiar faces along the way, too.

Illial, the speckled gray centaur, was in his usual spot on the outskirts of the square, puffing his pipe, his head surrounded by a haze of blue smoke.

"Maggie." The centaur nodded as she passed by. "Does the Endless Sea sparkle this morning?"

"It does every morning." Maggie shook her head, laughing. "You should come and see for yourself. Some fresh air would do you a bit of good."

"When the sights of the square no longer hold my fancy, I will try the sea as a thing to watch."

"Perhaps tomorrow then?" Maggie waved as she moved on, knowing full well that Illial wouldn't be coming to the rocks by the sea the next morning, just as he hadn't for the last few months. At least she thought it was months. By the time Maggie had wanted to keep track, she couldn't be sure how long she had been there anymore. Seventy-two notches marked the pole in her tent. Seventy-two sunrises she could count.

The smell greeted Maggie before Rushna came into view, sitting outside a tent, eating as usual. The female troll wore her usual tablecloth-sized loincloth. A beautiful man who was almost as tall as Rushna sat beside her, gazing lovingly at the troll as she ate.

"Morning, Rushna," Maggie called as she passed.

Rushna nodded but didn't look away from the beautiful man. Maggie walked a little faster, not trusting herself to hide her giggle. There was something to fit every desire in the Siren's Realm.

Maggie turned a corner and cut down a side alley, avoiding the green tent where the minotaur stood guard, then up another lane.

"Fresh roasted meat!" Gabriel's voice carried down the street.

A small crowd had gathered around Gabriel, ready to trade magic for a hot meal.

Watching the people in line ready to give their magic away made Maggie queasier than the stench of fish that incessantly clung to her.

Finally, she was the only one left standing in line.

"Busy today," Gabriel said when he looked up to find her his sole remaining customer.

"Lots of trade."

"You hungry, too?" Gabriel asked, giving her a hard look. "If we were outside the Siren's Realm, I would worry about you starvin' to death or freezin' come winter."

"Then I guess I'm lucky winter never comes." Maggie grinned, holding out her hand. The instant Gabriel took it, a dull sting ached on her palm. The feeling was there for only a moment. As soon as their hands parted, the stinging disappeared. Maybe that's why people were willing to part with their magic so easily. It only hurt for a second.

Gabriel handed Maggie a big leg of fowl before biting into one himself.

"Are you still all right, livin' down there on them rocks?" Gabriel's weathered forehead wrinkled with concern. "I don't know if I like the idea of a young thing like you livin' so far from the others like us."

"I'm fine there. I like the quiet."

"But the others like us," Gabriel said, "we all live together, and we keep each other safe."

"I am safe. It's the Siren's Realm."

"I know, I know." Gabriel shook his head, and Maggie waited patiently for him to continue.

She knew what he was going to say. He had been saying the exact same thing for months. But deep down, Maggie liked Gabriel's dire warnings. Just the same as she liked Illial's blue smoke, Rushna's smell, and Mathilda's chatter. She knew them, and they knew her. If she didn't show up one morning, they would notice. Gabriel might actually miss her. It was a strange sense of belonging, but it was the best she had.

"And when the magic folk get jealous of us earnin' a livin', that's when the trouble will start again," Gabriel was saying in a guarded voice.

Maggie nodded. She had missed the first part of the speech but knew it well enough to know when to nod.

"Then the Siren will get angry, and it'll be a bad day for all of us."

"But why?" Maggie asked, knowing what the answer would be, but willing to let Gabriel enjoy his speech.

"Because when magic folk come to the Siren's Realm, they have only what magic they bring in with them. When it's out, they're done. Nothin' to give to the Siren and nothin' to trade with the lot of us."

"Like a battery that can't recharge."

"Yeah, like a battering." Gabriel nodded solemnly, and Maggie hid her smile. "And when enough of 'em run out, they'll come after us that have worked hard to earn our way, us that didn't never ask to come here." Gabriel's gaze drifted up and down the street before he whispered, "And that times a comin', and it's a comin' soon."

"What?" Maggie said, almost dropping her meat. This was a part of Gabriel's dire warnings she hadn't heard before. "What do you mean?"

"I've seen three in the last few days," Gabriel whispered. "Ragged folks in clothes what looked like they should have been nice before. Hungry look in their eyes just wanderin' around."

"But only three," Maggie said. "That's not very many compared to how many people live here. I mean, how many of us are there anyway?"

"Three is more than there should be," Gabriel said. "The Siren, she hides people who can't give no more. Lets 'em survive out of the way. But she won't trap 'em. She isn't cruel. If a few have decided to come out, more will follow. And it'll be folk like us they'll come for first. Seen it twice before in my time, and it's ripe to happen again." Gabriel took Maggie's hand in his.

"I just don't want to see you hurt, girl. Storm's a comin'. I spent my days on a ship before I ended up here. You might not be able to scent it yet, but I'm tellin' you, girl, one of the Siren's storms is fixin' to blow us all away."

Something in the way Gabriel spoke sent a chill down Maggie's spine. "It'll all be fine. And if things get bad, we just keep our heads down, right?"

"I've got a feelin' you don't know how to keep yer head down, girlie." Gabriel laughed, but the usual glimmer didn't appear in his eyes. "You slipped into the Siren's Realm during a battle. But this is a fight none but the Siren can win."

"It all seems like false advertising," Maggie said, pausing to think while she finished her last bit of meat. "Because if this really were a paradise of joy and pleasure, there would be nothing to worry about. Not ever."

"It's not paradise," Gabriel whispered, leaning in close to

Maggie's ear. "It's the Siren's Realm, and she'll do with it what she pleases. And no one knows what the Siren will choose to bring with a storm." Gabriel scanned the street. "Go on, girl. Best to get back to your tent before the sun is down. The Siren's will will be done."

There were still hours until sunset, but something in the way Gabriel spoke made Maggie want to be back in her blue tent on the rocks.

"See you tomorrow," Maggie called as she hurried down the street.

"If the Siren wills it."

Cold settled into Maggie's chest at his words. She spun to look at Gabriel, but he had already disappeared.

CHAPTER 5

*H*er net clutched tightly in her hand, Maggie made her
way through the winding streets of tents. She had
meant to stop and buy bread before making her way back to the
rocks, but Gabriel's words had frightened her. Now the late
afternoon sun seemed tainted by something darker than the
approaching night. Whispers on the street sounded more urgent
than the usual intrigue and gossip that flowed from the open
tents.

"Wine for sale," a man in a crimson robe called as he made his
way down the lane.

"I'd better not," the man closest to Maggie said to his compan-
ion, "best to be cautious at the moment."

Only a few people had moved toward the man with the wine.
The rest stayed warily away.

Maggie took off at a run. If they were going after humans,
they would come after her. *You were born a witch, you stupid girl!*
the voice in Maggie's head shouted. But it didn't matter. She had
told everyone she had no magic of her own. And it was a lie she
wasn't willing to break.

She rounded the corner to the last short alley she would need to take to reach the shore. Standing right in the center of the narrow road was Bertrand Wayland, his long hair pulled back in a slick ponytail, his shoes shined, and his clothes perfect. He walked calmly down the road alone.

Maggie had often seen him on the streets and always ducked away before he could catch sight of her. It was easy when he was surrounded by his usual gaggle of beautiful women. But he was utterly alone today, not even speaking to the people he passed.

Maggie froze for a moment, her desire to get home warring with the urge to put as much distance between herself and Bertrand Wayland as possible.

She made the decision to hide in the shadows and wait for him to pass a moment too late.

"Miss Trent." Bertrand bowed and walked quickly toward her. "What a pleasure to see you again." There was an urgency in his tone not reflected in his smiling face. "I was actually hoping to run into you this afternoon. I was—"

Maggie turned on the spot and ran, cursing herself as her fishing net slipped from her fingers but not daring to pause to retrieve it.

"Miss Trent," Bertrand shouted after her, "I only wish to speak to you for a moment!"

She had spent every day in the Siren's Realm avoiding Bertrand Wayland. She wouldn't speak to him now. If trouble was coming, the last thing she needed was someone questioning how she had fallen out of a wizard's battle without being a witch.

Maggie turned onto a street she had never seen before, then down a wide lane with flowerbeds on either side. The packed dirt path narrowed so she couldn't avoid stepping on flowers that had left no room for her feet.

Tall tents lined the flowered lane, and centaurs milled about. Maggie glanced over her shoulder. There was no sign of Bertrand, only an elderly centaur who seemed angry at Maggie for crushing the flowers. Still, Maggie kept running, and running.

Soon, the tents grew even taller, and the street became wide and hard. The tents changed from bright colors to gray, and then the gray canvas turned to stone.

Great houses with iron bars crisscrossing their windows lined the cobblestone walk. Maggie screamed as she tipped forward, pitching toward the canal that ran between the homes. Gasping, Maggie staggered back, leaning on the cool stone of a building as her head spun and her lungs stung.

The streets were empty though light shone through a few of the windows. Faint music floated down a nearby street. A violin playing a slow song. The first few notes were beautiful and calm. Like lovers would be riding the soft current of the canal in a graceful boat, listening to the peaceful music. But the more Maggie listened, the more wrong she knew she was.

The song wasn't about love. It was about fear. Quiet, penetrating, inescapable fear.

A shadow passed by a window across the canal, and Maggie clapped a hand over her mouth to keep herself from screaming. This wasn't the part of the Siren's Realm she belonged in. She belonged on the sunny rocks with her tiny tent. The people here, who protected themselves with stone and iron, couldn't possibly want someone with no magic of her own hiding in the shadows of their streets.

The violin music played faster now, making Maggie's heart race more quickly than the running had.

Bertrand Wayland or not, she needed to get home. Back out to the tent on the rocks where she could wait out whatever storm was coming.

"Make it through the night, Maggie." She dug hers nails into her palms as she turned back the way she had come. "Get home and make it through the night. You've made it through worse, so just do it, you silly girl."

Not allowing herself to run, Maggie headed back up the street. The glimmers of light from the windows were disappearing quickly, as though those hiding within the thick stone walls didn't want to give any sign they were there.

"Get to the tent." Maggie pushed away the dread in her chest shouting that if the people in the stone houses were afraid, her canvas tent would be anything but safe.

The gray tents had come into view when she heard the first scream.

"Please, someone! Help me!"

Instinct told Maggie to hide in the shadows, but she ran toward the anguished cry.

"No! No!" the voice called desperately.

Maggie tore down the row of gray tents and turned toward the sound, freezing as the terrible sight came into view.

Four ragged, pale people stood over a man who lay shaking on the ground.

"Please don't." The man screamed as one of the four—a woman with matted hair hanging to her waist—reached down and seized the sides of the man's face.

A pale, silver light glowed under the woman's palms as the man screamed again.

His magic. She was stealing his magic.

"Stop!" Maggie shouted.

The woman's head snapped up to look at Maggie. The magic thief's face had regained its color, and her black hair was no longer matted but shining and sleek.

"Leave him alone." Maggie forced the words past the knot in her throat.

The other three turned their attention to Maggie.

"Please," the man on the ground groaned. "I have to be able to give. Leave me something to give."

The biggest of the ragged group kicked the man hard in the stomach.

"Stop it!" Maggie shouted over the man's scream of pain. "What has he done to you? Why would you hurt him?"

"Not hurt," one of the ragged people said, taking a step toward Maggie. The man was short and missing patches of hair. "We're taking what he shouldn't have in the first place. It only hurts because he doesn't want to give it up."

"Give what up?" Maggie asked, her gaze darting between the four as they crept toward her.

"Magic," the short man said, his tone so loving it made Maggie's skin crawl. "He's been hoarding it. There's only so much to be had, and if some keep it all, the rest of us have nothing to give."

"But you can't just take it." Maggie took a step backward as the man smiled at her.

The four laughed together.

"We can," the woman said, "and it doesn't hurt us at all. No, it feels so good. Let me show you, pretty girl."

The woman launched herself forward, arms outstretched, her nails scraping Maggie's face as she leapt backward and ran.

A screaming cackle followed Maggie as she sprinted back down the row of tents.

"Stop her!" one of the ragged men shouted, and four sets of pounding feet followed Maggie.

Maybe he'll get away. Maybe that poor man will be gone by the time they're done with me.

Maggie raced past the row of gray tents and down another avenue she had never seen. Bright white tents dotted with rainbow colors sat in a long line. She had no idea where she was going. But the screams of the black-haired woman followed her, so she kept running.

Night was coming fast. Soon it would be dark, and she could find a place to hide. Her lungs ached, pain shot up her legs, but she kept running.

The white tents turned back to gray. Whether from the fading light or actual color, Maggie didn't know. The lane twisted, and Maggie's feet hit hard stone, sending her tumbling forward. Pain shot through her hands and head where they struck the cobble-stone street.

"Just give us a taste, and we'll let you go!" one of the men shouted.

Maggie leapt to her feet, sprinting between the stone buildings, desperate to find a place to hide. How could people so sickly-looking run so fast? But the doors were locked and barred. If she had been able to use magic, she could have thrown open one of the doors in an instant.

Maggie rounded a tight corner, careful not to tip into the canal that reflected the stars up above. The gaps between the stars caught Maggie's eye as she kept running. Clouds covered the night sky. The storm had arrived.

"A place to hide," Maggie muttered. "I want a place to hide."

A hand shot out of the darkness and closed around her arm, dragging her into the shadows.

CHAPTER 6

a hand covered Maggie's mouth before she could scream. "Do not make a sound, or they will find you, Miss Trent," a voice whispered urgently in Maggie's ear. "I don't fancy fighting four Derelict when the Siren has chosen to bring a storm upon us."

"Mmmhmmnaa," Maggie tried to speak against the hand.

"I will release you, Miss Trent, but I do insist you remain quiet."

Maggie nodded as much as the stranger's grip would allow, turning to see who had grabbed her the moment she was free.

Bertrand Wayland held a finger to his lips.

Maggie swallowed the urge to scream or punch him.

"Why the hell did you grab me like that?" Maggie hissed.

Footsteps and shouts sounded from the corner not ten feet away. This time Maggie didn't fight as Bertrand pulled her farther into the shadows.

"Come out, come out, little one!" the short man called, flecks of spit flying from his mouth. "It won't hurt for more than a minute. And when it's done, it's done."

"We want what's ours!" the woman screamed.

They were coming closer. Shadows or not, they would see her and Bertrand hiding. Maggie took a breath, getting ready to step out into the open to fight.

Bertrand took her hand and pulled her farther back than it seemed the shadows could go.

"Move quickly," he whispered.

Several things happened at once. A *whine* of old metal hinges came from behind Bertrand, a patch of light appeared, the woman screamed, "We've got her!" and a bolt of lightning burst through the sky as thunder shook the building.

Before Maggie had time to decide which thing was the most threatening, she had been yanked off her feet and landed on her back in a dimly lit room. A *slam* shook the floor as another *clap* of thunder rumbled outside.

Maggie lay on the floor, gasping. The sound of a heavy lock being turned made her look toward the door. Thick and wooden with bars across, it looked like the doors at street level. Someone pounded on the door to come in. Maggie scrambled to her feet.

"They won't get through the door," Bertrand said calmly. "I'm quite sure of it. Two of the best things about living on the stone streets—doors that lock and much more privacy." He leaned back against the stone wall.

They weren't trapped in a tomb as Maggie had feared. It was more like a narrow entryway with a much less battle-worthy wooden door at the far end.

"The people here don't tend to be nearly as neighborly," Bertrand said. "There isn't the sense of blissful freedom as in the Textile Town, but it is worth it when the Derelict come."

"Derelict?"

"The ones with no magic left. They've used all they have, and when the drabness of nothing becomes too much, they steal from those who have something left to give." Bertrand moved toward the other wooden door. "It really is a pity to see. I've been here for quite some time, however, and it happens again and again. Would you like to come in, Miss Trent?" Bertrand gestured to the door. "The storm is arriving, and I think it will be quite some time before you will safely be able to travel home."

"I can wait here," Maggie said.

"I would prefer you didn't." Bertrand opened the door, and warm light poured into the entryway. The smell of fresh baked bread and herbs filled the air. "If you were to wait in the dark hall, I would feel obligated, as your host, to wait with you. And since the storm is here, I would much prefer to wait by the fire."

As though to emphasize his words, more thunder shook the stone walls.

"Fine." Maggie moved toward the door. "Thank you," she added grudgingly as she went through the door and up five stairs to enter the main house.

It was unlike any other house Maggie had ever seen. The walls were made of stone, giving the whole place the look of a fortress. The windows were set chest high to be above the eye level of anyone on the street. Rain pounded against the glass, nearly obscuring the thick metal bars on the outside of the windows.

With the sound of another lock scraping shut, Bertrand followed her up the stairs.

"This way please." He turned the corner, and Maggie followed, examining the worn, wooden floor as she went.

The wood was grooved with the wear of uncountable footsteps. How old was this house? Or had Bertrand merely wanted worn floors?

Bertrand stopped in a room that looked like a fancy living room from an old movie. A bookshelf stood against one wall away from the barred windows. A fireplace was nestled in the corner, and after a glance from Bertrand, a fire sprang to life.

Maggie flinched. How much magic had it cost him to start the fire? Would it have been less or more to just ask the Siren for matches?

A large painting of a glade in the woods hung above the crackling fire. White trees surrounded a patch of sunlit grass.

"Please do sit." Bertrand nodded to the large red sofa in front of the fire before moving to a tray in the corner.

Maggie sat, watching him work at the tray. Less than a minute later he pressed a cup of steaming tea into her hand. The scent of lavender made Maggie's shoulders relax before she even knew what was happening.

"It is excellent tea." Bertrand nodded. "There's a lovely woman on the market lane—"

"I don't want tea." Maggie set the cup down on the table beside her. "I'm just going to wait here for the storm to pass, and then I'll go home."

"To the tent on the rocks?" Bertrand asked. "Do you really think your tent will still be there after the storm, Miss Trent?"

"How do you know where I live?" Maggie glanced down at the talisman on her wrist out of habit. But she wouldn't be able to defend herself with magic here. Why had she let him lock her in?

"I've been keeping an eye on you," Bertrand said, apparently not having noticed Maggie searching for an escape. "It seemed to be the kind thing to do after your unexpected arrival. It's not often that we have someone fall into the Siren's Realm by chance. And I think in your case it might not be chance at all."

"I—what?" Maggie asked, Bertrand's words distracting her from planning her escape.

"I simply mean, Miss Trent—and I do hope you'll forgive me for being so forward—for a girl who is clearly a witch to fall into the Siren's Realm and pretend to have no natural magic? That's not a thing one forgets quickly."

"I'm not a witch." Maggie's mouth had gone completely dry. "I'm human."

"Miss Trent, even if you weren't wearing a Clan symbol on your wrist—"

Maggie clapped a hand over her bracelet.

"—I knew the first time I shook your hand you were a witch. And a strong one at that," Bertrand finished.

"How did you know my Clan's crest?" Maggie asked, giving up on the lie.

"I came from your world, Miss Trent." Bertrand smiled gently. "Unlike your friend Gabriel, whose world is far from ours, we may have walked the same streets centuries apart. Still, the Clans of my time are the Clans of your time as well."

"Why didn't you say something?"

"If you were determined to lie about being a witch, I assumed it must be for a good reason." Bertrand sipped his tea. "Though, of course, with a lie as dangerous as that, it was clearly my duty to make sure you remained safe."

"Why is saying I'm human dangerous?" Maggie ran her hands through her hair, wondering if it would be worse to be out in the pouring rain than stuck in a warm sitting room with Bertrand Wayland.

"I would have thought you had reasoned that answer out by now, Miss Trent. In a realm where magic is all important—"

"But you can't even do spells here! If I could—"

"Then I am sure those Derelict would never have been able to chase you. But it isn't the spells that are important in the Siren's Realm." Bertrand stood and began to pace the path of a particularly deep groove in the floor. "Some places, they trade gold, or livestock, even bits of paper. Here, we trade magic. Magic is our currency. Ask the Siren for something, she will take a bit—buy something on the street, the vendor will take a bit.

"Everyone takes until there is nothing left to give. Once a person is Derelict, the Siren in her mercy moves them to the shadows where they can exist without needing anything. But nothingness is boring, and once in a great while they find their way back up onto our streets. Then the fighting begins, and the storm blows. The Siren will rinse her realm of anything that does not fit into the order she has created."

"Wait," Maggie said, leaning forward, "so the people out there, the Derelict, is the Siren going to just blow them away?"

"I would be terribly surprised if they were still in the Siren's Realm come morning."

"Where is she going to send them?" Maggie pictured the terrible blackness that had greeted her in the Siren's Realm. Would that be the fate of the Derelict? Did they really deserve something better?

"One problem at a time, Miss Trent." Bertrand held up a hand. "There is nothing more offensive to a Derelict than someone with no natural magic who manages to survive in the light of the Siren's Realm. Those who have worked hard to earn magic for trade are considered usurpers. Those who came in with magic but have managed to gain more than their original share are hoarders. The Derelict will seek to take it all. And a young girl who seems to have usurped so much so quickly would of course be a target for theft."

"But if I had told them I came in with magic, that I'm a witch," she choked on the word, "they would have left me alone?"

"That is a story many human-born have tried to tell." Bertrand sat on the opposite end of the couch. "So, no, I don't believe it would have saved you."

"Do you do this a lot? Stalk people just in case crazies come up from the shadows and try to steal their magic?"

"No. You are a special circumstance. Generally, I try not to bother with what others are going about. My life is enough of an adventure that others' business is rather mundane."

"But I'm not?" Maggie asked, trying to decide if she should feel offended or not.

"On the surface you most definitely are." Bertrand examined her. "But there is something more to you than a girl with a fishing net. You come from my world, a world I fought desperately to leave long ago when the fate of magic seemed bleak beyond all redemption. Yet Magickind continues. You were born and lived a life grand enough for the Siren to rip you from the grips of a battle and drag you into her realm."

"I wasn't ripped. I fell." Maggie ground her teeth, her desire to be inconsequential warring with the need for abandoning her friends to mean something.

"Are the two so very different? No, Miss Trent, I cannot allow the Derelict to get you before I discover what your fate here is."

"Thanks."

"If you wish to thank me, please drink your tea." Bertrand pointed to her abandoned cup. "The storm has yet to begin, and it would be a pity to waste such a fine cup of tea."

Maggie picked up the cup and took a sip of the hot liquid. The vague sweetness and earthy brightness made her breathe a little easier. "Thanks," she muttered, watching the rain lash against the window as the wind began to howl.

CHAPTER 7

*H*er cup was empty, but Maggie still clutched it in her hands. It wasn't even warming her fingers anymore, but she was afraid if she let go, her hands might tremble, and then Bertrand would know the storm was scaring her. The winds had picked up over the last hour, blowing the pounding rain down in horizontal sheets.

Underneath the wind's howling, the rain striking the window, and the thunder crashing, was another noise. A steady thumping that grew louder with the wind's increasing strength. Maggie took a breath, willing her heart to slow. It wasn't until her sixth deep breath that she realized the sound wasn't her heart.

"What's that noise?" Maggie turned to Bertrand, who had moved to an armchair by the fire, sipping his tea and watching the rain disinterestedly.

"Hmm." He sat up straight and set his tea on the table. "By *noise* you could mean the rain, thunder, or wind, or even my sipping my tea, though I do pride myself on excellent table manners. But judging from your frightened tone—"

"I'm not frightened."

"—I must conclude you're speaking of the waves in the canal

pounding at the rocks that hold this house above water." Bertrand regarded Maggie for a moment. "And I hope you don't believe I was implying your fear was out of place. On the contrary, there are many times when fear is a very reasonable reaction. The Siren's storms would definitely qualify as one of those situations."

"Should we be sitting here drinking tea?" Maggie asked, ignoring Bertrand's condescending tone. "If the rocks under this house are being battered by the storm, shouldn't we go to solid ground?" Maggie set her cup on the table harder than she had meant to and stood.

Surely the Derelict had gone. She could get back to…to where? Bertrand had been right—her tent wouldn't be safe in this storm.

"The Siren's will will be done," Bertrand sighed. "If she wanted to be rid of you, she would be. If she wanted to be rid of your tent on the rocks and you happened to be in it, you would be gone with the tent. We are but fleas to the Siren, tiny beings that inhabit her realm."

"So if she wants to be done with this house, then we drown?" Maggie tore her hands through her hair. "I've tried to get used to surviving here—I swear I have—but this is too much. Calling up a storm and getting rid of anything she doesn't like?"

"Miss Trent, I don't think you have ever tried to get used to surviving here. Hiding on the rocks and pretending you have no magic. I'm not casting blame"—he held up a hand, silencing Maggie's protest—"I don't know how often a witch has slipped into the Siren's Realm without wanting to be here, and to be pulled from a battle, leaving your friends to fight without you—"

"Leave that out of this."

"You knew nothing of the Siren when you arrived," Bertrand said. "I chose this path, and I have still found it to be trying. The sacrifices we make to live in the beautiful Siren's Realm are much like the sacrifices made to live anywhere. It is only much easier to see the rules here, and seeing makes accepting so much more difficult."

"So we're just supposed to sit here and hope the Siren doesn't blow us away?" Maggie said, hating the panic that surged through her chest.

"Miss Trent, please." Bertrand took her hand, and Maggie didn't have the will to be bothered to pull it away. "I would not have rescued you from the Derelict only to bring you somewhere unsafe. I have lived through five of the Siren's storms. During the first I was out in the Textile Town—"

"Where?"

"The tents." Bertrand gave a dull laugh. "You really should learn more about your new home. Merely surviving isn't what you are meant for. The Siren's storms are terrible in the Textile Town. After that first dreadful storm, I made the choice to move to the Fortress. These stone walls were standing long before I arrived in the Siren's Realm, and I can assure you they will last through the night."

"Unless the Siren decides to kill us."

"If you wish to speak crudely, then yes."

Maggie watched the storm outside the window. Gabriel would be in his tent. If the Derelict hadn't gotten him…

Bile rose in Maggie's throat.

"Miss Trent," Bertrand said gently, "I know this must all be very disturbing to you. Come down to the kitchen. The noise of the storm won't be as frightening, and I have the feeling you could use a good meal."

"I don't want to eat."

"That's usually the time you need food the most." Bertrand bowed and gestured for her to exit the sitting room the way they had entered.

Maggie bowed back before walking into the hall, half-hoping Bertrand would get angry at her for mocking him, but if he noticed, he showed no sign.

They walked down the stone hall with the worn floor. A streak of lightning sliced through the sky, and Maggie jumped backward, covering her eyes against the bright flash of light, and bumped straight into Bertrand.

He caught her under the arms when she was halfway to the floor and set her easily back up on her feet. Maggie's face burned, and she knew it was red. She hated blushing. It was the curse of being pale.

"Careful, Miss Trent." Bertrand took the lead down the hall. "I pride myself on ensuring the safety of my guests."

He opened a door that led down steps like the ones they had come up from the entryway. But these steps went down farther. By the time they reached the kitchen, the sound of the rain was a dull hum, and the thick layers of rock had muted the thunder. The only hint at the ferocity of the storm was the slapping of the waves against the stone.

The kitchen was simple with no windows to be seen. A metal cauldron hung in a fireplace so large it took up a whole wall. Cabinets sat against the two walls beside it, and in the middle of the room was a scrubbed, wooden table. It looked almost homey.

Images of water pouring in through the rocks swam unbidden into Maggie's mind. She swayed for a moment before realizing Bertrand was staring at her.

"I'm fine," Maggie growled.

"You're not, but I would be more concerned if you were." Bertrand strode to a cupboard in the corner, chose a bowl, and placed it on the table. "I think a hot bowl of hearty soup will do you a world of good." In an instant, steaming, brown, beef stew filled the bowl.

"You could have made the stew," Maggie said, not sitting at the table. "It takes less magic to find the things to make soup than to wish it into being."

"You are a clever girl." Bertrand smiled as he sat at the table with his own bowl of bright orange soup. "It does cost more to ask the Siren's favor in giving you something than to seek what you wish for from the other occupants of her realm. But I assume the markets are closed at the moment. And I've always been a terrible cook besides."

"What about this house?" Maggie stepped toward the table. "How much magic did it take to get this place? How come you aren't living in the shadows with the Derelict?"

"There are ways to enjoy all the pleasures of the Siren's Realm without ending up in the darkness. And I have never stolen magic. I hope, Miss Trent, you would never believe that of me. Though I will admit I have had an unusual amount of good fortune in the Siren's Realm."

"Were you just a really strong wizard back home?" Maggie sat at the table, the smell of the soup and her curiosity overpowering her desire to reject anything Bertrand had to offer.

"I was," Bertrand said, "and remain a very strong and rather clever wizard."

"But you can't do magic here." Maggie took a bite of her stew. The taste made the fear that had clung to her chest melt away.

"No."

"And when you're out of magic, you're out," Maggie said.

"Did someone tell you that, or did you figure it out for yourself?" Bertrand tented his fingers under his chin, leaning across the table to examine Maggie.

"I felt it," Maggie said, "the first time I asked for anything here. I felt the magic go out. And then nothing replaced it."

"Then you are as clever as I hoped you would be."

"But you must be out of magic, then." Maggie looked down at her stew to avoid Bertrand's gaze. "All this? If you haven't stolen magic and aren't a secret silk trader, you can't have much left."

Bertrand was silent for a moment. Maggie looked up to find him staring at her as though trying to read a book in a language he didn't quite understand.

"There is a way to refill the cup of magic," Bertrand began

slowly. "The Siren has her rules, and magic that comes here with her travelers is finite."

"But you said—"

"There is no rule against bringing in more magic from the outside."

"What? You like, put in a FedEx order for more magic?"

"I'm not sure what you mean by that." Bertrand shook his head. "But no. You cannot ask to have more magic brought in. You can, however, go and fetch it for yourself."

"You can leave?" Maggie dropped her spoon, not caring when her stew sloshed onto the table. "You can get out of the Siren's Realm?"

"I said as much when we first met, Miss Trent." Bertrand furrowed his brow. "I thought you had been listening."

"I was, but you said it took a lot of magic if the Siren was even willing to send you back home."

"I never said anything about fetching magic from home." He smiled sadly. "To get to one specific world would take the help of the Siren. But going home has never interested me. I have already lived in our world. There are, however, ways to slip through the stitches that join the Siren's Realm to the worlds that surround it."

"Worlds?"

"Miss Trent." Bertrand leaned across the table, staring directly into Maggie's eyes. "There is much more to this pale existence than merely surviving. I have always been one for adventure, and the Siren has provided that to me in abundance."

"But you leave?" Maggie gripped the edge of the table so hard her fingers hurt.

"I do, Miss Trent, but the cost can be terribly high. I saved you from the Derelict and the Siren's storm. It is my hope you will learn to do more than survive here in the Siren's Realm. You are far too interesting to be condemned to the shadows."

His eyes searched Maggie's as though he were seeing into her very soul. Examining every fear that had plagued her since she was trapped in the endless darkness. Or maybe even before. Since the battle. Since birth.

"You are not meant for that kind of danger," Bertrand whispered. "Not all of us can be."

"Wait, what?" Maggie asked, but Bertrand had already stood up and strode to the door.

"You should finish your stew before it gets too cold, Miss Trent. I would offer you the guest room upstairs, but I do feel you would be happier down here away from the storm. I shall see you in the morning, Miss Trent. The sun will rise when the storm has passed."

Without another word, he turned and walked up the steps, leaving Maggie alone in the kitchen.

CHAPTER 8

*M*aggie lay curled up on the floor by the kitchen fire. The floor was hard, but the heat of the fire had warmed the stones. And the crackling of the flames made the pounding of the waves seem less ominous. She closed her eyes, willing sleep to come. Surely it was almost morning. But that wasn't how it worked in the Siren's Realm. The sun would come up when the Siren wished for the storm to be over. It could be weeks.

Maggie pressed the heels of her hands into her eyes.

She wasn't meant for danger?

She gritted her teeth. She had been fighting in a battle when she fell into the damn Siren's Realm to begin with. She had been willing to die. But an adventure was too dangerous for her?

Okay, so maybe she had never been the type to seek out adventure. She had been too busy trying to survive her Clan, and then the Academy. She had probably fought more terrifying things than Bertrand Wayland ever had. Choosing to give up on his world to come live a life of pleasure.

"Quitter," Maggie mumbled. "He quit his whole world, and *I'm* not meant for adventure?"

But maybe that was it. She hadn't wanted to give up her world. She had been fighting to save it. And even here in the Siren's Realm, she didn't want to give up her own magic to pay for pleasure. She had spent her days fishing and living off of bread and meat.

But she was being frugal. Keeping what was hers instead of using it to buy fancy silk dresses and beautiful things.

She hadn't wanted to risk her own magic. Hadn't wanted to give up what she had.

Maybe that's what Bertrand had meant. She didn't want to sacrifice what she had for a chance at something different.

Maggie massaged her cheeks, willing her teeth to unclench.

There was nothing wrong with wanting to keep what you had.

But what if there was a chance at something better?

The circle kept going around in her head as the crashing of the waves grew slower and the dull pounding of the rain disappeared.

Maggie stared at the wooden boards of the ceiling, expecting the storm to start howling again or for Bertrand to come down the stairs.

Minutes slipped by. Part of her wanted Bertrand to come dashing into the kitchen to give her another lecture on what the Siren's Realm was really like. Or maybe explain why she wasn't meant for danger.

But the waves grew calmer still, and Bertrand didn't appear. It took Maggie a while to force herself to roll over and stand up. Fatigue weighed on her limbs, and dread of what she would find up the kitchen stairs didn't help her move any faster. Only the thought that if she left immediately she might avoid seeing Bertrand made her climb the steps. Bright sunlight poured in through the iron barred windows, casting the stone walls in a warm glow.

Tiptoeing across the wooden floor, Maggie crept toward the window, holding her breath as she looked outside.

Bertrand had been right. The stone buildings of the Fortress had made it through the storm. But the buildings looked newer now. Cleaner and brighter. The water in the canal shone a gentle blue in the crisp sunlight.

Glancing up and down the hall to make sure Bertrand was nowhere to be seen, Maggie ran as quickly as she dared for the stairs to the entryway, not realizing she might not be able to get through the door to the streets until her hand was already on the big iron handle. But with a tug, the door to the outside burst open, and Maggie darted out onto the walk, pausing only to shut the door before running down the street.

The canal looked beautiful enough to swim in. The windows behind the iron bars were no longer draped with curtains. The Siren's Realm was bright and new and ready for a glorious day.

Through the stone houses and out into the gray tents, she ran. The tents didn't seem any newer or brighter like the Fortress, but they were still there, unmoved by the storm.

The wide row of centaur tents came next. The flowers seemed to have grown in the night, nourished by the storm, while the weeds had drowned, leaving the gardens pristine.

But the centaurs outside their tents didn't seem to be enamored of the flowers.

"The winds of the Siren can be cruel," a speckled male centaur spoke to a dainty-looking female. It wasn't until Maggie was only ten feet away that she noticed the distress on the female's face.

Maggie slowed her run, trying to look like she wasn't listening as she passed.

"It is a part of the path laid by the Siren." The male's deep, resonating voice chased Maggie down the street. "She grants our wishes, but we live only by hers."

Maggie wanted to turn around and ask if one of the centaurs' camp had been washed away by the storm, but it seemed too cruel.

If they really had lost a friend, the last thing they would want was a stranger intruding.

If one of her friends had been lost...

Maggie's heart skipped a beat as fear surged through her.

Gabriel.

He had no magic of his own. What if the Derelict had gotten him, or the Siren had decided she didn't want him around anymore?

Maggie ran as fast as she could, her legs burning as she tore down the streets.

She passed unfamiliar tents and people. One row of tents was so short, those living in them wouldn't be able to stand up right. A long line of black and red tents sat across from a high grass mound.

Fear lodged itself in Maggie's throat. The prickle of tears in the corners of her eyes made her stop running. She would not cry on the streets of the Siren's Realm. Not because she was afraid or lost.

Not for anything.

Maggie took a deep breath. "I need to find my friends. To find out what I lost."

Her hands tingled as magic was pulled from her fingertips.

Closing her eyes, Maggie spun on the spot. After a few turns she stopped, swaying dizzily.

A tiny part of her hoped to hear Gabriel call from down the street, *"What are you doin'? Have you finally lost yer mind to the Siren?"*

But no one called her name. Maggie opened her eyes. Directly in front of her was a row of tents she hadn't noticed before. Low to the ground and sandy brown, they looked like they were meant to be camouflaged on the beach.

Without pausing, Maggie ran forward, searching every

shadow for a sign of Gabriel, Illial, Rushna, or Mathilda. She was so busy hunting for a familiar face, she didn't know she had reached the edge of the Endless Sea until she was standing on the sand.

Maggie sagged, her hands on her knees, gasping for air. Gabriel didn't live by the sea. He lived in a tent...somewhere. She had never seen it. He lived with others who had fallen into the Siren's Realm. He had asked her to come live with them where she could be safe. If only she had gone with him to see the place, then maybe she could have found it.

Cursing to herself, Maggie looked up and down the beach. There were a few people around, but no one she recognized. Off in the distance was the outcropping of rocks that hid her tent.

"Gabriel will be on the same street at the same time as always." Maggie started down the beach. "Follow the routine, and you'll find the people." Her words sounded much surer than she felt.

A middle-aged woman lay on the sand right before the stone began to take over, turning the beach into a rocky shore. Basking in the warm rays of the sun, she beamed at the bright blue sky.

"Good morning!" she called to Maggie as she passed.

"Morning," Maggie said, not halting her stride.

"And what a fine one it is," the woman cooed. "I haven't felt a morning like this in ages."

A shiver shot through Maggie's spine as she wondered if the woman hadn't felt the sun because she had been hiding in the shadows with the Derelict.

Maggie didn't look back as the woman called, "Enjoy the blessings of the Siren, little one."

The rocks were already warm from the sun. Maggie scrambled up them, using her arms to pull herself onto the high, flat level. The storm had washed away the usual layer of sand, leaving the stone smooth and clean. Maggie crouched, running her hand on the smooth rock. The Siren had cleaned all the filth away.

"No." Maggie squinted into the distance, searching for a sign of her tent. "No, no, no!" She ran full tilt across the rocks. She leapt over cracks, barely giving herself time to find her balance. Before she had even reached the edge of the high rock, she knew her tent was gone. The peak of the blue canvas should have peered up over the edge.

But maybe it had just been blown over. She could set the tent back up—she'd done it before.

She stopped, her toes right at the edge, and looked down at the place that had been her home. The rock was flat and shining with no trace a tent had ever been there.

Maggie covered her face with her hands, willing herself to breathe and not let panic take over.

"It'll be fine," Maggie whispered, not caring if the Siren heard her. "Everything will be fine. You've dealt with worse before."

Slowly, she opened her eyes, blinking at the bright sun.

The tent really was gone. Right along with her cot and table. There was no debris in the water, but why would the Siren have let that survive the storm?

It was gone. All of it.

Everything she owned had been washed away by the Siren's storm. All she had left were the clothes on her back. No net to catch fish, no bed to lie down on while she tried to figure out what was next.

Maggie climbed down to where her tent had been. At least the rock was there. She sat on the very edge, dangling her feet over the shallows.

She knew it was foolish, but the rock felt like her front porch. Her home.

A plume of water shot into the air a hundred yards out to sea.

"Mort!" Maggie called, laughing tiredly as the whale's back breached the surface. "You made it, buddy. I didn't know if the Siren was going to let you stay."

The whale said nothing, but lay lazily in the water.

"Are there still fish out there for you? Well, there will be more since I can't fish now." Maggie dug her nails into her palms. "I don't have a place to live anymore. I lost my net, so I can't earn enough to buy another tent."

Maggie paused, hearing the whales imagined response in her mind. *You're a witch, silly girl. And a good one at that. You've plenty of magic to ask the Siren for a new net and tent.*

"And let my tent be blown away next time a storm comes? If I had been here"—she shivered in the warm morning air at the thought—"I might have been washed away with the tent. No, I don't want to move into the *Textile Town.*" She held a hand up to silence the whale's protest. "Who decided to call it the *Textile Town?*" She said the words again. Somehow the name felt right in her mouth, and she hated herself for it.

"I don't want to live crowded in with people," Maggie said. "I like it out here. I like the rocks and the sea. It's home. My home, and I want to stay!"

The whale rolled onto its back, showing his stomach to the sky.

"This is where we live, and we're going to stay here. I just have to find a way to earn enough magic to build a Fortress of my own."

Maggie sprang to her feet, newfound determination flooding through her. She knew what she wanted, and she was plenty strong enough to earn it.

"Thanks, Mort!" she shouted over her shoulder as she climbed the rocks toward the Textile Town. "Good talk!"

CHAPTER 9

The market square was her first stop. She had walked quickly through the streets, partially due to her newfound determination, mostly because the streets didn't seem like a good place to linger. The tents were all there—the Siren's cleansing hadn't reached into the town itself—but there was a low rumble in all the conversations she passed. A sense of dread and grief.

"I've never seen it so bad," a beautiful young woman with flowing red hair said to the minotaur who guarded the vivid green tent. The line to get in was longer than usual. "I don't know if it's safe to be here."

Making a split-second decision, Maggie turned and walked back to the girl.

"I'm sorry," Maggie said to the girl, bowing to the minotaur before continuing, "but I'm pretty new here. I've never been through one of the storms before."

The girl stared silently at Maggie with her startling green eyes.

"I just," Maggie began, "I couldn't help but overhear. What have you never seen so bad?"

The girl looked up to the minotaur. He looked down at Maggie, considering her with his jet black eyes before nodding. At the minotaur's approval, the girl spoke.

"The Derelict," the girl said, her voice still as loud as it had been before. Maggie wished the girl would speak more softly so the entire street couldn't hear what she was saying. "There were more of them out last night than I've ever seen before. And not just roaming the lanes looking miserable. They were attacking people."

"The ones with no magic of their own."

"Those," the girl said, "and others. They stole magic some people came here with. But the problem is," the girl spoke even more loudly, shouting so everyone waiting in the line could hear, "there's no way to tell who has stolen magic. So the scum get to walk the streets and come into our tent. Filthy, disgusting thieves."

"Enough," the minotaur said, his low voice shaking the inside of Maggie's chest.

With a nod of her head, the red haired girl turned and walked past the line and into the green tent.

"Take heed," the minotaur said.

Maggie watched his mouth move. He had the head of a bull, and there was something comical in seeing his lips form the dire words.

"The street will be dangerous for some time," the minotaur said.

Maggie bit her lips together to keep from smiling.

"Those who have stolen magic will be eager to lose it. And some will try and steal more before they are forced back into the shadows."

Maggie nodded, not trusting herself to open her mouth without laughing.

"If you need a safe place to stay, or a way to earn, Lena would let you in. She has spoken of you before, Maggie Trent."

Maggie took a step back, startled at the sound of her own name. "Thank you." She turned and walked away as quickly as she dared.

Hurrying through the murmuring crowds, Maggie arrived at the market square. Trade was going on as usual, but the mood was solemn.

Nearly everyone was silent and tense except for a group of young men in front of the tent that sold ale. They were sitting at a fine wooden table that was new to the square, laughing loudly.

One of the men leapt unsteadily onto the table and shouted, "A toast! To the greatness and mercy of the Siren!" He thrust his glass to the sky, slopping ale down the front of his shirt.

His friends laughed as he tried to climb off the table, tripping and falling to the ground. He lay on the dirt road, howling with laughter as two of his drunken friends tried to get him to his feet.

Turning away from the raucous men, Maggie walked toward Mathilda's tent, keeping her head low as the murmurs around her shifted from solemn to angry.

Mathilda's tent came into view, and Maggie held her breath, waiting for Mathilda's bright white mobcap to appear.

Sure enough, as the drunken men burst into song, Mathilda popped her head out of the shadows, glowering at the men.

"Mathilda!" Maggie cried so loudly the people near her spun to glare at the noise. "Sorry," Maggie mouthed before ducking into the shadows of the tent.

Mathilda stood behind her row of goods, deep in the shadows and out of sight. On a normal morning, she would have been standing on the street, greeting everyone who walked past, trying to tempt them into buying something.

But today she stood, arms crossed, as though waiting for something she dreaded to happen.

"Mathilda," Maggie said, much softer than she had the first time, "you're okay."

"Of course I'm okay." Mathilda waved a hand. "I was always

going to be okay. I was rather worried about you. Waiting through the storm on that rock you call safe."

"I wasn't"—Maggie began before changing her mind—"I found a safe place to wait out the storm."

"And the Derelict." Mathilda *tsked*. "Coming into town. That lot out there, they'd better be careful." Mathilda waved a finger at the men, one of whom was now lying on the table and serenading the sky. "As if we don't know why they're celebrating. Sitting in the market square, throwing magic at the most absurd things. As if they think we won't know why they have so much magic to spare.

"Give me your fish, and you'd best be on your way. People are fearful this morning, and it won't be long before someone decides the square would be safer without that lot. And I can't say as I disagree."

"I don't have any fish," Maggie said, her stomach suddenly feeling hollow as she again remembered the loss of her net. "My net got lost in the storm. My tent, too. Everything really."

"What? Oh, poor child." Mathilda furrowed her brow. "Are you able to give?"

"Yes, ma'am." Maggie nodded. "I just don't know where to go."

"The Siren is the best way for it," Mathilda said. There was no hint of regret at her words. "As long as you can give to her, she'll be the best for those sorts of things. If you wanted a glass of the finest wine or even a fancy silk dress, I could offer some suggestions for where to go, but for this, the Siren."

Maggie hated the thought of the magic flowing freely from her, not knowing how much it would take to get what she needed, but if Mathilda said it was the best way, there was nothing else for it.

"All right," Maggie said, "I'll ask the Siren for it. Thank you."

"Of course, child," Mathilda said as Maggie walked around the table and back onto the bright square. "Wait." Mathilda picked up a piece of bright purple fruit from the table. "Take this.

You need to eat." She smiled kindly. "I'll be expecting fish tomorrow."

"Thank you," Maggie said, warmth spreading through her at Mathilda's kindness. She wasn't used to people being kind without reason. But Mathilda didn't ask for a draw of magic or anything in return. She only shooed Maggie away with a smile.

Maggie cut across the square, making her way toward where Gabriel would be. Her path led her near the pack of men. Their stench of sweat and ale turned her stomach.

"Pretty one!" one of the men shouted as she passed. "Come join us!"

Maggie kept her head down, not acknowledging the man's words.

"Come and have a laugh!" the man shouted, his tone growing more insistent.

Just ten more feet, and she would be level with the table. A few seconds and she would be past them.

"I said join us," the man said. "I'm offering—"

But what he had to offer, Maggie didn't hear. The man reached out and grabbed Maggie's hand as she drew level with the table.

With no thought for wishing she could do a spell, Maggie punched the man hard in the face. Pain shot up her arm, but she kept her fist tight, ready to strike again as she yanked her arm free from the man's grasp.

"Oy!" One of the other men shouted. "What's the matter with you!"

The man she had punched stepped toward her. Maggie dug her heel hard into his toes before running down a side street, diving into the shadows as soon as she could. She waited, huddled behind a barrel, for the men to chase after her.

Shouts carried from the square. Angry shouts from more people than had been in the drunken group. Maggie stayed where she was as the noise from the square grew louder.

Maggie took a bite of the purple fruit. It was sweet, thick, and juicy. She hadn't realized how dry her mouth was until the juices flooded it.

Someone was screaming in the square now. It sounded as though a fight had broken out. Maggie stayed in the shadows until the fruit was gone. She cleaned her hands on the grass before leaning out of her hiding spot to scan the street.

The narrow lane was nearly abandoned. An old woman who looked like she might be deaf toddled down the street, but everyone else had disappeared. Maggie couldn't blame them. She wished she could be hiding far from whatever was happening in the square, too. But there was nowhere for her to hide. Her home was gone.

In one swift motion, Maggie leapt to her feet and began jogging down the street. Illial hadn't been puffing on his blue smoke pipe in the market square. But that didn't mean anything. What with the fighting, he was smart to avoid it.

The smell hit Maggie's nose before she reached where Rushna should have been. The tent was there, but the flaps were tied very decisively shut.

"Rushna," Maggie called softly. "Rushna!" There was no answer. But that didn't mean anything. If the tent wasn't selling food, why would Rushna be there?

Maggie walked swiftly. The noise of the fighting in the square had disappeared, and there were people out on this street. A girl near her own age lay in a hammock by the side of the lane, playing with a cat who sprawled lazily on her stomach. Neither the girl nor the cat seemed to be upset about anything. But then they were both there in the Siren's Realm safe and happy.

Maggie wondered if the cat had been wished into being or slipped through the stitches like she had. But there was no way to know. Maybe one day she could wish a cat into being for herself.

Rounding the corner onto the street where Gabriel sold his roasted meat, Maggie's heart soared into her throat.

Gabriel and his cart were in the middle of the lane, surrounded by hungry people. The crowd wasn't as large as usual. But they were still there, waiting for the legs of meat Gabriel passed around.

"Gabriel!" Maggie called from behind two men who vied for the largest piece of meat.

"What do you know? She's alive!" Gabriel's face split into a wrinkled grin, but his smile didn't hide the fatigue in his voice. "I was afraid you hadn't made it through."

"I did," Maggie said, scooting around the men to get a closer look at Gabriel. "My tent's gone, but I was safe inland. What happened to you?"

Gabriel gave the tiniest shake of his head as he passed meat to the last of his customers. Bickering like old women, the two men walked away.

"The good fer nothin' folk who live in the shadows came up to our part of town last night," Gabriel growled. "Busted into our tents just before the storm was comin'. Drove people out into the rain and then attacked 'em. Stealin' the magic others worked hard for." Gabriel's shoulders sagged, and a shadow passed over his face.

"Did they…" Maggie wasn't sure how to ask, or if it was even right to ask. "Did they get to you?"

"One of 'em tried." Gabriel rubbed a leathery hand over his mouth. "Bunch came into my tent carryin' sticks, chasin' me out into the storm. The wind was howlin' somethin' fierce. One of 'em knocked me face-first to the ground right into the water from the storm.

"I felt the magic rippin' out of me like someone was tryin' to pull my skin all off. Lightnin' was strikin' all around, and the wind was terrible. I think they thought I'd be too scared or confused to fight back. But I spent my life before here on a ship. I'd seen worse storms and fought nastier folk."

"So what happened?" Maggie asked. "How did you get away?"

"Rolled over, knocked the bastard off of me, an' pummeled him till he stopped fightin' back," Gabriel said matter-of-factly. "Left him out in the rain, and he wasn't there when the sun finally come up. Don' know if the Siren took him or if he walked away on his own."

"I'm sorry," Maggie said. "Did they get many of your friends?"

"A few," Gabriel said, "but we managed to fight 'em off. That's the good of bein' one who has no magic of their own. I was in plenty of fights before I ever came here, and I never used magic to win any of 'em. I have enough to earn. I'll make do. I'm just glad they didn't get you."

"Thanks," Maggie said as Gabriel handed her a turkey leg. "When do you think it'll happen again? The Derelict attacking and the Siren making a storm."

"Eh." Gabriel shrugged. "Could be a thousand sunrises, could be tonight."

"And we're just supposed to sit and wait for it to happen again?"

"Aye. It's the best we can do."

Maggie took Gabriel's hand, giving him more of her magic than usual. "Then I guess I had better get ready for the next storm."

CHAPTER 10

*M*aggie took the long way back to the rocks by the Endless Sea. Getting lost in the maze of streets had made her determined to learn her way to all the hidden places she could find.

She had been existing, moving from one day to the next, enjoying the sun and stability. Always fish in the sea, always food for her stomach. But her life hadn't been stable at all. She had been living at the mercy of the Siren without even realizing it. The only power she had was in the magic she possessed.

She found her way back to the Fortress and considered walking along the canals. But Bertrand Wayland strode by, a look of fierce determination on his face, and Maggie walked quickly in the other direction rather than risk having to explain disappearing from his kitchen.

There were no Derelict on the sun-bathed streets, though wariness and solemnity were everywhere.

When it was only a couple of hours before sundown, Maggie returned to her rocks. They were still there, and there was still no trace of her little home.

Maggie lay down on the rock, imagining the blue of her tent

above her. The breeze from the sea would rustle the fabric. The morning sun would peer through to wake her.

But it wasn't safe.

Stone. She needed a stone house. But at what cost?

Maggie laughed to herself, imagining shouting *can I get an estimate on a stone house?* to the sky, but too afraid to say it out loud for fear she might actually get an answer.

"Well," a voice said from above.

Gasping, Maggie rolled backward, hiding in the crevice of the rock.

"It seems you have wiped the slate clean again, sweet Siren."

Maggie recognized the voice. Bertrand Wayland stood on the rocks above her.

"You have smoothed out some of the cracks, and hidden the tiny stitches," Bertrand called out to the sea, "but not all. And I will find more. I suppose you would stop me if you wanted to. But I think we both know better than that.

"I will venture out again and bring back more riches for your realm. But I do ask…" Bertrand paused. "Try not to blow Miss Trent away if there is a storm in my absence. I can see you've ruined her home. She's probably living with those who have no magic of their own now. Dear Siren, don't let the poor girl's lie destroy her. And don't let my journey destroy me."

Maggie held her breath as faint footsteps moved away from her.

Bertrand had come here to make sure she was okay.

Weird.

Bertrand thought living with the others she pretended to be like was going to get her taken by the Siren.

Probably true in the long run.

Bertrand was going to go through one of the stitches and bring back more riches. Since you could only bring the clothes on your back to the Siren's Realm, riches meant magic. Magic to build a stone house on the rock by the sea.

Brilliant.

Rolling back out of the crevice, Maggie sprang to her feet and climbed up onto the high rock. Bertrand was three hundred yards ahead, striding toward the city. Glancing around the deserted cliff to be sure no one was watching, Maggie ran after him.

Half-formed plans rolled through her mind. He had said she wasn't strong enough to go with him to wherever it was he went. But what did he know about her? He had figured out she was a witch. So what? She was braver than he knew. Stronger, too.

She would go out, get some magic, come back and build her little stone house.

But what if he wouldn't let her come with him? What if she didn't know how to get back? What if the whole thing was a trap? Or they died trying to find some great adventure? What if she didn't know how to get more magic to bring back in?

Maggie's steps faltered, and she slowed to a trot, keeping Bertrand in sight but never gaining on him.

He didn't seem to be in a hurry as he walked down the lanes. Past the jewel bright tents and on to the gray ones. Maggie had expected him to turn onto the stone streets of the Fortress. But instead, he pressed onward down more long rows of tents.

Soon, the tents weren't so close together. There were spaces between all of them like little yards. Bertrand nodded at people as he passed in his easy manner. Somehow, his nodding to strangers made Maggie angry. Like he thought he was a local celebrity.

But as Maggie passed the people on the spread out streets, they nodded to her, too. Smiling kindly at her. This was the first place she had been since the storm where no one seemed tense.

If Bertrand was looking for some sort of illicit adventure, surely he had gone the wrong way. But he kept walking. He was only a hundred feet in front of her now, but she had to stay that close to keep him in sight as the grassy yards turned into a forest dotted with tents.

The air here smelled damp with earth. Musky leaves added their scent. A log cabin stood in the distance, its chimney merrily puffing smoke.

"What the hell is this place?" Maggie muttered. How could she have spent so much time in the Siren's Realm, talked to so many people, and no one had bothered to mention a forest?

Not that she would have wanted to live there. To some, the woods might feel liberating, but to her the trees felt like a crushing cave. Maggie took a shuddering breath and pushed down the memories of blood, screams, and a bright green light.

She was so occupied with trying not to think she almost didn't hide in time.

Bertrand stopped in the middle of a stand of bright white birch trees. All of them bent gently toward the earth as though they were trying to listen to its secrets.

Peering out from behind a thick-trunked oak tree, Maggie watched as Bertrand paced inside the circle of white birches. He was saying something in a low voice that Maggie couldn't hear. After a minute or so, he began running his hands along the trunks of the trees, as though searching for some kind of hidden catch.

But he didn't seem to find what he was looking for as he moved from one tree to the next. He made his way back to the center of the circle, tenting his fingers under his chin as he gazed through the white branches up to the sky.

Then, without warning, he walked out of the circle of white trees to a large, barren tree three feet to the left. Maggie hadn't noticed the barren tree before. It was so dark and ordinary next to the clearly magical trees Bertrand had just been examining. Bertrand smiled as he stepped toward the tree, and with a bright flash of green light, he disappeared.

Maggie yelped and leapt back, falling to the ground. Something cut into her palm, but she didn't bother looking at it as she sprang to her feet and ran toward the tree.

Bertrand was gone. There was no trace of him. It was as though the tree had swallowed him whole. With trembling fingers, Maggie reached for the tree. She half-expected it to grow teeth and eat her with a tongue of green light, but nothing happened. She ran her fingers along the bark. The rough surface felt warmer than it should have in the shade of the forest. But there was no knob, or instructions. Nothing to say how to follow Bertrand.

Maggie went to the center of the white trees, following what Bertrand had done—searching the trees with her fingers, muttering inventive curses the whole way. If the trees wanted a spell, she didn't have one to give. She stood in the center of the clearing and looked up through the branches. But there was no hidden password or spell written in their leaves.

Maggie jammed her fingers through her hair, willing her brain to come up with a solution.

But there was nothing. She didn't know how to find a way out of the Siren's Realm, let alone what to do once she did. The best thing she could hope for was for Bertrand to make it back alive and then maybe she could convince him to take her with him the next time he left the Siren's Realm.

Maggie's heart sank. She hadn't even really wanted to go, but now knowing she couldn't...

"Nope," Maggie said to the empty woods. "I'm going. I am figuring this thing out, and I am going."

She strode over to the barren tree. There was something there she hadn't seen before. A dark crack, barely big enough to be noticed. Yet the closer she got, the wider it seemed. Almost large enough for her to slide through.

Maggie reached her hand out toward the darkness inside the tree, wondering if she would find only shadows or something living inside. The instant her fingers grazed the darkness, the world disappeared in a bright flash of green, and she was falling.

CHAPTER 11

*C*old crushed her lungs, pushing out her last precious bit of air. Whether she was falling or the world around her was moving, she didn't know.

Death.

This can't be death. It wasn't before.

Maggie's brain felt as though it might burst from lack of air.

Maybe she had done it wrong. She hadn't found a way through one of the stitches that led to a faraway world, and now she would just be trapped in the darkness forever.

She opened her mouth to try and ask for a light, but in the void, speaking was impossible.

Dying in battle would have been better.

Just when Maggie had decided that this was, in fact, the end, bright light shone around her, and she was plunged into cold darkness.

But it wasn't like before. This darkness had texture. Flowing around her. Maggie opened her mouth to try to breathe, but water flooded her lungs, burning worse than the nothing had.

Spots danced in front of her eyes. Up, she needed to find the way up. But the world had gotten twisted around, and she didn't know which way might lead out of the water.

Forcing herself to relax, a gentle wave pushed her up the tiniest bit. Fighting with all the strength she had left in her limbs, Maggie kicked up toward the surface.

Bright light and warmth greeted her as she reached the open air, coughing and retching the water from her lungs. Her arms ached as she fought to keep her head above the water, gasping for breath as her head spun. It took nearly a minute for the world around her to begin making sense.

She was in a lake of some sort. Vast though the water was, she could see land on all sides.

The water wasn't freezing. That was good. It was cool and still, almost comfortable to be in.

The shore was covered in trees so thick it looked like a jungle. Faint rustling and hooting sounded from deep within the shadows. High stone cliffs cut through the water, some reaching around to corners and disappearing, some rising like tree-topped spires isolated in the lake.

Luckily, the shore nearest her sat low at the edge of the water. Trees rose up behind, masking the landscape between Maggie and the cliffs in the distance.

Taking one last deep breath, Maggie swam toward the shore. Something brushed up against her leg, but she didn't dare stop to see what it was. If something wanted to eat her, there wasn't a thing she could do about it anyway. The shore was farther away than it had seemed, and by the time Maggie pulled herself belly first onto land, she was gasping for breath again.

"This," Maggie panted, still face down on the ground, "is bullshit."

"On the contrary, Miss Trent"—a voice came from above—"I think you've done quite well."

Maggie rolled onto her back and looked up at Bertrand Wayland.

He wasn't drenched or puffing. He didn't look like he had just fallen through the rabbit hole of doom into some unknown world with creatures shaking the branches twenty feet away. Bertrand Wayland was bone dry, perfectly clean, and smiling.

Maggie lay on the ground, glaring up at him.

Bertrand didn't seem to notice. "I did think when it took you so long in getting here you might have changed your mind and decided not to follow me, which, of course, would have been quite understandable given the nature of our adventure. And you did make it out of the water remarkably calmly. I was prepared to go in after you, but I supposed you must have lived your whole life near the water since you seem so attached to the Endless Sea now."

"What the hell," Maggie growled, pushing herself shakily to her feet, "makes you think you know anything about me?"

"Well, Miss Trent"—Bertrand grinned—"I understand you well enough to know you would be following me today. Well, yesterday for me. I have been here since last night."

"What?" Maggie wrung the water out of her hair. "I was only ten minutes behind you."

"But that is the rub in leaving the Siren's Realm," Bertrand said. "I have never known if the Siren doesn't understand time as we do or if she simply doesn't care to bother with it. But time inside and outside of the Siren's Realm never do seem to line up."

Maggie's mind raced, trying to think of how long she had been in the Siren's Realm. "So ten minutes in the Siren's Realm means a day outside?" She had been in the Siren's Realm for months. The battle at Graylock would be long over by now. Everyone she knew could already be dead.

"Oh no." Bertrand shook his head. "Nothing nearly so simple. Sometimes it will be only a few moments' difference. I was gone from the Siren's Realm for nearly a year once. I came back, and it was only just after lunch.

"There is no way I have ever seen to calculate how much time has passed within the realm when I'm without. It is never less on the outside. Sometimes much more. It is the way of the Siren, and we poor mortals must accept it is her will. Though I did truly hope I wouldn't have to spend a month waiting for you to come after me."

"What made you think I would come after you?" Maggie took off her boots and dumped the water out of them.

"I made sure you knew the lure of what I was adventuring toward and even visited your home so you would know to follow me."

"You wanted me to come!" Maggie screeched, sending something in the woods scurrying for cover. "You're the one who told me it was too dangerous! You're the one who said I should make do in the Siren's Realm!"

"I gave you very practical advice. I only hoped you wouldn't follow it. Now put on your shoes, and let us move along. Adventure is waiting somewhere in this forest, and I intend to find it."

"What do you mean?" Maggie hopped after Bertrand, jamming on her boots. "You *hope* to find adventure?"

"Well, we cannot simply wait by the shore and expect something worth seeing to find us." Bertrand didn't turn to face Maggie as he spoke. He plowed into the jungle, not even checking to see if Maggie would follow.

"You don't know what's here?" Maggie pushed her way through the brush to follow Bertrand.

"No."

"Then how did you know we'd land in water?"

"I didn't."

"But what if we had fallen onto rocks?"

"It would have hurt significantly more."

"I've just followed a madman into a world neither of us knows anything about," Maggie muttered.

"And you don't know the way home, so keep up!" Bertrand shouted back from forty feet ahead. The trees had become so thick she could barely see him.

Branches and brambles tore at Maggie's clothes, ripping the thin fabric and scratching her skin. The air inside the trees was thick and humid. Within minutes, Maggie was puffing and covered in sweat.

Bertrand led them in a straight line, but toward what, Maggie couldn't tell. She wanted to lay down on the ground and rest, but the shaking of the tiny leaves near her feet made her sure bugs of some sort waited for her down there.

Soon, Bertrand began leading them steeply uphill. Maggie scrambled after him. He gradually slowed his pace as the climb became more difficult and finding purchase for their feet took more time. Maggie was ruefully grateful he had stopped climbing so quickly. Her breath came in shallow gasps, and her head pounded from heat and exertion.

She tried to take her mind away from her pain by examining the trees they passed. They were thick and tall with leaves that sprouted high over her head. They were definitely different from the trees she had been around growing up. But there was nothing otherworldly or innately magical-looking about them.

The leaves overhead were large, thick, and a deep green. Maggie gazed longingly at them, wondering if there might be clean rainwater nestled in their crevices she could drink.

With a hoot and a squeak, something launched itself from one tree to another, soaring high in the sky right above Maggie's head. Maggie squealed and dropped to the ground, covering her head for protection.

"What?" Bertrand asked, sounding mildly curious. "Is something wrong, Miss Trent?"

"There are animals up there," Maggie said, keeping one arm over her head as she pointed to where the beast had disappeared. "One jumped through the trees."

"Oh good." Bertrand beamed. "Always comforting to know living things are about. It means something has managed to survive. Now come along, Miss Trent, we have a ways to go before night catches us."

He turned to keep climbing. The way in front of them was steeper than the hill they had already climbed. She would have to use her arms to pull herself up.

"No," Maggie said. "I am not going any farther."

"Really?" Bertrand furrowed his brow. "You run so frequently through the Siren's Realm, I didn't think you would have a problem with our climb."

"It's not boiling hot in the Siren's Realm. There's water in the Siren's Realm. I'm not going any farther until you tell me where the hell we're going."

"Ah." Bertrand nodded, pulling a thin, silver bracelet off his wrist. "It is a bit hotter here than the comfortable climate the Siren so lovingly provides. I can understand how you would become thirsty." He pinched one side of the loop between the fingers of both hands. The silver of the loop grew as he pulled his hands apart, forming a silver tube. When the tube was about seven inches long, he stopped pulling, set it open-side down on his right palm, and tapped it with his left finger. With a sympathetic smile, he held the silver thing out to Maggie.

Pushing herself laboriously to her feet, Maggie examined the smooth silver sides. "A cup?" she asked, looking inside at the solid, silver bottom.

"A very fine cup." Bertrand nodded. "It cost a dear amount of magic to get something of this nature from the Siren that I could slip through the stitches with. But it has proven invaluable." He handed the empty cup to Maggie.

"Do you have any water?" she asked, her throat suddenly dryer than it had been before, now that water was so nearly within her grasp.

"You did say you were a witch, didn't you?" Bertrand asked, bemused. "I assume you know how to create water?"

Rolling her eyes at Bertrand's smug smile, Maggie said, "*Parunda.*" The tingle of magic flew through her body, and the cup was filled with fresh, clean water. But she was filled with magic as well. Filling the cup hadn't drained her of anything. Maggie smiled down at the cup. "I can use my magic here. And I won't lose all of it?"

She looked hopefully at Bertrand as she took a long drink of the cool water in the cup, reveling in the chill as it flowed down past her lungs, making it easier to breathe in the heavy air.

"Yes and no." Bertrand frowned. "Now come along. We have a long way yet to go."

"But you haven't said where we're going," Maggie said, starting to follow. "*Parunda.*" She filled the cup again.

"I don't know where we're going," Bertrand said, choosing a path that would allow Maggie to climb beside him, "but the best way to find adventure is to find the people of this strange world. And to find the people, we must see the landscape."

"So we get up high and see what there is to see."

"Correct, Miss Trent." Bertrand smiled, apparently pleased she had caught on. He began climbing the boulders that led up the side of the mountain. "Keep up!"

Maggie took another long drink of water before pressing lightly on the rim of the cup and hiding her smile as it collapsed back into a bracelet. "Neat."

The water had helped. Her head was no longer pounding so badly she couldn't see straight. But she was still drenched in sweat, and in a few minutes her arms ached in protest at the constant work of pulling herself uphill.

With a burst of rustling branches, another one of the things flew through the trees overhead. It was close enough that she could see a little more of the animal this time. It looked rather like a monkey.

Another tree rustled, and Maggie searched the treetops. She felt her fingers slip from the rock she clung to, teetered for a moment, and fell backward.

A sharp pain shot through her shoulder. With a cry, she fell sideways, rolling off the next boulder. Jamming her fingers into a crack in the stone, she caught herself and, with a horrible jerk on her shoulder, broke her fall.

"Oww, oww," Maggie groaned, pulling herself to sit on the rock. She flexed her fingers and wiggled her toes to make sure nothing was broken.

"Are you all right, Miss Trent?" Bertrand jumped down to where she sat, looking genuinely concerned.

"I'm great," Maggie said through clenched teeth. She raised her arm, and pain shot from her shoulder.

"What made you fall?"

"I saw a monkey." Maggie rolled her eyes at her own stupidity.

"I have seen a few little furry things flying through the trees." Bertrand knelt to examine Maggie's shoulder. "But you really should be more careful." He took Maggie's arm and began twisting it around.

"What the—Gah!" Maggie yelped as her shoulder popped back into the socket.

"We'll have to climb a bit more slowly now, as you'll need to be kind to that arm, Miss Trent."

"Be kind to my arm?" Spots danced in front of Maggie's eyes from the pain.

"It will take a while to heal," Bertrand said, already ten feet above her on the rocks.

"Why can't I just use magic to heal it?" Maggie growled as she climbed painfully to her feet. "In fact, why don't we use a little magic and get ourselves up this mountain in half the time?"

"It won't work," Bertrand said in such a matter of fact tone, Maggie had to take a deep breath before she dared to speak.

"Why won't it work? I made water in the cup." She jiggled the silver bracelet on her wrist at him. "We have magic here. Wasn't that the point of coming?"

"My dear Miss Trent, I think you are a bit new at this to be deciding the point of anything." Bertrand smiled sympathetically. "And water is one of the constants. So you can easily form a cup of water."

"Constant whats?" Maggie moved to run her hands through her hair and instantly regretted it as a dull ache throbbed in her shoulder.

"In every world, there are three things that remain constant." Bertrand beckoned for Maggie to keep climbing.

Grudgingly and painfully, she did.

"In every world I have visited that is, which is not to say these rules will always apply. I would never assume myself to be that grand."

"Really?" Maggie's voice dripped with sarcasm. "You, not grand?"

"I said not *that* grand, Miss Trent," Bertrand corrected, apparently unaffected by her tone. "There are three constants. Water, shelter, and fire. Which means to say the spells I know for each from my time in our former world—"

"You mean Earth?"

"Those spells that I am familiar with from my early training work wherever I go. *Parunda* will consolidate water into a glass. *Primurgo*, or *primionis*, will create a shield, which becomes your shelter. And *inexuro* will light an acceptable fire. Everything you need to survive."

"But food. You need food to survive, but there's never a spell for that," Maggie said, now climbing right next to Bertrand despite the pain in her arm.

"But it is helpful to be able to cook whatever you can find," Bertrand said. "*Inexuro* creates a reasonable flame you can cook over."

"But you're on your own to figure out what's edible? Awesome."

"It is as you say, Miss Trent, awesome." Bertrand grinned. "Or as I prefer to call it— *adventure*."

They climbed without speaking for a while, listening to the hooting and the cawing in the forest as Maggie's mind raced through what she could do with water, fire, and a shield spell.

"But how do you know?" Maggie asked. "How do you know a levitation spell won't work?"

"I don't. But it is a fairly good assumption based on previous experience."

"Then shouldn't we try it?" A bubble of excitement grew in Maggie's chest. "I mean, what if *adsurgo* works here? What if it works better here?"

"By all means, please try it, Miss Trent." Bertrand sat on a rock facing her, an ill-concealed smile on his face.

"You're setting me up." Maggie narrowed her eyes. "It won't work, and you want to laugh at me."

"It doesn't matter if I am setting you up or not, Miss Trent. You are bound to try it for yourself anyway."

Maggie opened her mouth to argue, but he was right. So with a shrug she said, "*Adsurgo.*" It was as though someone had knocked her feet out from under her with a stick. She was airborne for only a split second before she tumbled face-first to the ground.

"And now I hope you see why I didn't try to heal your arm with magic." Bertrand stood and brushed himself off, ready to climb again. "As you can see, the results might have been disastrous. I might have accidentally removed your arm entirely."

"Right." Every muscle Maggie had ever felt, and several she hadn't, ached as she followed Bertrand up the mountain.

"And we really must work on your sword play, Miss Trent," Bertrand called back. "I do beg your pardon if I am making any false assumptions concerning your aptitude, but having skill with a sword can be vital if you cannot use magic to fend off an attacker."

"Nope." Maggie grimaced. "They definitely didn't teach us swords at the Academy."

CHAPTER 12

*M*aggie had gone numb by the time they neared the top of the mountain. There was nothing but moving forward one more step. Then another. Then another. She had long since stopped looking up to see how close they were to the top. There was no point. They would get there when they got there.

She didn't even look anymore as things rustled in the bushes nearby.

"If you want to eat me, just do it," Maggie growled at the trees.

"I'm sorry, what was that, Miss Trent?"

"I said—" Maggie looked toward Bertrand, but he wasn't climbing a few feet ahead of her. He was standing on the top of the mountain ten feet above her. "We're here?" Maggie's words came out as a whimper. "We're done climbing?"

"For now, Miss Trent." Bertrand lay on his stomach and reached down, catching the hand of Maggie's good arm as soon as she was near enough and dragging her to the top. "And for the evening."

Maggie rolled onto her back, panting and staring up at the darkening sky.

"We do have an excellent vantage point. Though I don't see any people at the moment," Bertrand said.

"Mmmhmm." Maggie closed her eyes and let the breeze play across her face.

"There is a decent ridgeline we can follow tomorrow if we still can't see anything from here."

"A ridgeline sounds great." She raised her hand and gave Bertrand a thumbs up.

"I must say—" Bertrand bustled around, breaking sticks.

Maggie unwillingly opened her eyes.

"—you have done better than I thought you would, Miss Trent." He piled the sticks on top of a flat rock. "I was afraid you might not make it up the mountain, or you might decide to turn around and head right back to the safety of the Siren."

"I don't know how to get back." Maggie sat up and watched as Bertrand built a fire. It had gotten so dark Maggie blinked at the sudden light of the flames. "And I came here to bring more magic into the Siren's Realm. I'm not leaving without it."

"But you've already, shall we say, refilled your magic stores." Bertrand took off his jacket and began pulling things out of his pockets. "So you could go back whenever you like."

"I what?" Maggie said, watching quasi-disgusted as Bertrand pulled two large fish from his pockets.

"You have what you came for," Bertrand repeated as, with a horrible squelching noise, he casually shoved a stick lengthwise through the first dead fish. "You can go back whenever you like."

"Next you're going to tell me to click my heels three times and I'll be back by the Endless Sea."

"I know nothing of clicking heels, Miss Trent," Bertrand said, looking at Maggie as though afraid the heat had done something to her brain, "but you could slip back through the stitch and take what magic you've gained with you."

"Then why the hell did we just climb up a freakin' mountain!" Maggie screamed, her voice bouncing out into the darkening air.

"Because, Miss Trent, I hope for more from you than simply sneaking into a world, stealing a bit of magic, and returning home a little richer but none the wiser. You are in a world neither you nor I have ever seen. Magic connected the Siren's Realm to this place. Only something fiercely magical could have made an opening we can travel through. I mean to find that magic and discover what secrets it holds.

"We would not have fallen into this place if there were no reason for us to be here, Miss Trent. Magic has called us to this world, and I intend to discover why. And if you are the person I believe you to be, I have no doubt you will be following me around this maze of a lake come morning."

Maggie buried her head in her hands, taking a few shuddering breaths before speaking. "I really have no idea who the hell this person you think I'm supposed to be is, but I'm pretty sure I'm not her."

"Self-deprecation is hardly a virtue, Miss Trent. You are important enough to have been drawn into the Siren's Realm, smart enough to respectably make your way in the Textile Town, caring enough to befriend the misfits you meet, and brave enough to defend a stranger against the Derelict. Really, I am beginning to suspect I know you better than you know yourself."

Maggie squeezed her eyes shut against the night as she pictured herself throwing Bertrand from the top of the mountain.

"Would you like some fish?" Bertrand asked. "You will need your strength come morning. Unless, of course, you want to run back to the Siren's Realm simply to prove me wrong."

Pain shot through Maggie's jaw as she clenched her teeth. She slid the bracelet from her wrist, and turned it back into a cup. "*Parunda.*" The cup filled with water. "Cheers to adventure."

"Brilliant, Miss Trent." Bertrand beamed, spreading his arms wide as though embracing the dusk. "And what a wonderful place we have found for an adventure!"

Maggie looked out over the edge for the first time. Barely visible in the shadows were more cliffs and spires she hadn't been able to see before. The lake wasn't round, but built like a true maze with canals and offshoots going in every direction and disappearing into the darkness.

"Wow," Maggie breathed. There was a remarkable beauty in the brokenness of the lake.

Impossible to navigate. Water and rock surrounded by thick forest filled with unknown things. For the first time in a very long time, Maggie felt small. Small enough to curl up in the back of a closet and hide until the darkness was gone.

"How are we going to find anything in that maze besides water?" Maggie asked.

"We wait for daylight, Miss Trent." Bertrand slid the first roasted fish from its spear and handed it to Maggie. *"Primionis."*

The air shimmered as the shield blossomed around them.

Maggie took a bite of the fish, her stomach rumbling its appreciation of the food.

"Eat and sleep well, Miss Trent. For tomorrow morning, the true adventure begins."

~

*S*leeping in the jungle was not nearly as simple as Maggie had imagined. As night fell, the animals that hid in the trees seemed to decide it was time to come out. Leaves rustled, and unseen things growled and snorted. The fire still burned between Bertrand and Maggie, keeping away the chill that had crept over the mountaintop.

Maggie inched closer to the embers. It seemed wrong that a few hours ago she had been sweating to death and now she was too cold to sleep. A simple spell could have fixed it. But it could have melted her skin off, too.

Maggie stared up at the sky, blocking the haze of the firelight with one hand. Stars peered out from the black, but they weren't stars she had ever seen before. There were no constellations she recognized. Seven stars seemed to be brighter than the rest. Maggie wrapped her arms around herself, trying to squeeze out the thumping in her chest that shouted she was too far from home and the horrible notion that the Siren's Realm had somehow become home. She fell asleep, trying to remember what constellations she had been able to see out her window at the Academy.

"Miss Trent," a voice pulled her from sleep. "Miss Trent, the sun has begun to rise."

Maggie's eyes fluttered open. Bertrand knelt next to her.

"We must begin our watch of the lake." Bertrand's face beamed with excitement. "I have a distinct feeling people are moving about the lake. We need only spot them."

"What?" Maggie rubbed her face. "Why do you feel like there are people moving around?"

"There." Bertrand pointed to a distant patch of low-lying trees. Their leaves were a bright red that was nearly swallowed up by the deep green of the taller trees around them.

Just as Maggie began to wonder what sort of trees could be so red, a flock of birds burst from the branches, cawing their fear before settling into another patch of trees down the lake.

"So there's a predator out there." Maggie shrugged. "It could be jungle cat or bear or whatever they have around here."

"I have discovered in my many travels that whenever one suspects the presence of a predator, it is best to assume the threat is a person until you discover otherwise. People are the most dangerous thing to have creep up on you unexpectedly. And the thing you least want to find you in the dark is usually what is lurking in the shadows."

"Thanks for that." Maggie walked to the edge of the cliff and sat, her feet dangling over the side as she scanned the trees, searching for more patches of red. "You really made me feel better about this whole *finding adventure* thing."

"Miss Trent," Bertrand said from his post facing the other side of the lake, "it will never be my intention to make you *feel better*. It will always be my intention to keep you alive."

"Well, I guess there's something in that."

The morning sun glistened on the lake, showing more of it than Maggie had been able to see the night before. The sight was not comforting. The maze of cliffs and islands reached out to towering mountains in the distance. Once the twists and turns of land covered the water, there was no way to know how much longer the lake went on for.

"We need a map," Maggie said. "Even if we see someone, there'll be no way to follow them without a map. We'll get lost in the maze."

"That is a problem," Bertrand said, "but first we must see where we want to go. Then we will worry about the details of getting there."

Trees stirred on the other side of the lake. Maggie sat up straight and squinted into the distance. Nothing as large as a person appeared. Small brownish things moved along the edge of the water, grazing on something.

"How deep do you think the water is?" Maggie asked. From the top of the mountain, there was no sign of shallows near the shore. The lake simply began in a deep blue, becoming ever darker toward the middle.

"Knowing how magic works in most parts, I would say extremely deep. Deep enough to hide something terrifying in its depths. Or, alternatively, about four-and-a-half feet."

"When I fell in, I went more than four-and-a-half feet down."

"Then we must assume terrifyingly deep is the correct assessment."

They settled back into silence. Maggie's mind wandered as she stared out over the unmoving lake. A bird flew nearby, pale blue, his wings tipped with bright purple. It circled lazily overhead, spiraling higher and higher into the sky before diving into the trees.

A squawk of terror and squeak of pain were followed by silence. Maggie shuddered and turned back toward the lake.

Dead ahead, a boat glided smoothly across the lake's surface.

"Bertrand. I see people!"

Bertrand was by her side in two long strides.

"Should we shout for them?" Maggie asked.

The boat was gliding past them. One person at either end held a long paddle, steering the boat quickly toward a clump of spires.

"They wouldn't be able to hear us from all the way up here," Bertrand said. "We shall watch them as long as we can and do our best to mimic their path."

"But we don't have a boat," Maggie said, feeling minimally guilty at pointing out the obvious flaw in Bertrand's plan.

"Luckily," Bertrand said as the boat slid out of sight, "our slice of land will bring us far enough to be even with where they disappeared, and then it's only a matter of crossing to the spires and seeing what we find."

"So swimming in the terrifyingly deep water that might have something awful in it?"

"Precisely. Now come along, Miss Trent, we have a ridge waiting for us to walk it." He pointed to the rocky ridgeline that led parallel to where the boat had disappeared.

"At least it's not climbing straight up." Maggie sighed as she followed him.

CHAPTER 13

*T*he mid-afternoon sun was beating down upon them when Bertrand finally decided it was time to head back down to the water. Maggie's momentary relief at being out of the sun was drowned by the staggering weight of the humid air in the trees.

Rocks tore at her hands as they struggled back down the steep slope, and once she no longer needed her hands to keep balance, she kept the cup constantly filled, passing it back and forth to Bertrand.

"You know," Maggie puffed, "it's good to know you're human."

"I am not human," Bertrand said in a moderately offended tone. "I am a wizard. But wizards still need water."

"And food," Maggie added. "Food would be great."

"If you insist, Miss Trent." Bertrand looked up, searching the trees.

Maggie stood next to him, trying to see what he was looking for. All she saw were trees.

"There." Bertrand pointed after a moment.

The leaves rustled, and one of the monkey-looking things burst into view.

"There is your food."

"You want to eat a baby monkey?" Maggie asked.

"No, Miss Trent," Bertrand said, "I want to take whatever the monkey is eating."

He walked through the trees to where the monkey had appeared.

"But how do we get it?" Maggie asked. "We can't levitate, and we can't use a summoning charm."

"Climb." Bertrand took off his jacket and handed it to Maggie.

"You're going to shimmy up that tree like a *wizard*-sized koala and steal food from monkeys?" Maggie asked as Bertrand ran and leapt at the tree, wrapping his arms around it and beginning to climb the tall trunk.

"That is exactly what I intend to do, Miss Trent."

"What if you fall?" Maggie said. "The monkey was really high up. I can't heal you here!"

"Then I shall not fall, Miss Trent."

"This is great," Maggie muttered. "Really freakin' great. He's going to die, and I have no idea how the hell to get back to the Siren's Realm."

A branch broke not ten feet behind her.

Maggie spun to see who was there, but before she could make sense of it, something thick and dark had covered her head.

Maggie screamed as arms wrapped tightly around her. "Bertrand! Help!"

"Hold her still," a voice growled.

"No. Please!" Maggie yelled as something cut into her wrists, binding them together.

There was a bellow and a *crash*.

"Unhand her at once!" Bertrand shouted.

A muffled grunt of pain was followed by the smack of flesh hitting flesh.

Something hard knocked into Maggie, sending her tumbling sideways.

"We are not here to hurt—"

With a horrible *crack*, Bertrand fell silent.

"Bertrand!" Maggie tried to find her footing and shake off whatever was covering her head. "Bertrand! Leave him alone!"

"Shut her up," a woman ordered. A hand touched Maggie's neck. She crumpled to the ground before she could scream.

~

*P*ain climbed Maggie's wrists. Not a mind-numbing pain or a hateful pain. Just an ache, which seemed to assure her that if she tried to move, something much worse would follow. She was tied up, her back pressed against something hard and straight. Her face was still covered, and the heat of every breath made it more difficult to breathe.

She listened closely in the darkness. The sound of water lapping came from beneath her. The rhythm of steady breathing came from behind her. Movement in the corner. Not constant. Like someone was shifting their weight, uncomfortable from sitting in one place for so long.

"You know," Maggie said as carelessly as she could, "I have to stop waking up like this. Darkness, not knowing where I am. Last time was bad enough. Eternal darkness with nothing to mark time. But this. This is almost worse. Being tied up, my head covered. The person who's keeping me here listening to me rant and not saying anything." She paused for a moment.

"I suppose it would be too much to ask for kidnappers to be polite. That's fine. But, it would be *nice* of you to tell me where I am, you know. I really don't know that. I assume I'm still by the lake, because I can hear the water and"—Maggie paused again —"yep, I can feel the floor moving. So I'm going to say boat or raft."

Maggie leaned her head back, resting it on the surface behind her. "I know you can understand me. Because I could understand you when you decided to attack my friend and me and knocked me out. I assume my friend is the one passed out behind me. It's probably good he's sleeping. I don't think he'll take being kidnapped very well, and I would hate for him to hurt you.

"Of course, it's probably rude of me to assume you're the asshole who decided to use magic on me to bring me here. Especially since I've been lecturing you on manners. But it's hard to have a nice conversation with someone who won't let you see them and won't even answer your questions. I don't even know what it is you think we've done that gives you the right to hold us like this. It must have been something bad—"

A sharp guttural noise sounded from the corner.

"Oh," Maggie said. "You think we've done something *very* bad. You're mad at us."

Something moved in the corner.

Maggie held her breath for a moment, wondering if she had gone too far, waiting for another touch of a hand to knock her out. But nothing happened.

"Whatever it is you think we've done, you're wrong," Maggie said. "We didn't mean to end up here. We don't even really know where *here* is. My friend caught a few fish, we climbed a mountain, slept there, came down, and then you caught us. Are any of those things why you're mad? Are the fish sacred or something? Because we really didn't know."

The person in the corner stayed silent.

"So it wasn't any of that," Maggie said. "Then whatever you're mad at us for, we didn't do it. And if I have to wait here until you believe me, so be it. I doubt your plan is for me to die of starvation and dehydration if wherever we are requires us to be guarded. I mean, that would be a terrible waste of time and resources. So, since you're planning to keep me alive, could I please have some water? Food would be great, too."

Nothing.

"Okay fine," Maggie said, "I'll wait here until the guards

change or your leader wants to talk to us or whatever. But I promise you, I'll be much nicer about all of this than my friend. So you'd be better off explaining why you've kidnapped us before he wakes up, because after…well, ropes and bags on our heads or not, you'll be in huge trouble."

The floor in the corner creaked, and footsteps moved around the room.

"My name is Maggie, by the way," she said as the footsteps got farther away. "Maggie Trent. I'm from Virginia in the United States of America on a world called Earth where our stars are very different from yours. I fell into the Siren's Realm in a flash of green light. That's where I met my friend Bertrand Wayland. He told me there were ways to fall back out of the Siren's Realm into worlds I had never seen before. We did slip back out of the Siren's Realm, and we landed here.

"I don't know what this world is called, or why you're so afraid of us. We're only adventurers. We want to explore, not to hurt anyone. But if you try to hurt us, we will fight back. You may not believe me now, but you don't want to fight me. Because I will win, and I will hurt you if you make me. So whoever it is you're going to tell about the prisoner who won't stop talking, make sure you mention that. We managed to find a way out of the Siren's Realm. We can find a way out of this."

The footsteps moved away. The tone of them changed after a door closed. The ground where the person had gone was hollower, like a ramp. A ramp between rafts.

"Bertrand," Maggie whispered. "Bertrand Wayland, wake up."

The sound of steady breathing continued behind her.

Maggie closed her eyes, listening carefully to everything around her, waiting for some new sound to tell her more about where she might be. Far away there were sounds of people. Faint conversations she had no hope of hearing. The bindings on her arms were warm. Warmer than her skin. Maggie twisted her hand so she could feel the rope. A faint tingle hummed in her fingers as soon as she touched it. The rope was laced with magic.

"Bertrand," Maggie whispered, knowing full well he couldn't hear her, "does this seem like a good time to risk a spell from home and hope it doesn't go too badly wrong, or are we not that desperate yet? Didn't think so."

Maggie sat waiting.

"I really hate waiting. It's the worst part of bad things happening. Because there isn't anything you can do, you know? You just have to sit and wait for the world to come crashing down."

Footsteps echoed on the thin walk outside, more footsteps than had left before. Three different voices were conversing softly as they drew nearer.

"Abeyla," a man's voice said, "if you had heard her, you wouldn't doubt me. I don't think they are Enlightened."

"Then how did they get here?" a woman asked.

"She says they fell with a green flash of light," the man said.

"An Enlightened wouldn't know about the Land Beneath," a second man said.

The door creaked open, and the sounds of the footsteps stopped right in front of Maggie.

A hand grazed the top of her head as the bag was pulled away.

Maggie gulped in fresh air, blinking in the dim light before looking at the people who stood above her. Two men flanked a gray-haired woman. All three of them glared down at her.

"She isn't old enough to have been sent out by Jax," the first man said. He was young, not much older than Maggie. Too young for the lines of worry etched around his eyes. His tan face was framed by light blond hair so pale it made his bright blue eyes look even more dazzling.

"Wow," Maggie breathed.

The woman stepped forward. She was older with the same bright blue eyes as the boy and a terrifying scowl. "If Jax was assuming his spies would be killed, then it would only make sense to send someone he hadn't wasted training on."

"But if they weren't meant to survive, then why send them at all?" the second man said. He appeared nearly as old as the woman, but his hair was still solidly black. "How would they report back?"

"He could be assuming that if they don't, we've killed them," the woman said. "Then he would find us by default."

"That seems like a wasteful plan," the first man said. "They could have been killed by animals as easily as by us. It's a waste of life."

"Jax Cayde has never been concerned with the loss of life," the second man said.

"If it helps," Maggie said, "I don't actually know who this Jax dude is and have a strong resentment to being called cannon fodder."

The three of them stared at her for a moment.

"Cannon fodder?" Maggie repeated. "You don't have cannons? It means I don't like the idea of being sacrificed...basically."

"Who are you?" the woman asked.

"I already told the person who was in here." Maggie looked at the younger man, whose neck tensed. "I told you."

"Maggie," the man said. "She said her name was Maggie Trent."

"And what's your name?" Maggie asked.

"We will be the ones asking questions," the woman said, shooting a withering glare at the young man.

"Sure." Maggie shrugged. "I have nothing to hide, but I am hungry and thirsty, and my friend is probably dehydrated as hell. So how about we compromise? You give me some food and water, have someone check on my friend, and then I will happily tell you whatever you want to know."

The woman locked eyes with Maggie for a moment, appraising her.

"Very well." The woman turned to the young man. "Tammond, get the prisoners food and water. Lamil, take a look at the other one."

The blond boy, Tammond, gave a quick bow before opening the door and slipping outside. Through the dazzling sunlight, Maggie caught a glimpse of the lake outside before Abeyla closed the door.

"Bertrand Wayland," Maggie said as Lamil, the black-haired man, moved behind her. She twisted, but the bindings around her middle were too tight for her to see where he had gone. "My friend's name is Bertrand Wayland."

"I thought you weren't speaking until you were fed," the woman said.

"Call it a show of good faith," Maggie said. "But if you want information about this Jax person, you'll be disappointed, because I've never even heard of her."

"Jax Cayde is a him," the woman said. "And we all wish we had never heard his name. Perhaps you truly have been that fortunate."

The woman turned and walked out of the room, closing the door firmly behind her.

Maggie examined her prison. It was made of roughly hewn wood with bamboo braced across the walls like rungs of a ladder. A tiny window sat atop each of the walls, filtering in dim light under the thatched roof. The thick wooden pole Maggie was tied to was the only thing in the room.

Sounds of Lamil moving slowly came from behind Maggie, but she couldn't see what he was doing.

"Is he okay?" Maggie asked when Lamil had stopped moving for nearly a minute.

"He'll be fine," Lamil said.

"Thank you." Maggie sagged back against the pole. "You might not believe me, but we really didn't come here to spy on you."

"I'm not the one you should be worried about," Lamil said.

"Even spies whose masters don't care if they die aren't likely to keep a fire burning on a mountaintop in the middle of the night."

"You saw the fire," Maggie said, feeling stupid for not having figured it out sooner. "That's how you found us. How long were you following us in the woods?"

"Long enough to know that, sent by the Enlightened or not, you and this Wayland could be a danger to us all."

"In that case, thank you even more for helping him."

"I do as Abeyla commands," Lamil said before walking out the door.

A brief view of the sparkling lake outside was all Maggie saw before the door slammed shut behind him.

CHAPTER 14

"*B*ertrand," Maggie whispered. "Bertrand, wake up. Bertrand!" Maggie shouted.

"For the goodness of the Siren, Miss Trent, please do not scream at me," Bertrand muttered from his side of the pole.

"You're awake?" Maggie twisted fruitlessly, trying to see him.

"Apparently so," Bertrand said. "Have we been captured?"

"No. I just thought getting tied up in a raft hut would be a great thing to add to our adventure."

"Sarcasm is unbecoming when the person you're speaking to has a terrible headache."

"I'm sorry your head hurts." Maggie took a deep breath, willing herself not to scream just to make Bertrand's head pound. "But we've been kidnapped. They think we're spies from some guy named Jax. I told them we aren't even from this world so I don't know what they're talking about."

"And how did they take that bit of information?"

"They didn't kill us, and I made them agree to feed us before we'd answer more questions."

"Interesting," Bertrand said. Maggie could almost hear his

forehead wrinkling as he thought. "That would definitely give the impression that we have, in fact, been captured by the good guys."

"Why? 'Cause they used magic rope to tie us to a pole instead of just beating the answers out of us?"

"Because hunger is an excellent tool when trying to persuade someone to give up their secrets. It implies they really don't want to hurt us." Bertrand paused. "Or they intend to hurt us so badly hunger will no longer matter."

"You're right," Maggie said through clenched teeth. "We're definitely being held by the good guys. Is this a normal part of what you do?"

"I mean, I cannot say it hasn't happened before," Bertrand said in a tone so calm Maggie wanted nothing more than to reach around the pole and shake him, "but every world is different. I've been declared a god twice, king four times. Imprisonment is sometimes easier than being declared ruler. It's so much harder to slip away when people are trying to protect you."

"You have got to be kidding me."

"Oh no. There were statues and everything."

Before Maggie could contemplate the horror of people worshiping a statue of Bertrand Wayland, the door had swung back open.

The man called Tammond entered, carrying a bucket of water with one hand and balancing a tray of food with the other.

"Who's come in?" Bertrand asked.

"Tammond," Maggie sighed, only realizing her tone once the word was said and instantly hating herself for it. "Tammond," Maggie said again, this time hiding the fact that his dazzling blue eyes were making it hard for her to breathe, "is the one who agreed to bring us food before we answer questions."

"Ah good," Bertrand said. "Wonderful to meet you, Tammond. My name is Bertrand Wayland. As I assume Maggie has told you, whether or not the disclosure was wise we have yet to see, we are not of your world. We slipped here from a different realm. The

Siren's Realm. Perhaps your people have a legend about such a place. Pure delight and endless joy?"

"I am here to bring you food," Tammond said, "not to discuss the Land Beneath."

"The Land Beneath?" Bertrand said. "Ah, fascinating."

"Thank you for the food," Maggie said, leaning forward to look at the tray as Tammond set it on the ground. Neither of the men seemed to notice.

"And who is it you're fighting here?" Bertrand asked.

"I already told you," Maggie said. "Some guy named Jax."

"Abeyla will speak to you once you've eaten," Tammond said.

"Is Abelya in charge here?" Bertrand asked.

"Abeyla is the leader of the Wanderers."

Tammond set a carved, wooden plate of food down on Maggie's lap just within reach of her fingers.

Maggie managed to get a piece of pink fruit covered in soft spikes in her hands.

"The Wanderers," Bertrand repeated as Tammond made his way to the other side of the pole. "That's you. And Jax's people are?"

"Are you sure you don't already know?"

"Oh yes, quite sure," Bertrand said. "But I do think it wise to stay abreast of local politics when one is being held prisoner."

Bending her head as far down as she could, Maggie raised the fruit to her mouth. The skin was thick and didn't have a real taste. But the meat inside the fruit was amazing. Juicy and sweet, lighter than air in her mouth. She let out a little moan.

"Miss Trent, are you all right?" Bertrand said sharply as Tammond's head poked around her side of the pole.

"I'm fine." Maggie wiped the juice from her chin. "It's just really good food, and I was really hungry."

Tammond smiled, and for a moment Maggie forgot to breathe.

"I'm glad you enjoy it," Tammond said, lifting the bucket of water for Maggie to drink.

His fingers grazed her face, and he froze, a faint bit of pink creeping into his perfect cheeks. "You should drink, Maggie."

The water was cool and had a faint hint of earth. This water had not been created by magic.

"What's the fruit called?" Maggie asked.

"Fire fruit." Tammond moved to the other side of the pole with the bucket.

"Why fire fruit?" Maggie asked, hoping he would look back around to her side of the pole.

He did, giving Maggie an intrigued look.

"You really don't have it where you come from?"

"Nope." Maggie shook her head before taking another heavenly bite.

"The trees the fruit grow on, the leaves turn red. When they are as bright as fire, the fruit is ripe."

"Fascinating," Bertrand said in a tone that clearly said fruit was the least of his concerns, "but I think knowing who we are accused of spying for would be a much more interesting topic of discussion."

"I'll tell Abeyla you're ready for her," Tammond said, giving Maggie one last drink of water before leaving the hut.

"Well, Miss Trent, I suppose I should be grateful."

"That I convinced them to feed us instead of kill us? Yep, I'll take that gratitude." Maggie stared at the door, willing Tammond to come back in and look at her with his unnaturally bright blue eyes. It was at the same moment that she realized she was willing her sexy captor to come back that self-loathing set in and Bertrand spoke.

"No, I doubt they would have killed us. Having brought us all the way here, they would have wanted to speak to us both before resorting to murder. I am speaking of your affinity for the blond boy. I must admit when deciding to allow you to travel with me, I was concerned you might decide you had feelings for me, and I'm afraid that would be impossible."

"What?" Maggie coughed through her mouthful of thick, seedy bread.

"I'm not one to be tied down, Miss Trent. Not to a place, nor to a person. Adding to that the fact you are several centuries younger than me in experience if not in appearance, I hope you can see how impossible an arrangement that would become. And I am glad you moved on so quickly."

"You're right," Maggie said. "I'm really good at moving on."

"I'm so glad," Bertrand said. "But do be careful not to become too attached to the locals. It becomes difficult upon departure, and you can never be too sure what their local laws of modesty might be."

"Girls trying to marry you in all the realms, huh?"

"You haven't any idea, Miss Trent. I am so glad I don't have to worry about that with you."

"Happy to help."

They sat in silence. The longer Maggie listened, the farther away some of the sounds seemed to be. Voices that had shouted to each other earlier were now barely loud enough for her to hear.

Footsteps came up the thin ramp, and Abeyla murmured to someone.

Lamil was the first in the door, then Abeyla. Maggie's heart sank when Tammond didn't reappear. She rolled her eyes at her own stupidity as Abeyla began to speak.

"You've been fed. Now tell us what Jax is planning."

"Ah, you must be Abeyla," Bertrand said pleasantly, "the woman in charge. I am thrilled you came to question us yourself."

Abeyla moved to the side of the pole so she could see both Bertrand and Maggie at the same time.

"You know my name?" she asked, her eyes narrowed.

"Well, the nice blond boy, Tammond, said Abeyla was in

charge, and I assume that is you," Bertrand said. "It really is an honor to be questioned by the leader of a group. Things tend to stay so much more reasonable."

"If you would like me to remain reasonable," Abeyla said in a low and dangerous tone, "then tell me what Jax is planning."

"We don't know," Maggie said. "Sincerely, we don't."

"Even if you are not one of the Enlightened—" Abeyla began.

"So, that's what his people are called," Bertrand cut across.

"Everyone in Malina knows Jax Cayde is the Master of the Enlightened," Lamil said.

"And here we have found the answer," Bertrand said. "We are not from Malina. We are from another world far from here."

"The Siren's Realm." Abeyla glared at Maggie.

"Yes, Ma'am. Tammond said you call it the Land Beneath."

"It seems Tammond said a lot of things." Abeyla's face was set so tightly, Maggie couldn't tell if she was starting to believe them or not. "What is this world you come from called?"

"The planet?" Maggie said. "Earth."

"What land?"

Maggie swallowed the urge to say Disney as Bertrand answered, "It was the British Colonies when I left, but Ms. Trent came to the Siren's Realm quite a bit after my time."

"The United States of America," Maggie said, an unexpected pang hitting her chest. "I was born in Virginia. My family was of the Virginia Clan, but I grew up farther north at the Academy. It's a school. Well, prison-slash-school. It's where they put kids with magic who don't have anywhere else to go. That was in Delaware. But I guess you don't know where that is, so I don't suppose it matters."

Abeyla knelt down, her face not a foot away from Maggie's, and stared directly into her eyes. "Why did no one want you? How did you get sent to this Academy?"

"I lost my family." Maggie pushed the words past the lump in her throat. "There's always been disputes about who should be in charge of the Virginia Clan. My family had a blood feud with another family, so there was always fighting.

"My father wanted control of the entire Clan. He attacked the people who were in charge, but the others from the feud, the ones who had always hated us, they joined with the people my father was fighting. My mother sent me to the Academy right after the attack. Within five days of my getting sent away, my whole family was dead. And who wants to take care of a kid from the wrong side of a blood feud?"

Maggie bit her lips together. The metallic taste of blood flooded her mouth, ridding her of the unbearable urge to cry.

"I'm so sorry, Miss Trent," Bertrand said from the other side of the pole.

"Don't be," Maggie said. "People die all the time. Mine just died all at once."

"I didn't know being a witch in our world had stolen so much from you. I can understand why you wanted no part of magic in the Siren's Realm."

"I don't think that worked out so well," Maggie said.

"That has yet to be seen," Bertrand said.

"And the decision seems to lie with me," Abeyla said. "A lost orphan wound up on the Broken Lake—it has happened before, but what about you?" Abeyla narrowed her eyes at Bertrand.

Maggie wished she could see Bertrand's face as Abeyla stared him down.

"What is your story?"

"I lived in a land where magic was forbidden and we were all meant to live like humans. With no joy or laughter, suppressing our magic until we died of awful mundanity. I refused to live my life in breathless boredom, so I left. I found the Siren's Realm and have been living there quite happily ever since, with the occasional exploration of other lands, of course."

Maggie couldn't shake the feeling there was more to the story than Bertrand let on, and Abeyla seemed to agree.

"A man who runs from his world in search of pleasure?" Abeyla stood. "Even Jax Cayde wouldn't want you."

"I take it I've proven my point?" Bertrand asked. "That we are not, in fact, spies or enemies, only travelers?"

Abeyla looked at Lamil for a moment. He gave a small nod.

"I believe you," Abeyla said, "because if Jax had spies coming for us, the simplest lie for you to tell would have been that you had come here to train with the Wanderers. Jax would have found such an elaborate lie distasteful. And I'm sure even Jax's most dispensable spies wouldn't dare do something to displease him."

"Even to save their lives?" Maggie asked. "Jax sounds like a real asshole."

"A lovely description, Miss Trent."

"Jax is a terrible man," Abeyla said, "and I am afraid you might be in more danger here as travelers than as captured spies. If Jax comes, he will not care if you are a Wanderer or not. He will slaughter every living thing in the Wandering Place."

"Great." Maggie leaned her head against the pole. "Can we get untied? That way we won't die strapped to a pole."

Bertrand gave a low laugh.

"Of course." Abeyla raised her hand slowly through the air, and the ropes lifted away as if they had never been tied at all. "But I am afraid you will have to stay with us until morning. You are far from where we took you, and night is nearly here. You could never find your way through the maze alone, and I won't risk my people escorting you in the dark."

Lamil nodded. "A wise choice."

"You will be our guests until morning, then I offer you transport back to where we found you. I suggest you take it. We have not seen Jax or the Enlightened on the Broken Lake yet, but the waters are too vast for us to see all. And I assure you, Jax is coming."

Maggie's heart raced at the finality of Abeyla's words. "Thank you for your hospitality."

"Tonight we shall celebrate the travelers from the Land Beneath." Abeyla turned toward the door. "Every moment that can be celebrated must be cherished." She walked out of the room. Lamil followed her. This time, they did not shut the door behind them.

CHAPTER 15

"The Land Beneath," Maggie said, more to push Abeyla's parting words from her mind than anything else. "It sounds like we crawled up from Hell, doesn't it?"

"It wouldn't be wise to make the Siren's Realm sound too appealing." Bertrand stood up and peered out the door. "I've always suspected that is why there are so many from our world in the Siren's Realm—the stories sound so forbidden and enticing. I don't know how anyone resists."

"She also likes to drag people in, remember?" Maggie got stiffly to her feet, rubbing the sore places on her arms where the ropes had bound her.

Looking through the door, Maggie couldn't have said how far from where they had been they currently were, only that they were someplace different.

Surrounding them were high walls of sheer rock, which came down to the lake with no beach to keep the water from lapping gently at the cliffs. Out in front was a channel that curved slowly until it blocked the view of whatever lay beyond. The sky had turned a dusky blue, and soon, even the nearby cliffs would disappear into the darkness.

"I think it's time for a bit of exploring, Miss Trent." Bertrand stepped out the door and onto the ramp.

Maggie nodded before following. Even knowing Bertrand couldn't see her, the silent affirmation that she was choosing to explore and not being dragged into the darkening night was comforting.

The ramp—well, walkway really—was made out of thin bamboo tied together with the same brownish-green rope that had bound them to the pole. The gentle sway of the water beneath was just enough that Maggie could feel herself move.

Bertrand was already ten feet down the walkway, striding forward with confidence Maggie was unsure she could match. Four steps out onto the ramp, she looked to her left and gasped.

She stood, staring for a moment, trying to force her brain to register what it was she was seeing.

Houses.

A hundred houses floating on platforms made of the same bamboo planks she was standing on. Walkways led from one house to another, wrapping around the sides, cutting across open water, looping to go over the roofs of the houses.

And people everywhere. Sitting on docks outside their front doors, paddling their boats in for the night. A group of children were swimming in the water with an elderly man keeping watch from the side. A little boy not more than three splashed the old man, who pretended to try and dodge the deluge of water, laughing all the while.

In the center of the houses was a structure larger than the rest and a full story taller. The thatched roof seemed to have been peeled away and lay against the sides of the building. Through the gaps between the houses, more people could be seen, surrounding the large building. Young people, around Maggie's age, but they weren't laughing like the children.

Each of them had a look Maggie knew very well. The look of someone who was preparing to fight and knew that a fight might mean saying goodbye to everything they held dear. Even their own lives.

"We should go there." Maggie jogged on the walkway to catch Bertrand, hating the feeling of the ground bobbing under her feet.

Bertrand didn't even look where she was pointing. "Of course we're going to the center of it all, that's why we're here. The center of the wheel might not be where adventure lies, but it is where one can best see what trouble there is to get into."

"But didn't you hear Abeyla?" Maggie whispered, keeping as close to Bertrand as the narrow walkway would allow. "These people are about to be attacked by a very bad man. This isn't an adventure, it's a battlefield…battlelake…you know what I mean."

"Adventure often comes in the midst of battle, Miss Trent." Bertrand glanced at her with a gleam in his eyes. "Why do you think there are so many heroes who carry swords?"

"But this isn't an adventure for them. It's their lives." Maggie grabbed Bertrand's arm, forcing him to stop mid-step.

Slowly, he looked down at her fingers clasped around his arm. Without a word, he peeled her fingers away and placed her hand back at her side.

"My dear Miss Trent, I think we must come to an agreement." Bertrand's tone was so patronizing Maggie wanted nothing more than to shove him into the water and see if he ended up back in the Land Beneath. "We both agree we are here to gain a little magic and have a wondrous adventure if this land will allow it. I believe we are both individuals with enough conscience not to want any harm to befall the good people who call this floating village their home.

"But, and this is a very important *but*, Miss Trent, we do not know this world. We do not know the history of their fight with Jax Cayde. They might very well have been in the wrong and are now criminals forced into hiding for doing unspeakable things."

"But you said—"

"People change." Bertrand held up a hand to silence her. "I hope that will be one of the first lessons you learn, Miss Trent. Hopefully for the good, but some inevitably for the bad, people change. We cannot help people when we don't know whom we are helping. I will not hurt people if there is a chance they might be innocent. We are here to learn and to have an adventure. Not to save people who have embroiled themselves in a war we know nothing about."

He paused, staring so intently at Maggie, it took all her willpower not to look away.

"You're right," she said finally. "Maybe Jax is a real live Robin Hood and the Enlightened are his Merry Men. But then what are we supposed to do?"

"We go to that big building, see what there is to see, learn what we can learn, and hope adventure presents itself."

"But what if these really are the good guys?" Maggie asked. "What if our adventure is helping them survive whatever Jax is sending after them?"

"Then what an adventure it shall be."

CHAPTER 16

*S*tares followed them as they made their way through the town. Children were pulled out of their path by adults, and whispers seemed to move faster than the wind.

They had started moving in the direction of the large building, but the ramps didn't make sense.

Some houses were attached by the ramps to the ones catty-corner to them, but not the ones next door. A high ramp, held aloft by thick staffs of bamboo, looked like it should lead them directly to the roofless building. The thing shook so badly as they crossed its narrow slats, Maggie wasn't sure it was actually meant for people to stand on.

Her nails biting into her palms, she took deep breaths, telling herself this would be the last walkway and then they would be at the big building. But when they reached the ground level, they were on another platform ten feet of open water from where they wanted to be.

"I say we swim." Maggie shrugged. "It's not too cold to get wet."

Maggie moved to sit on the edge of the dock, hoping the

water here wouldn't be any colder than the part of the lake she had landed in.

"Maggie!" a voice called from across the water. She pitched forward, swinging her arms wildly to catch her balance.

A strong arm wrapped around her middle and yanked her back, landing her right on her butt.

"Careful, Miss Trent," Bertrand said over her muttered, "Ow."

"Are you all right?" a voice called from across the water.

Tammond. Beautiful Tammond, his hair glowing even in the setting sun, was ten feet away from her, looking terribly concerned.

"Fine!" Maggie said, adding in a whisper, "I'm just going to jump in and drown myself now."

Tammond stood in front of the large building. The people around him stared at Maggie, too. Heat crept into her face as she blushed.

"We got a little turned around trying to find a way there." She pointed at the big building, not knowing its name.

A girl with bright red hair leaned in toward Tammond as she giggled.

"The paths can be complicated." Tammond smiled. "Wait there. I'll come and get you."

"Great!" Maggie's voice squeaked as she spoke. "Thanks."

Tammond cut through the crowd and out of sight.

"Miss Trent," Bertrand said, taking her by the elbow and helping her to her feet, "I think it would be best for us to explore separately this evening as there is so little time to discover if there is an adventure here for us. In fact, we only have one night. One brief night, Miss Trent. If you need me please do come and find me."

"Thanks," Maggie said. "Not sure how I'd do that, but sure."

"And remember, Miss Trent, your virtue is your own, but I do hope you'll protect it."

"I—wha—"

"Maggie." Tammond rounded the corner in the opposite direction of the large building. He beamed at her. Like the sun. Her own personal blond-haired, blue-eyed, muscular sun. "I'm glad to see they've decided you aren't here to betray us."

"Yeah," Maggie said breathlessly. "Not evil traitors makes things good."

"How eloquent, Miss Trent," Bertrand said.

"Are you trying to get to the Fireside?" Tammond asked, not looking away from Maggie.

"Is that the big one?" She pointed stupidly across the water, silently cursing her finger for doing something so mundane as pointing.

"It is, and I would be honored to escort you there."

Maggie blushed and followed as Tammond led them back the way he'd come.

"Is that your primary gathering place?" Bertrand asked, breaking the glorious silence Tammond had left in his wake.

"It is our library, our school, our meeting place, and where we gather in the evenings when the village must go dark. It's where the children ride when we travel."

"A simple *yes* truly would have sufficed, but I appreciate your thoroughness."

"What do you mean *travel*?" Maggie asked as Tammond led them down one dock barely wide enough to walk on and onto another that cut through the center of a shop filled with tools.

"You have much to learn, Maggie." Tammond looked over his shoulder with a charming smile. "The Wanderers' home may be small, but it is a place filled with wonder."

They walked across loosely-tied bamboo that sat barely above the water.

Tammond reached back and took Maggie's hand, steadying her as the bamboo swayed.

A thrill shot up Maggie's arm and filled her chest with a warm and brilliant buzzing. "Thank you," she murmured as her cheeks flushed.

"Here we are." Tammond swept an arm through the air. "Welcome to the Fireside."

It was larger than it had looked from far away—three stories high and made of thicker wood than the other buildings in the village. Up close, Maggie could see ropes tied to the roof, which had been peeled away. Wide doors opened out onto a walkway broad enough to allow people to stand five across.

"Impressive." Bertrand examined the peeled-away roof. "Why the moveable covering?"

"To let the sun in during the day for the school children. We tip them up to cover the firelight at night. For rain and moving, we shut the roof tight. We can't afford to have extra rooms, and this is the simplest way to ensure we can use the Fireside for whatever we need."

"Awesome!" Maggie said, her stomach sagging as Tammond looked at her confusedly.

"Great." Maggie corrected. "It's a really great idea. Having one room that does lots of stuff. Like classes and fires…"

"May we see inside?" Bertrand asked.

For once, Maggie was relieved Bertrand was talking.

"Please." Tammond bowed then led them through the crowd.

People gawked as Maggie and Bertrand passed.

It was strange. There were people near Abeyla's age and people near Tammond's age, but there didn't seem to be anyone in the middle. As though for twenty years no one had joined their village.

Before Maggie could begin to come up with a reason why there were no thirty-year-olds, they had entered the Fireside, and she forgot to think.

The four walls were lined with books and shelves reaching

from the floor to the eaves right below where the ceiling would have been. Tables with long benches sat along the walls, waiting patiently for students to take their seats. But the fire was what drew Maggie forward. In the center of the room was a metal disk twelve feet wide, holding a swath of low-lying flames, which danced hypnotically, casting the shelves of books in their warm glow.

"Wow," Maggie whispered. "This is not like school back home."

"Not like school anywhere in Malina," Tammond said. "It was never really meant to be this way. The Wanderers were never meant to live all packed together like this. But this is how we've survived. And for the younglings, it's home."

Twin boys around ten-years-old entered the Fireside, carrying trays of food. Both looked terrified, and after a silent battle, one inched forward and spoke so softly to Tammond, Maggie could barely hear from three feet away.

"Abeyla told us to bring food to the spies." The boy's voice wavered as he spoke.

"They aren't spies," Tammond said kindly. "They are only travelers."

"But they're strangers," the other twin squeaked, looking terrified at his own boldness.

"Child," Bertrand said, bending down to look straight into the boy's eyes, "strangers can often be the best sorts of people. You see all those people?" Bertrand pointed to the Wanderers peering in through the doors. "I assume you've known them your whole life."

Both boys nodded.

"You know their stories, you know their ways. But there is the rest of the world to greet. Many, many worlds to know. If you are terrified of anything you have never seen before, how are you to learn about any of it?

"The secret isn't to be afraid of strangers. It's to love the strangeness. Love the challenges it brings. Once you do that, you'll see the dangers that are real. And how much safer will you be if you spend your time fighting those who mean to bring harm rather than those whom you simply do not know?"

"That was actually really good," Maggie said.

"I am quite aware of my aptitude in dealing with children, Miss Trent."

One of the twins passed his tray smilingly to Bertrand while the second shoved his in Maggie's direction, not even bothering to look away from Bertrand as he did it.

"Children are the ones who will tell the most about what's happening in a place," Bertrand said. "They've been too busy learning to walk and speak to have perfected lying. I really should have found a way to bring you a book to write everything I say in, shouldn't I? I am teaching you invaluable things every minute, and I sincerely doubt you are remembering all of it."

"Thanks?" Maggie followed Bertrand to a table. He sat on one side and Tammond on the other.

"If you don't mind," Bertrand said, "I would love to hear more about Jax. Anyone who can be a threat to a group in such a remote location must be either very smart, or very evil."

Maggie stood looking at the two vacant seats left at the table. If she sat next to Tammond, she could be near him while she ate. But if she sat next to Bertrand, she could look at Tammond while she ate.

"Jax Cayde is a terrible combination of both," Tammond said, his voice lower than before, as though he had aged ten years in saying that short sentence.

If she sat across from Tammond, he would watch her eat. She sat down next to him as he began to speak.

"It all began—"

"I do love a good origin of strife tale," Bertrand said, not touching his food as he leaned forward, intently listening to Tammond.

"It all began," Tammond said again, "long before I was born. In some ways, even before my mother was born. Magic has always been a part of our blood in Malina. The same as has the water and the wind. Some have more magic than others, but the power has always been there, since the first stories of the river carrying our land forward. Magic has always been taught to all. It was a right of birth.

"The Wanderers were the teachers. Those most skilled would be trained at the University. When they had finished their studies, they would go out into Malina, stopping in villages and passing on what they had learned." Tammond dug his fingers into his beautiful blond hair. "It may not seem like the best way to people who have seen the Land Beneath."

"It does seem like there are rather large gaps for students to fall through if teachers are simply wandering through towns, teaching what they like." Bertrand tented his fingers under his chin in his now-familiar thinking gesture.

"Every summer, all the Wanderers would travel back to the University. The greatest among them would teach classes. Maps were drawn up, deciding who would go where and what they would teach," Tammond said. "It was planned to the last detail. All to be sure every person would have the opportunity to learn."

Bertrand nodded, Maggie stared, and Tammond continued.

"Thirty years ago, Jax Cayde took up the position as head of the University. He had been one of the greatest Wanderers. Never afraid to climb high into the mountains if there was one person living in the snow who wanted to learn. Everyone was thrilled, thinking Jax would bring a new age of enlightenment to Malina." Tammond paused, studying his hands, which were gripped tightly together on the table. "It began slowly at first. Not allocating the senior Wanderers to poor towns. Then not sending them as often.

"In his fifth year, he decided at the summer meet not to send any Wanderers at all. Teachers protested. Who were they to decide who should be able to learn the ways of magic? But Jax was persuasive. He told them the Wanderers were the most valuable resource in Malina and their lives couldn't be risked traveling to remote areas. Children should be brought to learn at the University. Some Wanderers refused to obey, and Jax told them to do as they pleased, but they would receive no help from the University. Over the next year, those Wanderers vanished. Some killed by villagers, others disappearing in the wild. All of it seemed to confirm what Jax had told them. No one suspected he might be behind it."

"Jax killed his own people?" Maggie asked, the rich orange pudding she had been eating suddenly tasting foul.

"He did," Tammond said. "But it took people a long time to see what was happening. Jax started by offering for all children to come to the University to study. But the cost of sending a child far from home and losing their labor was too much for most families to consider. The teachers tried to find ways to help, to make it easier for children to make the journey, offering to collect them themselves. But Jax wouldn't allow it. And when a few poor children finally managed to make it to the gates of the University, Jax turned them away, calling them unworthy of the great legacy of magic.

"The Wanderers revolted, declaring magic a right of all in Malina. Jax gave a speech under the painted window in the great library. He told them magic was meant for greater things than to ease the tilling of fields, and as long as they allowed magic to remain common, none would ever grow to reach his full potential. Magic was not meant to serve Malina, but to rule it. He showed the Wanderers magic like they had never witnessed before."

"And the Wanderers believed him," Bertrand said darkly.

"But how?" Maggie asked. "If it was going against everything they believed in?"

"You would be amazed the insanity one impassioned speaker

can turn a reasonable crowd toward," Bertrand said. "But Jax didn't convince them all?"

Tammond shook his head. "Of the four-hundred Wanderers, more than sixty left the University that night, determined to strike out on their own and teach all who wished to learn."

"Only sixty?" Maggie asked, her stomach sinking even further into that terrible sick feeling.

"A powerful man is hard to disbelieve, Miss Trent."

"The sixty organized and began teaching," Tammond continued, "always traveling in pairs now, recruiting new teachers whenever they could. Some expected Jax to make them all disappear as he had with the others who had gone against his wishes. But this time he worked through lies, telling the common folk the Wanderers were dangerous. That they were spreading falsehoods and teaching magic too perilous to be used. He said the Wanderers were thieves, stealing from the people they pretended to help. Making children who showed the potential to be greater than them disappear in the night."

"Did people believe him?" Maggie asked.

"Some, but the Wanderers pushed on. Their duty was to teach, and they were determined to fulfill their promise to the people of Malina."

"Whether the people were grateful for it or not." An angry knowing filled Bertrand's voice.

"For three years, the Wanderers taught, fighting to regain the people's trust. Gaining new members whenever they could. I think that's when Jax realized he wasn't going to be able to make them quietly disappear. He had been building his strength at the University. Demanding to be called *Master*"—Tammond said the word with disgust—"by all who studied under him. Giving the title of *Enlightened* to his followers. The Wanderers knew the Enlightened were strong and held no love for them, but no one thought they would attack. Magic being used in war was not a thing ever seen in Malina. Magic is a gift to be treasured, not abused for the terrible purpose of pain and death."

"If only more thought like you," Bertrand said.

"So they attacked and then what?" Maggie asked, wanting the story to be over as quickly as possible. Not because she didn't want to hear, but because the pain of it beat unbearably in her chest.

"The first attack came in the night during the summer meet," Tammond said. A chill swept through the room as though the night wind knew well the horror of which Tammond spoke. "They came in quietly, aiming to kill everyone without a fight. Maybe they had hoped the people wouldn't notice all the Wanderers were gone. But Jax had underestimated our numbers. A fight broke out, and most of the Wanderers managed to escape.

"Word of the attack brought more supporters to the Wanderers as people began to see Jax for the monster he was. They fought and fought. Innocent people were killed. Marcum, the leader of the Wanderers, didn't want any more unnecessary blood spilled. So he led Jax's army here to the Broken Lake for the final battle. Jax brought everyone he had from the University who could fight. Hundreds of his men came through the water to join the battle, with Jax Cayde himself at the helm."

Maggie pictured a man riding a wave of fire, power crackling at his fingertips as he shouted deadly curses into the night.

"It was too much," Tammond said, grief filling his voice for the first time. "Jax slaughtered the Wanderers. He left the lake glowing red with blood."

"I'm so sorry," Maggie murmured at the same time Bertrand said, "But then how did you end up here?"

"Twelve of the wounded managed to hide in the woods. Weak and beaten, they decided to stay here. They built their homes on rafts so they could move throughout the Broken Lake, finding new places to hide." Tammond smiled sadly. "But some were determined to find them.

"Family members who refused to believe those who they loved had been lost. Even if the ones they loved hadn't survived, when they saw what Abeyla had built here, away from Jax, they stayed. Some who wanted to learn from the fabled battle came. They stayed. Children were born, and our home was made."

"And no one who wanted to hurt you ever found you?" Bertrand asked.

"A few who couldn't be trusted have found their way through the maze to us."

"What did you do with them?" Maggie wondered how many others had been tied up in the little cabin.

"If they were confused or lost and meant us no harm, we pulled all memories of the lake from their minds and moved them to the other side of the mountain. If they were Enlightened, we took them far away and killed them."

Maggie swallowed. "Good thing we aren't Enlightened."

"Very good." Tammond turned his bright blue eyes to meet Maggie's, and for the second time, she forgot how to breathe.

"But why do you think Jax is coming now?" Bertrand asked. "You all seem to believe his invasion is imminent."

"Over the past few years—"

Maggie looked toward the sound of Abeyla's voice. As Abeyla approached the table, everyone she passed bowed their heads. Maggie hadn't noticed how many people were listening to Tammond speak.

"—we've been sending Wanderers back out to teach." Abeyla raised a hand before Maggie could even begin to ask a question. "We are meant to be teachers. What is the point in training a new generation if the knowledge never leaves these waters? It is our purpose, and the longer we hide here and do nothing, the stronger Jax Cayde's hold on Malina becomes."

"And he's found out you are once again trying to educate the masses?" Bertrand asked.

"He captured two of our Wanderers," Abeyla said. "They were

good people. But under Jax's torture, most would break in time. Our friends in the world have told us Jax is preparing the Enlightened. He's stopped teaching them normal magic. He now only teaches them to fight."

"So Jax finds out his old enemies have been prospering, hidden safely out of sight, and he decides it's time to come looking for you," Bertrand said.

"And to bring an army," Maggie added.

"Precisely," Tammond said.

"We don't know when Jax is coming," Abeyla said, "but we do know he has left the University with three hundred men and disappeared into the wild. There would be no reason for him to travel in the shadows unless he was coming for us."

"Then you should leave the lake," Maggie said. "Go somewhere he can't find you."

"If Jax can find us here," Tammond said, "there is nowhere in Malina he won't follow us. We move the village to many secret places on the lake. Even the people he captured wouldn't be able to tell him where in the maze to find us. So we keep moving and hope he doesn't catch up."

"And when he does?" Bertrand asked.

Maggie didn't miss the *when*.

"We fight," Abeyla said without a hint of fear in her voice. "He may be strong, but we are much stronger than the first time we met. He will be fighting on our waters. We may win."

"But what about the kids?" Maggie asked. "All the little kids. Where are they going to go?"

"There is a place for them to hide," Abeyla said. "A place where Jax will not follow them."

"Then why can't you all go hide there?" Maggie asked. "Why fight at all? Why not go to The Siren's Realm or the Land Beneath or whatever you want to call it?"

"Miss Trent," Bertrand said gently, "that battle you were taken from, when the Siren pulled you away. Would you have left your friends to fight without you if you had been given a choice?"

A cold fist closed around Maggie's heart. "No. No, I wouldn't."

"And would your friends have abandoned their cause to run away and leave their world a worse place without them to defend it?"

"Never."

"Then you cannot ask the Wanderers to run," Bertrand said so softly the bystanders a few feet from their table wouldn't be able to hear. "We are new to this world. Their war is just a story by firelight to us, but to them it is the truth they breathe. This is the world that gave them life. You cannot ask them to leave it to a man like Jax Cayde."

"I'm glad to know some truths hold fast even outside our land," Abeyla said.

"Some truths remain in every world I have seen." Bertrand bowed. "Abeyla, I will not try and persuade you to give up your fight. The spreading of knowledge is a worthy cause. I understand you wish for us to leave in the morning, and I respect your decision. But I have fought in many battles against many foes. Perhaps I can be of some assistance. If in no other way than giving advice before I leave. It seems to me the Wanderers have been a people of peace. There may be holes in the safety of your village you have not found."

Abeyla considered him for a moment. The flickering of the fire cast shadows into the gentle lines of her face, making her look twice her age. "I would be a fool to turn down help. When you're ready."

"Now is the perfect time." Bertrand stood. "There is never time to waste when battle nips at your heels." Bertrand looked to Maggie. "Stay here, try not to get hurt, and if battle does come, do remember not to use any magic here that might get you killed."

"Right." Maggie nodded, not sure if she should feel grateful for Bertrand's concern or punch him in the face for thinking she couldn't take care of herself.

"Don't worry," Tammond said, "I will make sure Maggie comes to no harm."

"Brilliant," Bertrand said dryly before following Abeyla out of the Fireside and into the night.

CHAPTER 17

*M*aggie sat at the table, not sure where to look. If she looked at Tammond, she might drool. If she looked at the people around her staring at her, she might run. So instead she looked at the books lining the walls.

"How did they all get here?" Maggie pointed to the shelves upon shelves of books.

"We brought them here," the girl with the red hair from outside said as though Maggie didn't understand things could be carried.

"The first Wanderers who came to the lake brought their books with them," Tammond said after glaring at the girl with the red hair, who huffed and stalked away. "Others who came to join brought more. A few times, we've sent people out to find new books, ones that were necessary to learn. All of the books we have in the village reside in this room."

"But," Maggie said, hoping her words wouldn't offend, "wouldn't it be safer not to keep all your written knowledge next to a giant fire?"

Sniggers floated around the crowd.

"The Fireside is safe." Tammond took Maggie's hand in his

and led her toward the fire. Heat rushed to her face, and she hoped the warmth of the flames would be a good enough excuse for the redness creeping into her cheeks.

Placing his palm on the back of Maggie's hand, Tammond moved her fingers toward the flames. Fear told her she would be burned, but Tammond stood close behind her, his steady heart-beat thrumming into her back. A foot before her hand reached the flames, her palm touched something soft—an invisible barrier as cool as the water of the lake, even as the heat of the fire passed through it to warm the room.

"Wow," Maggie breathed.

"The fire is safe for all of us," Tammond said.

Maggie turned to face him. His chest pressed into hers. He gazed down into her eyes.

"It's…beautiful."

Tammond smiled. "I have seen many beautiful things, but I had never thought to count the Fireside among them."

Giggles came from behind Tammond's broad shoulders. The group in the Fireside had grown. Teenagers and adults alike stared at Tammond and Maggie by the fire.

"Perhaps we should go." Tammond kept his voice low. "There are other beautiful things to see in our village."

Maggie nodded, not trusting herself to speak, and followed Tammond out into the dark.

The night had grown cool with the breeze across the lake. The surface of the water reflected the stars, and the moon gave depth to the mountains around them, casting their high peaks into silhouette. The roof of the Fireside had been raised up to block the light of the flames within. In the village no lights shone. No lamps peered through windows. No cooking fires crackled.

"Is everyone asleep?" Maggie whispered.

"Some are," Tammond said. "The rest are either at the Fireside or enjoying the darkness."

A thrill shot through Maggie's stomach as she wondered what *enjoying the darkness* might mean.

"Don't worry," Tammond said, taking Maggie's hand in his, "the stars and the moon will give us enough light to make our way through the village."

"I'm not worried." Maggie pulled her gaze from Tammond to watch where she was stepping. "It's just sad that you all have to hide in the dark."

"Only at night." Tammond gave Maggie a shining smile. "And to be free from the Enlightened, to be able to teach and learn, it's worth hiding our fires at night."

"Did you ever go out to teach?" Maggie asked.

He had led her away from the Fireside to a walkway that skirted the very edge of the village. This walkway was longer and more solid than the others she had seen.

"No," Tammond said, a hint of bitterness creeping into his voice. "You aren't to teach until you've reached twenty-one years. They won't let me leave the lake until next year."

"I'm sorry."

"It is as it must be. Besides, my mother has told me many times I am too rebellious to be trusted in the outside world. I would be too likely to fight someone who opposed free teaching, and then where would we all be?"

"Your mother gets to decide if you get to go?"

"If your mother is Abeyla."

"Wait." Maggie tugged on Tammond's hand, forcing him to stop. "Abeyla is your mom?"

"A fact the Wanderers will never let me forget." Tammond grimaced. "It's not easy being the son of your people's savior."

Maggie opened her mouth to say something comforting and brilliant, but, "No, I guess it wouldn't be," was all that came out.

The long path ended, and he led her up onto a high ramp. This one didn't sway as they climbed bamboo slats ten feet above the row of houses they had walked past.

"Why the ramps?" Maggie asked, wishing there was a bit more light to see where she was stepping and trying not to picture herself falling through someone's roof and into their bedroom.

"To see above the village, and hold the village steady when we travel." Tammond sat on the ramp, drawing Maggie down to sit with him.

"How does the village travel?" Maggie asked. Tammond's arm brushed against hers, and her stomach purred.

"If you stay a little longer, perhaps you'll see."

"Hmm." Maggie didn't trust herself to say words.

"It must seem small here to you," Tammond said, gazing at Maggie as though wanting to drink in every bit of her, "between your home and the Land Beneath."

Maggie clamped a hand over her mouth, trying hard not to laugh.

Tammond raised an eyebrow and smiled at her.

"I—" Maggie began, shoving aside the instinct that told her not to talk about anything that mattered, "I mostly grew up in a place about this size, but without the lake and mountains."

"At the Academy." Tammond nodded, taking Maggie's hand in his. "The school cared for you?"

The warmth of his touch made Maggie shiver. The cool night air suddenly seemed too cold to bear. Tammond wrapped an arm around her, pulling her close to his side.

"They didn't." Maggie searched for the words that would cause the least sympathy. "They didn't really care for us. They fed us, taught us, and kept us alive, but that's about it. We weren't allowed to leave the grounds. I didn't see the outside world for twelve years. Twelve years of gray walls."

"No wonder you decided to leave for the Land Beneath."

"I didn't decide." Maggie fought the images of blood and the scent of fire even thinking of the green mist brought flooding back to her. "There is a bad man—our version of Jax, I guess. He's evil and wants to kill a whole bunch of people. Not everyone in our world has magic, and he wants the people that do to be able to control the people that don't.

"Friends—well maybe not friends, but the people who let me out of the Academy—were going to fight the bad guy, and I volunteered to go with them. It was terrible. Fighting in the woods, people dying everywhere. Our people, the bad guy's people. And blood…so much blood."

Tammond pulled her closer, leaning his cheek against the top of her head.

"Then in the middle of it all, there was this green mist, and I saw someone in it, a friend of mine. I ran forward to try and help him, but he wasn't there. There was nothing but darkness in the mist, and then I fell. That's how I ended up in the Land Beneath. I didn't choose it."

"I'm sorry."

The honest sympathy in his voice made it hard for Maggie to breathe. "Don't be. I survived."

"I'm glad you did." Tammond looked down at Maggie. His face was so close to hers. Gently, he pressed his lips to her forehead. "And I'm glad you landed in the Broken Lake as well."

"Me, too." Maggie held her breath, waiting to be kissed again, this time preferably on the lips.

"I've never met someone like you. My whole life I've lived in a beautiful place with wonderful people. Always moving. Always surviving. I never realized…" Tammond brushed the hair from Maggie's face. "Maggie Trent, you are a blazing light in the darkness."

She stared at him for one heartbeat, then another. Forgetting to breathe as her mind raced, imagining what his lips would taste like. "Stars," Maggie gasped when her lungs finally remembered they needed air.

"What?"

"Your stars are different from ours," Maggie said.

You stupid girl, you ruin everything! Every good and beautiful thing! Now he hates you!

"I suppose all worlds have stars as unique as their people." Tammond lay back on the ramp, laying his arm down beside him to make a spot for Maggie.

Okay, maybe he doesn't hate you, but don't mess it up again.

Maggie took a deep breath and lay down, resting her head on Tammond's shoulder.

"I've only been here, the Siren's Realm, and home," Maggie said. "But all the stars have been different. When I was little, my dad told me people made up constellations and stories about the stars so they could feel close to home even when they were really far away. Now I understand why. Not seeing the stars I'm used to, it makes me feel further from home than anything else."

They lay in silence for a moment. The waves gently lapped against the village, which creaked softly with each movement.

"We have stories for our stars, too." Tammond's voice was as soothing as if he were telling a bedtime story. "Maybe if you know our stories, you won't feel so lost."

"I'd like that."

"The seven bright ones," Tammond said, pointing to each of them in turn, "are the captains of the seven ships that brought the first people down the great river to Malina from a land far away where magic only lived in the dark, hidden places. Right there"— he pointed to six stars that were close together, making a diamond with the two extra stars coming out the top—"is the great ship that came before the seven and discovered Malina."

"Imagine," Maggie said, "discovering a whole new world no one has ever seen before."

"You've found a whole new world." Tammond turned to face Maggie. "Do you wish there weren't people here?"

His lips were close to Maggie's...so very close. "Ummm. I..."

His lips brushed hers. Gently, carefully, as though afraid she might push him away. Pulling herself closer, Maggie deepened the kiss. His heartbeat echoed in her chest, racing as she twined her fingers through his hair.

"Maggie," he whispered as he pulled her closer, wrapping both arms around her as though he wanted to be sure she was real.

Maggie gasped, all thoughts of stars and faraway places gone. She was here with Tammond, and nothing else mattered. His hand found her hip, tracing a line up her side through her thin shirt.

"Miss Trent," a voice came from below.

Maggie squeaked and rolled away from Tammond. Her shoulder found the edge of the ramp, and before she could stop herself, her torso was hanging out over thin air.

"Maggie!" Tammond shouted, grabbing Maggie by the ankles to keep her from falling into the water below.

"Miss Trent," Bertrand said calmly, his upside-down face level with Maggie's as he stood on the roof beneath the walkway, "I see you have had a chance to explore the finer sights of the village."

So much blood had already rushed to Maggie's head it was impossible for her to blush. "What do you want?" Maggie snapped as the bamboo cut painfully into her back.

"We need to discuss our departure plans, Miss Trent."

"Now?" Maggie widened her eyes, hoping fruitlessly that Bertrand would understand and walk away.

"Yes, right now, Miss Trent," Bertrand said, "but I think it would be better if you either came down to the roof or went back up on the walkway. It would be rude to ask Tammond to continue holding you by the ankles when our discussion does not require you to be upside-down."

"You," Maggie growled at Bertrand as Tammond pulled her back up onto the walkway and lifted her to her feet in one swift motion.

"Thanks," Maggie gasped.

Tammond caught her around the middle to keep her from falling back over again.

"My pleasure," Tammond said. "I should let you two talk. The sooner you leave, the safer you'll be."

"But—" Maggie began, but Tammond leaned down and was kissing her again. Her knees melted as she leaned into his strong chest. Tammond pulled away, kissed her on the forehead, and walked down the ramp into the darkness.

"Well," Bertrand said.

Maggie spun to find Bertrand standing two feet behind her.

"Don't do that." Maggie grasped her chest. "Do not sneak up on people."

"In general or when they are doing illicit things in the dark?"

"I don't think that's any of your—"

"Whatever you do is my business as I am personally responsible for your safety while outside the Siren's Realm."

"What?"

"I brought you here, Miss Trent, and I intend to bring you back to the Siren' Realm alive. Which brings me to my next point —our departure."

"I think we need to stay—"

"We can't leave in the morning—"

"What?" Maggie said. "You think we should stay, too?"

"Certainly, Miss Trent. I've seen their guards. The sort of magic they use is fascinating and well worth exploring. But from the stories I've been told of this Jax, they are in no way prepared to handle that sort of attack. The Wanderers study magic for magic's sake. Jax studies magic to learn how to control and destroy. I don't think any of them even truly think they can win a battle against Jax. What sort of people would we be if we abandoned our hosts to such a terrible fate?"

"Terrible people," Maggie said more emphatically than she had meant to.

"And why do you wish to stay, Miss Trent?"

"Same reasons as you," Maggie said. "We can't let Jax destroy this place. That would be very bad."

"Good." Bertrand nodded again, apparently not having noticed anything strange. "Then the best thing we can do is rest. Abeyla has informed me the village will be moving in the morning. She will wake us in a few hours to watch the preparations. Once we are in the new position, we will help the Wanderers to train and prepare the village for war."

Bertrand strode down the ramp, not bothering to look back to see if Maggie followed.

CHAPTER 18

*T*he room they were given was better than where they had been held prisoner, though nearly as small and made almost entirely of bamboo. The walls, floor, and shutters were all made of bamboo of some kind. Even the bedframe was bamboo. Luckily, the mattress was something soft. Maggie didn't want to know what she was sleeping on badly enough to think of anything beyond gratitude it wasn't bare rock.

She lay staring at the thatched roof, trying to sleep. Bertrand was already breathing in a maddeningly steady rhythm. If only Tammond were here instead of Bertrand. Kissing her, holding her.

Dammit.

Every time she closed her eyes all she could see was Tammond. Smiling. His blue eyes sparkling.

She opened her eyes and looked back up at the crisscrosses of the ceiling.

Way to make out with the guy who kidnapped you earlier today. Good for you, Maggie. Awesome choices.

But then she closed her eyes, and Tammond was pulling her

close to his big strong chest. Holding her like he would never ever let her go.

Before she knew if she had actually fallen asleep, there was a knock at the door.

Maggie leapt out of bed and dragged her fingers through her hair.

"I didn't take you for an early riser, Miss Trent," Bertrand said as he pulled on his jacket.

"I'm full of surprises." Maggie yanked open the door to find a person a third of Tammond's size.

A little girl with big brown eyes stared up at Maggie.

"Excuse me," the little girl's voice wavered with fear. "Abeyla told me to come get you. You're to watch the traveling from the Fireside with us." The girl averted her eyes and gave a half-curtsey.

"Ah, perfect," Bertrand said over Maggie's shoulder. "And what is your name, little one?"

"Mina," the little girl said barely loud enough for Maggie to hear.

"Well then, Mina," Bertrand said, "lead on please. I don't want to miss any of this."

Mina smiled and reached through the door, taking Bertrand's hand in her own and pulling him past Maggie.

"They'll start as soon as the sun touches the mountains," Mina said, her voice quiet even in her excitement. "And we can see all of it from the Fireside. When I am big, I will be a rower like my mother. Now I am too small, but I watch with the others so I can learn."

"Watching is a very good way to learn."

Even though the sky was just beginning to turn gray, the village was already bustling with people, all moving silently in patterns that suggested they had done this very thing many times before.

"Mina," Bertrand asked, his voice matching the quiet of the morning, "how often do you move the village?"

"Used to be every six days." Mina led them down a path that cut below the short eaves of a building, making Maggie and Bertrand double over to follow. "But since the grownups have been scared of the bad people coming, we move every three. The runners go to the hills every three days now, too, to tell where we're going."

"Runners?" Maggie asked, but before Mina could answer they had reached the Fireside, and she had turned around to beam at them.

"I know faster ways than the big folks." Mina planted hands on her hips, her chin tipped up with pride. "I'm a good leader."

"You did very well, Mina." Bertrand bowed.

Maggie was glad he didn't mention they got there faster because they had climbed through places too small for *big folks* to fit.

"It's almost time," Mina said, taking Bertrand's hand again. "We can watch the unwrapping and moving from the deck if you like, but we have to stay here."

"That's fine," Maggie said. "Thanks for bringing us."

Mina didn't seem to notice Maggie had spoken. She was too busy staring adoringly at Bertrand.

A whistle sounded from the front of the village. Maggie peered through the houses but couldn't see the source of the sound. A shuddering of the deck below her feet was the first sign of what the signal had meant. Mina grabbed her and pulled her away from the edge of the dock.

"Don't fall in."

Maggie opened her mouth to say she wouldn't, but the words disappeared as the high ramp nearest them started to sink toward the water. Two men were removing the heavy poles that had held the walkway high in the air as a woman pushed another pole against the building opposite her. As the walkway lowered to the water, the houses moved away from each other, unfurling into one long line.

Moving carefully across the deck, Maggie could see the other high walkway being lowered. Low walkways were being tied together to lock the houses into place with the Fireside at the center. The village was transforming from a watery maze into a barge, solid and ready for travel.

There was no shouting of orders or panicked movements. Everything was fluid. From the knots being tied to make sure the ramps were joined, to the great poles being stored.

Soon, boats were being lowered into the water on both sides of the Fireside and tied to the edges of the walk. Maggie leaned out as far as she dared to see more boats being tied all along the village. Rowers climbed into their boats as others climbed onto the roofs.

As soon as the last boatman was in place, each of the people on the roofs raised a hand, and a voice from the front of the village yelled, "Forward!" As one, the rowers began paddling.

At once, the deck surged forward, jarring Maggie and making her stumble, but with the next stroke, the only movement she could feel was the steady momentum of the village.

"Amazing."

Maggie jumped as Bertrand spoke right over her shoulder.

"An entire village moving," Bertrand said. "Without threats or fuss. Just moving on to the next place."

"No!" A man paddled up along the side of the village. "Stop please! We can't leave. We can't!"

The man leapt from his boat and up onto the Fireside walkway. "Please stop this! Abeyla! Please!" The man's face was desperate and pale. Dirt caked his hair, and scratches bled on his cheeks. "Abeyla!"

"Elson." Abeyla appeared around the corner, her voice tense. "We can't stay. You know we can't stay."

"But my wife is still out there!" the man cried. "My wife, Abeyla!"

"I know, Elson," Abeyla said, "but for the good of the village, we must move on."

"My wife was out in the jungle for the good of the village!" Elson shouted. "Searching for resources for the *good of the village*."

"Lana knew the risks," Abeyla said. "She knew the risks as we all do."

"So we leave her behind? Two days gone, and we consider her lost forever?" Tears streamed down the man's furious face.

"She can find the watchers in the hills," Abeyla said, holding her hands out as she approached Elson. "The watchers always know where we are going. Lana knows to go there. She will find her way. But we can't risk the entire village to wait for one person."

"She's my wife."

"She knows the way to the watchers," Abeyla said, taking Elson's shaking hands in hers. "She can find her way home."

"And if the Enlightened have found her in the woods?"

"Lana is a brave woman," Abeyla said. "She would never betray the Wanderers."

Elson collapsed to the ground, shaking in his tears.

Abeyla knelt beside him. "It is not an easy path we tread. The life of a Wanderer is hard and long. Lana is a brave and strong woman. She holds magic deep within her blood. She will find her way to the watchers, and they will send her home. You must believe that."

"Yes, Abeyla," the man said weakly through his tears.

As if on a silent command, a big man appeared at Abeyla's side and half-lifted Elson to his feet before leading him away down the ramp.

Abeyla watched them for a moment before turning to Bertrand. "It may seem cruel to leave one of our own behind, but the best safety we have is in staying hidden."

"Protecting the many is not an easy task," Bertrand said. "Yours is not a place in which many could stand."

"No," Abeyla said, "but sometimes leaders aren't given a choice. When everyone else is gone, you must stand up and do your best to protect whatever is left." Without another word, Abeyla walked away toward the front of the village.

Through it all, the rowers had never stopped pulling the village forward. The boat Elson had rowed up was tied to the side of the deck, clunking uselessly along as they traveled.

A shuffling and sniffling from the opening to the Fireside caught Maggie's attention. The children were huddled in the doorway, fear on their faces. Mina stood at the front of the pack, her little eyes brimming with tears.

"You all right?" Maggie asked. She had never been good with the little ones at the Academy. They cried too much and worried too much about getting home. Maggie had learned the uselessness of tears years ago.

"I hate the Enlightened." Mina rubbed her nose with her hand. "They ruin everything. They make the runners go more. And make it harder for people to get home. And when they come, they'll put all of us in the dark place to hide."

"That does sound pretty scary." Maggie sat down on the deck as Bertrand gave a warning growl of, "Miss Trent."

"But I think you're pretty brave," Maggie said, "and when you're brave, it's okay to be scared of the dark and the Enlightened. But you don't let your fear stop you. Do you like it when the village moves?"

Mina nodded. "We're almost to the rocks. The rocks are the fun part."

Mina was right. The village had almost reached the rocks that curved a path to the rest of the Broken Lake. Maggie's heart leapt into her throat. They wouldn't be able to fit through the opening. The village would hit the rocks and crumble. They would all drown before the Enlightened even had a chance to reach them.

Maggie took a breath, making sure her voice would be steady. "Why do you like going through the rocks, Mina?"

"I like the rocks because it feels like the lake is hugging the village, like it's promising to protect the Wanderers." Mina gave a wet smile and pointed up at the rocks high overhead. "See? They're so tall they almost block out the whole sky. I bet if we stayed right here, the Enlightened would never find us."

"Why do you move?" Maggie asked. "Why travel the lake?"

"Magic leaves marks," a boy at the back of the pack said, clapping his hand over his mouth in astonishment at his braveness. It took him a moment to recover before he spoke again. "When we stay in a place, we fill it with our magic. And if we stay too long, the marks start to stay, and then it's easy for people to find us. We used to be able to stay longer, but now that we know we're being watched, we have to move more often to stay safe."

"Wow," Maggie said, not letting her gaze stray to the rock outcropping that jutted out over their heads. "Sounds like a great system. What kind of magic do you do here? I've seen the fire inside. How it's protected so no one can get burned, but what kind of magic do you do that makes a mark?"

The boy's face flushed with embarrassment as he made his way to the front of the children.

"I-I can do this." The boy smiled as his feet rose a few inches into the air before he landed back on the deck with a *thud*.

The children behind him giggled, and he turned to them, whispering angrily, "I'd like to see you do better."

"That was quite impressive, young sir." Bertrand nodded.

"Oh watch what I can do!" Mina ran through the other children and returned a moment later, holding a red flower the size of her hand.

Staring at the flower with such concentration her forehead wrinkled, the flower turned from red, to purple, to a bright pink.

Soon all the children were clamoring to show what magic they could do. One girl made herself light enough to climb the wall using only two fingers on each hand. A little boy juggled tiny balls of green fire. Maggie and Bertrand laughed and applauded as one child after another did their best magic to impress the guests.

The mountains slid by, and the rowers kept pulling, moving them to unknown parts of the lake. The people on the roofs directed the rowers with arm signals, slowly turning the village where it needed to go.

The children's display ended with one boy pelting rocks at a girl who would block the pebbles before they could reach her with the wave of a hand.

Maggie and Bertrand applauded along with the other children so enthusiastically the two sparrers bowed deeply before taking their seats.

"I think we have learned a great deal about your magic." Bertrand stood and bowed to the children. "You have given us an excellent demonstration, but now if Miss Mina will show us a place, I would like to get a higher view of our travel."

"Best go fast," one of the older children said urgently, "we'll be to our new spot soon."

"Then time is of the essence," Bertrand said.

Mina took his hand and led him from the other children with a look of great importance on her face.

She led them to the backside of the Fireside and pointed at the closest house. "You can go up there, but don't go farther. We aren't supposed to leave the Fireside while we're traveling."

"I assure you we shall stray no farther," Bertrand said, going into the house and straight up a ladder in the center.

"Thanks," Maggie said to Mina before climbing the ladder, more than a little grateful Mina didn't try to follow.

The ladder led up to a trapdoor, which opened out onto the roof, giving them a view of the lake around them. They were headed toward a narrow entry between two spires. Maggie could see the shore behind the spires—a gentle slope that led from the water to the mountain miles behind.

"I am pleased, Miss Trent," Bertrand said. "I didn't think you would be so good with children, and they have provided us a fount of information by your asking one simple question."

"What fount of information?" Maggie held her breath as the fronts of the boats that dragged the village passed between the spires.

"We now know they do not have a language for their spells," Bertrand began. "We've learned they train their children from a very young age. They use no talisman. We've also learned I was unfortunately correct in my assumption that they are sadly ill-prepared to fight Jax. The oldest of their children can do basic shielding against non-magical objects only."

"But it's still a shield," Maggie said. "I'm sure the adults can do more."

"The adults hide," Bertrand said. "The children can't defend themselves. As soon as the village is settled, I will ask Abeyla to meet with her best fighters. She knows I wish to offer my help, and, given their position, even the fighters should be glad to receive it."

"Okay," Maggie said. "You help them prepare for battle, and what do I do? Please don't say hang out with the kids more."

"You seem to have formed a, shall we say, close attachment to Tammond," Bertrand said, not pausing or even seeming to notice when Maggie blushed bright red. "I will ask Abeyla if he can train you in their ways of magic. Then, when the battle comes, you will be prepared to fight."

"What about you?" Maggie asked as the village reached the inside of the cove and, with a whistle from the front of the village, rowers climbed back up onto the docks. "Won't you need to know how to fight?"

"My dear Miss Trent, I have traveled to many places and am much more adept at picking up different forms of magic than you are. I appreciate your concern, but I assure you when the time comes, I will be more than capable of assisting in the battle. Let Tammond help you. I will learn by teaching the fighters."

"Fine," Maggie said, her stomach already fluttering at the thought of spending more time with Tammond.

"But do remember, Miss Trent, though our stay with the Wanderers may have lengthened, we remain visitors in their lives."

"Yes sir," Maggie said, wondering if Tammond would be able to find a private place to teach her the ways of the Wanderers' magic.

CHAPTER 19

"The magic is already in your mind," Tammond said. He stood right behind Maggie, his breath whispering on her neck as he gently covered her eyes. "Magic runs deep in your blood as it does in ours. Feel it pulsing through you."

Maggie took a shuddering breath, trying to focus on Tammond's words instead of how close he was standing.

"Feel the magic in your hands. Find its texture, its warmth."

Maggie's hands trembled in front of her. There was warmth—she could feel it. Like she was holding her hands on either side of a candle. But it didn't feel like magic. There was nothing leaving her body, no energy being lost. Only a pale heat that didn't feel like it had much to do with her at all.

"Find the fire. Nurture it, and allow it to grow. Let its warmth surround you. Let it fill you."

But she didn't want the warmth to surround her. She wanted Tammond.

Heat like embers flew against her palms.

"Ouch." She pulled her hands away.

Giggling sounded around the Fireside. Maggie moved her

head to look toward the sound, but Tammond kept her eyes covered.

"It's all right," he said soothingly. "Just try again. Concentrate."

"Wouldn't it be easier to focus if I could see?" Maggie growled to another round of giggles. "Or if I weren't being watched by an entire village worth of kids."

"It's nice to know some grownups aren't very good at magic either," a little voice said from the corner.

"Mina, be nice," another voice squeaked.

"Now try again," Tammond said.

"Are you sure we couldn't go somewhere else?" Maggie asked, knowing it would be no easier to concentrate on magic if she were alone with Tammond.

"We'll stay here for now," Tammond said. "This is the room for learning, so what better place to start? Now concentrate."

The sun had begun to drift down toward the mountains before Maggie managed to hold the light in her hands. It had taken her hours to manage it with her eyes closed, and it wasn't much easier to form the pale light with her eyes open. The sphere didn't have much distinction. It wasn't something that could be thrown or left to hover in the air and provide light. It was only a manifestation of magic.

Maggie wanted to shout that a manifestation of magic wasn't going to do any good when Jax came, but Tammond was determined this was the way she must learn. And he stood so close, staring at her with his bright blue beautiful eyes, she couldn't bring herself to argue.

Finally, when their lesson was done, he let her sit next to the Fireside while he collected food for them. There was a dull murmur from the adults in the gathering place Maggie wouldn't have noticed if she hadn't heard it before. Something had happened. Something the children weren't supposed to know about, and something they didn't want to tell her.

Maggie stared at her hands on the table. In the warm light of the fire, they looked normal. The faint scars from fishing in the Siren's Realm couldn't be seen. There was no mark to show she held any magic. Just two pale hands against the dark wood of the table. Back home, she could have thrown the table across the room. Burned it in an instant. Torn it apart and used the pieces to fight. But here she was helpless. Barely able to cast a basic spell.

And she and Bertrand were supposed to help these people survive. Suddenly their whole plan for adventure seemed the most horribly selfish thing imaginable. They wanted adventure, but the Wanderers wanted to survive. How dare they think they could help?

Maggie had just made up her mind to find Bertrand and tell him it was time to leave when a plate of food was slid in front of her. She looked up to find Tammond smiling down at her.

"You did well today." Tammond took a seat on the bench opposite her.

"I made a bit of light." Maggie ran her hands over her face. "I'm useless. It's a waste of time for you to even be trying to teach me."

Tammond caught her hand in his. "Learning is never a waste." He looked at her palm, tracing the lines that crisscrossed her hand.

A tingle shot up Maggie's arm.

For the love of God, girl, keep it together!

"And you are doing very well. Now eat, Maggie." Tammond pushed her plate closer to her. "There is still much for you to learn. A whole library's worth, in fact."

Maggie examined the shelves of books. They were worn and had strange leather patches in places, like ancient bound books from back home. The books even had titles embossed on their spines.

The Founding of Magic in Malina, A Light Within, The Magic of Others: Tales of Magic within Animals.

"I can read the titles," Maggie said, leaving her food

untouched on her plate and moving to the bookshelf. She pulled down *The Magic of Others* and opened to the first page.

Though magic has long been known to flow through the blood of Man in Malina, it is also known that animals who share our land...

"I can read the books." Maggie ran her fingers along the words.

"Reading is a fine skill to have," Tammond said.

"But I can read your words, and I can speak to you." Maggie shook her head, trying to think of her words before she spoke them to make sure it was English that was coming out. "Back home, there are hundreds of languages people speak, and I only know one of them. How is it that I fall from the Siren's Realm into another world and I can speak and read your language?"

Tammond considered for a moment as Maggie read another line in the book.

Old fables suggest in times long ago, animals that possessed magic would align themselves with men, becoming their partners in the creation of magic.

"Magic," Tammond said finally. "The only reason I can think of is magic. The Siren's magic allowed you to come to us. Magic has allowed you to speak to us."

A tingle shook Maggie's shoulders at the idea of the Siren herself watching, twisting the words in her mind so she could understand the Wanderers. Dread dripped into her stomach, forming a layer of trepidation that lurked beneath her fear of Jax Cade.

Slowly, she placed the book back on the shelf. "I'll have to ask Bertrand. He would know better. He's been so many places."

But the next moment all concern for magic controlling the words she spoke was washed away by a scream from the shore.

CHAPTER 20

"*H*ow dare you!" the voice screamed.

Maggie ran out of the Fireside, pushing past the children crowded by the door.

On the shore not thirty feet away, two of the Wanderers stood opposite a man dressed all in black.

"How dare you come to our village and make threats." The voice belonged to a man from the Wanderers. Rage contorted his face.

"I have not come to make threats," the man in black said. "I am a messenger of Jax Cayde. We have found your watchers in the hills. There is no one left to give you our warning. We have found your home." The man turned to face the village. "I have come upon your patrol without their knowledge. You cannot fight us."

"We will fight you," the second Wanderer on the shore spat. "All of us will fight you."

The man in black turned to the woman and smiled.

Rage filled Maggie's chest. Without thinking beyond wanting to stop the man from smiling as he made threats, Maggie walked to the edge of the docks and slipped silently into the water.

The water was cool and calm.

"Maggie," Tammond hissed, but Maggie didn't wait to hear what he was saying. Taking a deep breath, she dove beneath the surface.

The water was clear enough to see her way as she swam toward the shore, aiming behind the man in black. Months spent fishing in the Siren's Realm had made holding her breath easy, and before her lungs burned from lack of air, she had reached the shore.

Peeking up above the surface, she could see the man still facing the Wanderers.

"You have been given two days to surrender," the man said, his voice loud, clear, and full of confidence that not taking Jax's terms would mean certain death for the Wanderers. "Those not guilty of crimes against the Enlightened will be reeducated and allowed to join society. Those who have fought against the Enlightened will be tried for crimes against the great people of Malina."

The eyes of the male Wanderer caught Maggie's, widening as she raised her head above the water. Maggie pressed a finger to her lips, hoping it was a universal enough sign for him to know to keep quiet.

"You—" the Wanderer began, haltingly "You! How dare you come here and threaten the Wanderers? We are the true teachers of Malina. Our ways are older than yours."

Maggie pulled herself silently onto the bank, feeling the eyes of everyone in the village on her back.

"If you were so wise, old man," the man in black spat, "perhaps you would know when your time had passed."

A spell. One quick spell and the man in black would drop to the ground unconscious. Or a flower would grow. Maggie cursed to herself, wishing any of her sparring training were useful now. But it didn't matter.

"Two days, old man. You have two days to get your people in order."

A branch lay on the ground, smaller and lighter than Maggie would have wished for but she didn't have time to look for anything else.

"When the Enlightened fight, they fight to kill," the man said. "This is the only mercy you will see from us."

Raising her arms high, Maggie sprinted toward the man, bringing the stick down on his head with an almighty *crack* before he could turn to see what the noise was. The man crumpled to the ground, a look of surprise etched on his face.

"I've never liked other people's mercy," Maggie murmured as shouts rose from the village. "It always comes at too high a cost."

"Maggie!" Tammond leapt into the water, swimming quickly to shore.

"Miss Trent," Bertrand called from his spot on the docks, "you must be careful when doing such things."

"I really don't get a *nice aim!* or anything?" Maggie said.

"Oh, your aim was excellent, Miss Trent, and I agree—stopping his incessant threats was a valid choice," Bertrand said as Tammond emerged from the water and ran toward Maggie. "I am merely urging caution."

"Well, thanks for appreciating my valid choice," Maggie said as Tammond took her face in his hands.

"Are you all right, Maggie?" Tammond searched her face for some kind of harm.

"Yeah, I'm fine." Maggie looked toward the man on the ground. "He's the one who might not be okay. Is he still alive?"

The male Wanderer who had been shouting at the man in black knelt down next to him.

"Even if he is dead, you must not blame yourself," Tammond said, taking Maggie's hand as she leaned over the body.

"I wouldn't," Maggie said. "He threatened the village, and he threatened the kids. If I broke his head, it's no more than he deserves."

"He's alive," the Wanderer declared.

"I'll try harder next time." Maggie's voice was so cold, it nearly shocked her for a moment. But the moment was brief. There was no time to cry over a hurt person who wanted to hurt you. Her family had taught her that a long time ago.

"Get him in the boat." Abeyla had arrived onshore in a tiny boat rowed by Bertrand. "We need to get him tied up in the village. He may have information."

Tammond nodded and dragged the Enlightened to the boat, letting his head hit the rocks on the ground along the way.

"Sorry if I bonked him too hard," Maggie said as Abeyla turned her stern gaze to her.

"Don't be," Abeyla said. "You were brave and protected my people. We are not used to violence or conflict. It is not a thing we have resorted to in many years. But it would be impossible to argue the time has come to fight. I will not begrudge you drawing first blood. Perhaps we needed someone from the Land Beneath to show us how very close that time has come."

"So what do we do now?" Maggie asked, following Abeyla back to her boat. "You aren't going to surrender, right?"

"We have been given two days," Abeyla said. "We will move the village to the safest place we have and deliver the children to their refuge. When the Enlightened come, we fight."

"Great," Maggie said as Bertrand rowed Abeyla back to shore, leaving Tammond with Maggie. "I guess I should find myself a bigger stick."

"Maggie, you could have been killed," Tammond said.

"I've never been good at hiding when bad people come knocking at the door." Maggie shrugged. "We could all be dead in two days anyway."

"But I don't want you to be hurt." Tammond took Maggie's hand, pressing it to his chest. "This isn't your fight."

"So you want me to leave?" Maggie asked.

Tammond leaned down and gently brushed his lips against hers. Hoots and cheers sounded from the children on the dock. "I don't want you to leave. You are brave, Maggie. But bravery might not be enough to keep any of us alive."

Maggie smiled and kissed Tammond again, leaning in so his body pressed against hers. This time sounds of disgust were mixed in with the shouts from the children.

"I can take care of myself," Maggie said when she finally figured out how to breathe again, "and if I'm going to be here when the Enlightened come, then I'm going to fight. I'd rather get hurt than watch the people around me suffer."

Tammond smiled sadly. "I suppose it would be too much to ask for you to be so brave *and* willing to hide."

"Way too much."

"Miss Trent," Bertrand shouted from the dock, "could you please come back to the village? Battle is now imminent, and we have more pressing matters to attend to."

Bertrand's words froze the children in place, as though threats from the defeated man in black meant nothing, but Bertrand saying danger was coming had somehow made it real.

"Shit." Maggie let go of Tammond and waded out into the water. After about two feet of shallow shore, the water dropped off into blackness. Maggie stepped off the edge, letting herself fall for a moment.

The cool water surrounded her. No noise. No threat of battle. Only water. The water didn't care if she breathed or cried. The water wouldn't care who won the coming battle. Maggie loved it for its indifference. The water wouldn't even care if she decided not to find her way back to the surface.

"The magic is already in your mind. Magic runs deep in your blood as it does in ours. Feel it pulsing through you."

Maggie closed her eyes against the pressing darkness, ignoring the sting in her lungs. There it was. That hum she had felt her whole life. The essence of magic that flowed through everything she was. But it was different now. Without the crackling brightness that threatened to break her. A gentle part of her now, flowing softly with each beat of her heart. Unable to break her as she let it drift out of her hands, warming the water. A dim light shone around her, and instinct made it clear all she needed to do was let go. Let the light work its will.

With one tiny kick, Maggie flew through the water, bursting out into the fresh air and landing with a gasp on the dock.

Maggie stumbled, and strong arms caught her.

"Miss Trent," Bertrand said, steadying her, "I'm glad to see you haven't given up."

"Me?" Maggie panted, bending over to catch her breath. "Never. Just trying to figure out this whole magic thing before the big bad wolf comes knocking."

"Maggie." Tammond pulled himself from the lake up onto the deck. "That was amazing! I knew you could find your magic."

"It was easier in the water than with a bunch of kids watching." Maggie wrung the water out of her hair as a whistle sounded from the front of the village.

"It's time to move again." Tammond ran toward the raised walkways.

"We won't get where we're going before dark." Maggie followed him, dodging the others who sprinted to their positions. "Can't we wait until morning?"

"We have to get to the safe place," Tammond grunted as he hoisted one of the heavy support poles from under the walkway.

Maggie helped him lay it on the ground before he moved to the next pole.

"What about this safe place is so safe?" Maggie pressed herself against the wall of a house as a group of four men ran past, carrying a boat. "And if it's safe, why haven't you been there this whole time?"

"Safe doesn't mean we can't be attacked," Tammond explained. "It just means there will only be one direction for Jax to attack us from. And the dark place for the children is nearby. We have to leave the children in safety before we can go to the overhang." He moved to the edge of the raised walkway and began untying the ropes that bound it to the top of the dock.

"The overhang?" Maggie moved to the other side and dug her fingers into the ropes. The rope was warm, and the magic that flowed through it pulsed in her fingertips.

"The overhang is the safe place." Tammond leapt aside, pulling Maggie with him as two women pushed a long walkway into the water and bound it to the sides of the houses, making a solid ramp that bordered that section of the village.

Tammond ran toward the front of the village and, without pausing, leapt into a boat that waited in the water.

Seconds after he lifted his paddle, another whistle split the air, and, as one, the rowers began dragging the village.

"So what can I do?" Maggie asked, widening her stance to steady herself as the village surged forward.

"Nothing," Tammond said. "There is nothing any of us can do until the children are safe."

CHAPTER 21

*M*aggie sat with Bertrand in the Fireside. The children weren't running around or playing while the village traveled this time. Even the smallest among them seemed to know something terrible was coming.

"I hate feeling like this." Maggie tore her hunk of bread into tiny little crumbs. "I hate not being able to help. I wish we could at least row."

"We aren't as skilled as they are," Bertrand said. "They will move more quickly and safely without our help."

"Then what exactly are we supposed to help them with?" Maggie banged her fists on the table.

A tiny boy whimpered.

"Sorry," Maggie muttered, "but what exactly are we supposed to be doing to help? I'm just figuring out how to use magic here, we don't know how the Enlightened are going to attack, we can't even help row the damn boats." Maggie rammed her fingers through her hair.

"We help them to see the holes in their defenses," Bertrand said. "They've been planning to hide at the overhang for years. They might not see if it is a flawed plan."

"So we're just going to make sure the walls hold?"

"Miss Trent"—Bertrand leaned across the table, speaking barely above a whisper—"the village was threatened, and it took you with a stick to defend it. Like it or not, we have both seen more fighting than most of the Wanderers."

"I'll just run at Jax with a stick and hope he's caught unawares." Maggie took a bite of fruit, more to have something to do than because she was actually hungry. Something about knowing the time before battle was drifting quickly away made things like food seem irrelevant. But she would need food in her stomach when the battle came, even if she didn't know how she was supposed to fight.

A whistle from the front of the village made all the children freeze.

"I think we may have arrived." Bertrand stood up and strode to the door as Maggie scrambled over the bench she had been sitting on.

The air outside the Fireside had changed. It wasn't only the fear of the people who were scrambling out of the boats and back up onto the raft. There was something palpable in the breeze that drifted slowly by.

They weren't in an outlet of the main lake this time. They were stopped alongside a high and jagged cliff. Trees coated in layers of vines grew from the vertical surface, making it look as though someone had tipped the ground onto its side and forgotten to right it.

Parents of the children from the Fireside had come to the deck that surrounded it, hugging and kissing their children as though they would never see them again. The sun had already sunk low in the sky. Soon it would be too dark to allow the village to move at all.

"Quickly," Abeyla called over the crowds. "Get the children into the boats."

"But Abeyla," a young woman said, holding a crying little girl tightly in her arms, "we will have to stay here overnight. Let us keep the children with us tonight. They can leave in the morning."

"I will never be fool enough to trust Jax Cayde to keep his word," Abeyla said. Every face in the crowd turned toward her. "We cannot trust he will not attack before morning. The children will go to safety tonight. I will not risk their lives on the promise of a murderer."

The woman looked at Abeyla, her face stricken. But she nodded, kissing her little girl on the forehead before moving to the left side of the docks.

The largest of the boats waited along the side. One by one, the children were passed into the waiting arms of the rowers. Some screaming and crying, others resolute, knowing tears would make no difference.

"Maggie," Abeyla said under the noise of the departure, "you are going to the dark place with the children."

"What?" Maggie said. "I'm not going to hide with a bunch of kids."

"Not to hide." Abeyla held up a hand to halt Maggie's protests. "To learn. The dark place has magic hidden deep within its walls. Magic the Wanderers have spent many years exploring and molding. That is why the children will be safe there. The darkness itself will protect the innocent.

"What you did today was brave, Maggie, and you have clearly shown you have magic within you. We normally don't send one who has so much yet to learn into the darkness, but there is no time for you to wait. And you do not seem like one to shy from pain or fear."

"Sounds great," Maggie said.

"Go into the darkness, and you will come out capable of more than we could teach you in years of books and gentle magic."

"Trial by fire." Maggie nodded. "If that's the way it has to be, then Bertrand and I will get through it."

"I won't be joining you, Miss Trent," Bertrand said. "I'll be staying to help in guarding the village."

"But you're not from here either," Maggie said, feeling as though she might be getting the short and painful end of the stick. "Shouldn't you have to go through the fear-and-pain suffering training?"

"As I've said, Miss Trent, I've learned the language of many types of magic." Bertrand held out his palm, and a funnel of dark air formed instantly. Within seconds, lightning blossomed from the storm, lighting the dimming night.

"Nice party trick," Maggie snarked.

"Effective magic in this land," Bertrand said.

"Fine, so you just want me to go into the dark place with the kids and hope I find some suffering I can learn from?" Maggie asked. The boats carrying the children had cast off from the village and were rowing toward the cliffs. "Sorry, my mistake. I'll swim to the dark place and hope I don't drown."

"I'm taking you Maggie," Tammond said, appearing behind his mother's shoulder, his face covered in sweat from rowing. "Surviving the journey into the dark place is impossible without a guide you trust. So"—Tammond paused, his face flushing for a moment—"I thought it should be me."

The idea of being trapped in the darkness with Tammond made all Maggie's anger at being sent away fade.

"Sure," Maggie said, pleased her voice came out stronger than it felt. "Let's go."

"Abeyla," Tammond said, "if the Enlightened come, don't let us stay hidden in the dark. I would rather fight for my home than wake up in the morning to find I have no family."

Abeyla took her son's face in her hands. "If Jax comes for us, it will sound like thunder in the darkness. No matter what I want, you will know when the battle begins."

"Then I'll be waiting for the thunder." Tammond hugged his mother before turning to Maggie. "Let's go."

Maggie followed him to the edge of the deck where one, small wooden boat waited, bobbing in the gentle ebb and flow of the lake. Tammond held his hand out to help Maggie down into the boat.

Maggie paused, turning back to Bertrand. "Do me a favor. Make sure you live until morning, okay?"

"Have you grown attached to me, Miss Trent?" Bertrand asked.

"No." Maggie grinned. "But I don't know the way back to the Siren's Realm."

Maggie climbed down into the boat, and as soon as she sat, Tammond began rowing toward the cliffs not forty feet away.

CHAPTER 22

*M*aggie stared at the sheer rock wall Tammond rowed them quickly toward, his gaze fixed at a point near the base of the cliff. Maggie narrowed her eyes, trying to see what he saw in the shadow.

The darkness at the water's edge had depth, and the blackness seemed much thicker than any shadow she had ever encountered.

"Is that the dark place?" Maggie whispered.

"It is." Tammond held his paddle in the water, slowing them as the tip of their boat entered the darkness.

Maggie only had time for a quick glance behind before the shadow swallowed all the light.

"Tammond," Maggie whispered, grateful to hear her voice could penetrate the veil of blackness. "Tammond?"

"Yes," Tammond said. He was paddling again. The sound of his oar dipping into the water and the boat's movement forward were steady and sure.

"How can you see where we're going?" Maggie asked. "Or better yet the way out?"

"I can't see anything," Tammond said, and Maggie could hear the smile in his voice. "I can feel it. I can feel the magic in the walls that surround us, and I can feel the magic of those waiting for us up ahead."

"So you're just going to leave the kids in the pitch black for a few days while we have a little war outside?" Maggie asked, imagining how frightened little Mina must be. "Doesn't that seem a bit cruel?"

"Is hiding them more cruel than what Jax would do to them?" Tammond asked. "And there will be light for them. It's just in front of us. Close your eyes, Maggie. Try and feel where we're going."

With a sigh, Maggie closed her eyes against the darkness. The only thing she felt was the desire to not be moving toward something she couldn't see. She dug deeper, trying to remember what it had felt like just a while ago in the water. Magic inside her, surrounding her.

Tammond dug his paddle into the water, turning the boat.

"No," Maggie said, discovering the words as she said them. "You were right before. The kids are straight ahead."

"See, it's not so hard to see in here after all."

Maggie opened her eyes to find a tiny spot of light hovering ahead. As small and dim as a candle, flickering feebly in the distance. As they moved forward, the light grew larger and brighter much more quickly than seemed possible. In less than a minute the boat bumped into the edge of a rocky shore where the children sat waiting.

The people who had delivered the children were already getting back into their boats. An older woman stood with two teens not much younger than Maggie at the edge of the water, saying goodbye to the rowers, ready to take charge of the children.

The rowers glanced at Maggie and Tammond as they arrived before continuing to climb wordlessly into their boats.

"Maggie!" Mina burst out of the pack of children and ran toward Maggie as soon as her feet were on the rocky shore.

"Maggie, have they sent you to be safe, too? I will take care of you here. I don't know my way around yet, but I can figure it out very quickly so you should stay near me."

"She can't," Tammond said, lifting Mina under the arms and carrying her back to the group. "Maggie has to go deep into the darkness, and you can't follow her there."

"But why does she get to go and not me?" Mina's brow wrinkled. "I have been studying magic in the Fireside much, much longer than she has."

"Because," Maggie said, "I have to learn how to fight. That's my job. Your job is to stay safe here so you can grow up to be much stronger and braver than I'll ever hope to be."

"You think I'm brave?" Mina's eyes widened.

"Very brave." Maggie ruffled the little girl's hair. "Now you wish me luck being brave, because Tammond and I haven't got much time."

Mina threw her pudgy arms around Maggie's middle. "You'll be brave. I know you will be."

"Thanks, Mina."

Tammond took Maggie's hand and led her through the children, away from the water and toward the wall beyond. There were three openings in the cave wall. One was tall and wide with light shimmering in the distance. Another was narrow and pitch black. The third was jagged and had the air of being a place a person should not go. But in that tunnel there was a bit of light as well. Not shining to light the way, but glowing a pale blue that seemed to be more a part of the tunnel than an outside force trying to make it hospitable.

"Which way?" Maggie asked, hoping for the well-lit tunnel and knowing that wouldn't be Tammond's answer.

Without saying anything at all, Tammond led Maggie through the jagged entrance into the blue tunnel. Before they had walked ten feet, the voices of the children vanished.

"Creepy," Maggie muttered.

The light in the tunnel came from the walls themselves. A faint sheen that glimmered on the black surface of the stone, shifting every moment, as though millions of tiny little lights were moving about lives of their own.

"How does it work?" Maggie touched the wall. The instant her finger grazed the stone, the lights around it shone brighter and moved more quickly. Maggie trailed her fingers along the wall, laughing as the lights moved faster and faster.

"I don't know how it works," Tammond said, drawing Maggie away from the wall and guiding her farther down the tunnel. "I don't know if anyone does."

"So it's just magic then?" Maggie grinned. "Little lights that live in stone."

"Exactly." Tammond leaned down, brushing his lips against hers.

Maggie stood on her toes, lacing her fingers through his hair to pull him in closer. His fingers found the small of her back, and tingles raced up her spine. Her lips parted, and he deepened their kiss, holding Maggie so close she wasn't sure she would ever remember how to let go.

"Maggie," Tammond whispered, tipping Maggie's chin up so he could look into her eyes. "Maggie, I don't want to lose you."

"Then don't." Maggie leaned in to kiss him again, but Tammond pressed his fingers to her lips.

"Maggie, traveling through the darkness is frightening and painful—"

"So I've heard."

"You might hate me on the other side."

"No, I won't." Maggie took Tammond's face in her hands, reveling in the faint roughness of the stubble on his chin. "It's going to be terrible, but I'll just have to do it."

"Not if you stay here with the children. You could help guard them, and you wouldn't have to—"

"I'm never going to sit in the background while other people fight." Maggie took Tammond's hand and dragged him down the tunnel, walking more quickly and confidently than he had. "I'm not going to say it isn't nice to have someone who wants to keep me out of harm's way. It is nice, really nice actually. But it's not going to work. I hope you can handle that."

Maggie turned to Tammond, blushing in the dim blue light.

He ran his fingers through her hair. "You can't care for a bird and ask it not to fly." He pressed his lips gently to her forehead. "But please fly carefully, little bird."

"I'll try." Her heart racing, she turned and walked down the tunnel, knowing if Tammond started kissing her again she would forget what they were there to do.

Soon, the tunnel sloped downward. Maggie expected the lights to fade, but the deeper they went, the brighter and more vibrant the lights became. Ten minutes passed, then twenty. The tunnel twisted and turned but always moved downward.

"How much longer?" Maggie asked. It would be dark outside already. They couldn't afford to waste more of their precious night.

"When you're ready, we'll be there," Tammond said.

"Ready for what?" Sweat dripped down her back. "I'm definitely ready to get to where we're going. And if there's going to be lots of pain, I'd just as soon start now."

"Then we should be there soon."

Maggie wiped the sweat from her forehead, wishing the tunnel could at least have the courtesy to be cool. But the farther they walked, the hotter it became.

"You know, if we don't get there soon, we're going to boil to death." No sooner were the words out of her mouth than the lights in the distance began to change.

The dim, shimmering glow was replaced by something vibrant that coated everything in sight. The lights danced through the air, flashing as though their movements had purpose and meaning. Maggie ran forward, wanting to see the lights, to understand what they were saying. Tammond's footsteps pounded behind her, but he didn't call after her to slow down.

A cavern three stories high and large enough to fit half the village waited at the end of the tunnel. Lights danced across the surface of the rocks, speeding through the darkness like shooting stars. What Maggie had thought were lights moving through the open air were really bright reflections of the lights on the walls cast onto the haze that filled the air. The thick steam smelled like fresh summer fields, hot chocolate, and home baked bread.

Maggie gazed around the cavern, trying to find where the steam was coming from. It poured in from every direction, seeming to emanate from the walls themselves.

"Where is the mist coming from?" Maggie turned to Tammond, swaying as her head spun in the heat. Sweat dripped into her eyes, blurring her vision.

"I think it comes from the same place as the light."

Maggie wiped the sweat from her eyes with her shirt, blinking and focusing on Tammond, trying to steady herself. He stared back at her with concern on his face. His perfectly dry face, without a trace of sweat on it.

"You aren't hot?" Maggie's words wavered as she fought to pull in breath.

"No. I can't feel the heat. The steam feels like cool mist to me. Its scent and heat are only for you."

"So—" Maggie panted.

Tammond leapt forward and caught her around the middle as her knees buckled.

"So I'm just supposed to sweat the magic out of me? Well, it shouldn't take very long." The lights danced more quickly now, swimming through the stone overhead like a hundred shooting stars. "A meteor shower just for me. Too bad it's so hot. I don't like hot. I just want the…the stars."

"Let go, Maggie." Tammond's voice sounded far away as his

face faded into the darkness. "Follow where the stars are leading you."

"No," Maggie said, a cold hand clasping her heart as she understood. "No, I don't want to go. Don't make me go. Tammond!"

"Tammond?" The man next to her on the patchwork blanket turned to her. "Who's Tammond, sweetheart?"

"Daddy," Maggie breathed, reaching toward him with her pudgy child's arms. "Daddy!" She threw her arms around his neck, burying her nose in the collar of his flannel shirt.

"It's okay, Maggie," her father cooed. "You're okay. I'm here."

Maggie stood and wiped the tears from her eyes with the lacy sleeve of her nightgown. A shooting star flew by and then another. "The shooting stars, Daddy. We came out here to watch the shooting stars?"

"Of course we did, sweetheart." Her father rumpled her hair.

"Daddy, I had the worst nightmare," Maggie hiccupped, a fresh wave of tears streaming down her face. "I was grown up, and you and Mommy were dead. And I had lived someplace awful, and I never got to be with you."

"Maggie, darling." Her father took her by the shoulders, looking at his little girl with sympathetic eyes. "That wasn't a dream, sweetheart, and this isn't one either."

"What?" Maggie asked. The lace on her nightgown faded into nothing. "No, this has to be real. Daddy, I want this to be real. I want to see Mommy!" But before she could beg for her mother, the little girl Maggie had disappeared. Maggie herself sat on the blanket beside her father. Her clothes torn from the jungle. Her boots wet from the lake.

"I'm not going to see Mom, am I?" Maggie asked, her voice low, not meeting her father's eyes for fear of more tears coming.

"You will," her father said. "But not how you want to."

"Is this the pain they were talking about?" Maggie squeezed the sides of her head as though, by sheer force of will, she could push her thoughts into an order where any of this made sense. "I get to see you for a minute and then lose you again? Because that's really low."

"No darling. There is real pain to come. This is just an unfortunate side effect of what has to happen. You have to learn to fight. You have to learn now. And the best way the darkness knows how to do that is through fear. Fight when you're afraid, and the magic will learn how to come pouring out of you."

"What am I supposed to be afraid of?" Maggie looked around. They were in a field bordered by forest. The normal sounds of nighttime drifted through the trees. An owl hooted faintly, the tall grass rustled in the breeze. "Daddy, there's nothing here to fight."

A scream sounded from the corner of the field. Pitched high in terror, it was a voice Maggie would know even if she hadn't heard it for a thousand years.

"Mom." Maggie sprang to her feet. "Mommy!"

Maggie sprinted toward the scream.

"Fight, Maggie." Her father's voice trailed after her. But his footsteps didn't join hers. Maggie glanced behind. The blanket was gone. Her father had disappeared into the night.

"Daddy!" Maggie hesitated for a moment, wanting to run back and find her father. But another scream echoed, and she ran toward her mother.

The house was there. Just where it should have been—at the very edge of the field next to the trees. Strangers were outside the house.

And her mother was there, kneeling in the grass, defending something Maggie couldn't see as the attackers drew closer.

"*Terraminis!*" Maggie shouted the spell, expecting the ground around the feet of the strangers to crumble, but nothing happened.

Her mother screamed spells, shooting balls of fire and shards of lightning at the dark figures.

"Fulguratus!" Maggie screamed as her spell rebounded, knocking her back and shooting pain up through her arm and into her chest, streaking into her lungs so she couldn't breathe. "Mommy." Her lips formed the words, but she had no air to scream as the strangers moved in.

Her pulse quickened, her heart pounding against her ribs as her mind raced for an answer. Rolling onto her stomach, she dug her fingers into the grass, letting the anger and fear within her flow into the soil.

The ground shook, and one of the attackers fell over. Gasping for breath, Maggie staggered to her feet.

Her mother had seen her. Their eyes met for a moment.

"Maggie, help!" her mother screamed. "Help us!"

Us.

Her mother knelt hunched over something in the grass.

A body. Her father. Dead.

The men had killed him first. Maggie had known that. The other Clan had murdered her father and then killed her mother as she tried to protect her husband's body.

"No!" Maggie screamed, running full tilt toward the men. "Mommy, no! Run!"

Reaching deep down for the last bit of magic she could find, Maggie willed the energy into her hands, shaping it into magic strong enough to make the bad men go away. But she didn't know how. Didn't know what to make the magic do to stop them.

One of the strangers held his hand high. A spell crackled in his palm, just like the one Maggie was trying to create. But his magic came quickly, and before she could scream, the spell hit her mother.

Eyes wide and terrified, Elle Trent fell to the ground, dead.

"Mommy!" Maggie let the spell that had formed in her hands spill out into the night, burning everything in its wake.

ire burned through Maggie. She was not immune to her own magic. But with the pain came darkness. Her mother's and father's faces disappeared.

"No." Maggie felt herself saying the word before the world reformed around her. "No!"

But she wasn't at the old farmhouse anymore. Her parents were not there for her to save.

She stood in a hall with gray concrete walls. The Academy. Screams echoed down the corridors, and she knew before she moved what she would find.

Blood smeared on the walls and floor. Panic. Death.

Her feet carried her forward before she made the decision to move. A boy, Mark had been his name, lay dead on the floor. His stomach ripped open by claws.

Maggie took a shuddering breath. She couldn't save him. She wouldn't be able to save any of them. She could only sit and wait. Wait for the screaming to stop, for it all to be over. She knew how this ended. Blood in the night. Students—her friends—dead. The Academy destroyed.

"Help!" a voice called in the distance. She didn't even recognize who it was. But they were crying desperately. Maggie raised her hands to cover her ears.

"Someone please!"

Maggie ran forward, feeling the magic in the air and letting it flow into her. Fighting was better than waiting. Better to let the monsters hurt her than to listen to them hurt someone else.

She rounded the corner and found the beasts waiting. A little girl no older than ten—Vera, no, Ellen, that he been her name—was pinned against the wall. A black beast smiled as he drew closer to her, stepping over the bodies of the dead. The monster was only a man, really. A man whose skin had turned into black, shining armor and who had given up his hands for sharp talons that reached for Ellen's throat.

"Stop!" Maggie shouted. The word tore from her throat, bringing magic with it. The air pulsed with her breath, knocking the monster from his feet.

Maggie breathed the magic onto her hand, warming it, filling it with strength she had never known. She ran forward and grabbed the head of the monster, pushing it into the stone ground until, with a dull *crack*, the thing stopped moving.

"We have to go," Maggie said.

Ellen ignored the gore on Maggie's hand as she grabbed it, letting Maggie lead her down the hall.

"We need to get you to the cafeteria," Maggie said. "Everyone will be there."

"I want to stay with you." Ellen's voice shook. "Please don't let more of the monsters come."

At the girl's words, three beasts rounded the corner, their talons clicking as they slunk forward.

"Ellen, stay behind me," Maggie said calmly, not taking her gaze off the glistening, black beasts that approached.

"You fight us?" the closest monster hissed. "You know you cannot win. It is decided."

"Gonna try anyway," Maggie growled, feeling the magic in the floor beneath her. It hummed as though it were alive. A living force waiting for a command. Digging her hands into the air as though the magic beneath her were palpable, Maggie clawed upward. The ground trembled and rose, forming a wall blocking the path of the monsters.

"Ellen, we have to go the other way."

At Maggie's words, the little girl ran back down the hall and into the black talons that waited for her. Shining red poured onto the floor as Maggie screamed, and the scene disappeared.

"I won't."

She knew what was coming. She couldn't change anything that was about to happen. Wouldn't be able to stop any of it.

"Don't make me do this," Maggie whispered, keeping her eyes firmly shut as sounds emerged around her. "I won't do this. You can't make me."

Spells were being shouted. Screams of pain and rage carried through the noise of the battle. The *swoosh* of a sword close to Maggie's head didn't even make her flinch. That wasn't how it had happened. She hadn't been killed by a sword. She hadn't died in the battle at Graylock at all.

"Emilia!" Jacob screamed.

Maggie could picture him—running toward the girl he loved, bent on protecting her from every danger. But had he managed it? She hadn't seen everything that had happened. Hadn't been there to find out who had survived, if any of them.

Maggie opened her eyes. The battle raged all around her, spells shooting through the trees and shattering the rocks around the entrance to a cave. The entrance seemed so small. Such a strange place for power to be lurking.

But the Pendragon was there, fighting with his men. Determined to kill everyone who fought against them and to destroy the world Maggie loved.

Maggie walked slowly toward the cave, not flinching when spells streaked toward her, not stepping aside when a centaur ran past, whip flashing in his hand. She didn't care if they hurt her. It didn't matter anyway. She wanted only to see, to know what had become of them all.

The ground lurched and crumbled, dropping away to form a gaping hole in front of the cave. Green mist blossomed from its depths. Dexter. She had seen him in the shadows. That was why she had run forward, to save Dexter. But this was different, wrong.

Dexter wasn't standing in the mist—the mist was alive in its own right. It reached for Maggie with tangible tendrils, determined to pull her into the darkness. To drag her away so she would never know what had happened.

"Leave me alone!" Maggie turned and bolted through the battle. An arrow whizzed overhead. Maggie ducked but kept running, leaping over bodies, not looking closely enough to know if they were friend or foe. She could feel the mist behind her, drawing her back toward her fate.

A tree cracked in front of her and toppled toward the ground, blocking her path. Pushing the air with all her strength, Maggie shoved the tree out of her way. She ran farther, toward the edge of the battle. There was no one fighting here. Only bodies left to wait for the victor to deal with. A body lay between two trees. Eyes wide and blank as they stared at the sky.

"No!" Maggie paused. Only for a moment, but that moment was enough. The mist wrapped around her, dragging her toward the darkness.

"No!" There was magic in the mist, stronger than any she had felt before. Stronger than anything inside her. "Please don't!" But the mist had no pity for her screams. She reached out, grabbing a tree, trying to halt the terrible pull of the mist, but her hands slid uselessly across the bark.

Her hands dripped blood, which fell through the mist, not tainting its bright green with the deep red. The mist could pull her away, but a drop of blood could pass through. It couldn't hold everything. It wasn't all-powerful. Only magic.

Maggie closed her eyes and felt the magic swirling around her. Without caution, she drew the magic inside her. Letting it fill her until it burned, until there was no Maggie left. Only magic.

With a scream that drowned out the battle, Maggie threw her arms wide, severing the mist as though it had merely been a string trying uselessly to bind her.

She turned to the chasm that led to the Siren's Realm, toward the blackness that led to her fate. Magic crackled from her fingers, sparking brightly as the battle faded.

Scooping her hands through the air, she filled the pit with darkness, blocking her path to the Siren's Realm as the shadows surrounded her.

CHAPTER 24

Maggie lay gasping and shaking on the ground. The heat from the cavern had gone, and she was as numb as though she had been lying in snow.

"Maggie." Tammond knelt next to her.

Maggie blinked, trying to focus on his face in the dim, blue light.

"I'm back," Maggie croaked. Her throat hurt like she had been screaming.

"You never went anywhere." Tammond lifted her from the ground and cradled her to his chest.

He was warm, and Maggie pulled herself closer to him, shivering.

"I did," she said. "I did leave here, and I went to the worst places."

"I heard." Tammond held Maggie tightly. "I heard everything you said."

"And that's how you're supposed to learn?" Maggie asked, anger welling inside her. "You get to go revisit the worst moments of your life and watch helplessly as people die?"

"You go to the moments that will make your magic strongest. What they are varies with each person."

"I hadn't even seen it happen." Maggie crawled away from Tammond, afraid she might be sick on him. "I was hundreds of miles away when my parents were killed. Was that even how it really happened?"

"I don't know. The mist shows you what it must for you to learn. I don't know how much of it is true."

"Great. Torture as a tutor." Maggie rubbed heat back into her hands. "Does this mean we can go back up and fight Jax now? Am I all crazy powerful?"

"The powers you feel in the mist aren't what you'll really have, or I would be able to transform into a wild cat." Tammond smiled tentatively. "But you've felt the magic pour out of you, and now you'll be able to find it again."

"Awesome." Maggie pushed herself unsteadily to her feet. "All that so I can see how something feels. 'Cause I really needed all that pain for some freaking magic!" Maggie's voice echoed around the cavern. "That's great."

Tammond moved to wrap his arms around Maggie, but she stepped back.

"Don't." Her voice caught in her throat. "Thank you, but don't." Tears stung in the corners of her eyes. "I'm not really good with sympathy."

"As you wish." Tammond stepped back. "We can begin the next step of your training."

"Of course there's more. Now what? I walk on hot coals?"

"We go into the darkness and let your magic work."

"Doesn't sound as bad as the last part, so it's probably going to be worse."

"Not worse." Tammond took Maggie's hand and led her toward the back of the cavern. "Just darker."

The mist had cleared, leaving the blue lights still dancing on the ceiling. But their light didn't touch the hole in the back wall.

The opening was barely tall enough or wide enough for Tammond to fit through, but he crossed into the pitch black without hesitation, leading Maggie behind him.

"Are there monsters back here or something?" Maggie whispered, grateful to hear her voice sounding off the walls around them, carrying as though they were in a long narrow tunnel. "Or is it going to be more like jumping over molten lava?"

"It's different for everyone," Tammond said.

"But you're going to stay with me?" Maggie asked, tightening her grip on Tammond's hand without meaning to.

"I am," Tammond said. "You found the magic within yourself, but the way magic works in the dark dream is different from the way you can use it in the real world."

"*Dark dream* sounds right," Maggie said. "But real world might be a stretch. No offense but—"

Maggie fell silent and froze where she stood. Her voice had echoed as though she were in a vast place, larger even than the cavern where the mist had been.

"Tammond," Maggie whispered, but still her voice carried around the space, "where are we?"

"I need you to trust me, Maggie." Tammond slipped his hand from Maggie's, leaving her alone in the dark.

"I'm not really great with trust." Maggie stepped forward, but Tammond wasn't there.

"Where you were taught—"

"The Academy," Maggie said, moving to her left where Tammond's voice had come from.

"At the Academy"—he sounded like he was behind her now —"did they teach you to fight?"

"Yes, a bit." Maggie tensed, raising her hands, waiting for Tammond to strike. "I learned some on my own, too. Didn't have much of a choice, really."

"Then attack me." Tammond was back in front of her. It sounded like he was only a few feet away.

"What?" Maggie stepped backward. "I'm not going to attack you."

"I'll defend myself, Maggie." Tammond sounded as though he were mere inches in front of her. "But you have to attack."

Focusing all of her energy into her hand, Maggie pulled the air into her fist, compounding it into a sphere. Without a sound, she threw it as hard as she could at where Tammond's voice had last been.

"The spell was good," Tammond said from far behind her. "But you need to be able to sense where I am. You can feel the magic in you, in the air around you. Now feel the current I am creating."

"Don't you think when Jax attacks, I'll be able to use my eyes to see who's trying to kill me?"

"Jax Cayde can set fire to the water," Tammond began, and Maggie silently knelt, placing her palm against the stone floor. "He can fly without wings…"

Maggie pushed the magic from her palm into the stone, sending a ripple toward Tammond. Maggie pictured it. The rock made soft, moving in a wave, wrapping itself around Tammond's feet. A small grunt of surprise made her sure the spell had worked, but the sharp cracking of rock a moment later meant he had broken free.

"Nicely done," Tammond said. "But using my voice to find me wasn't what I asked you to do."

"Fine," Maggie growled, closing her eyes against the blackness. Sure enough, she could feel the magic moving through the air around her. Could feel it surging through her veins with every beat of her heart. And there was something in the vast swirling power of it all she was sure must be Tammond. Whipping her hand through the air as though grabbing a dart, Maggie hurled the spell at what she thought was Tammond.

A dull *thunk!* echoed through the dark as the spell struck stone.

"Better," Tammond said from the opposite direction.

Maggie ran her hands through her hair. If she only had a bit of light. Without thinking about how to form the light, a pale red orb shimmered into being right above her head. Maggie spun on the spot, looking for Tammond, but the light reached only a few feet in each direction.

"More light," Maggie whispered. Magic surged through her, and in a moment twelve orbs had split from the first, zooming in every direction, filling the cavern with their faint red glow. Tammond stood not twelve feet from her in front of a grouping of stalagmites ten feet wide that reached nearly to the ceiling. All around the cave as far as her lights could reach, stalactites and stalagmites showed the slow passing of time.

"You shouldn't have done that yet," Tammond said, worry filling his voice.

"Why not? It worked." Maggie pushed the air from her hands so it hit Tammond in the stomach. "Tag, you're it."

"But they come toward the light, Maggie." Tammond moved closer to her as a sharp clicking began in the shadows. "And they won't want you to see."

"They?" Maggie searched the shadows. "You never mentioned anything about a *they*."

"I said I would stay with you, and I will." Tammond squared his shoulders as though preparing to fight. "Wanderers never face the shadows until their training is complete. You weren't meant to see them."

"Well, then you should have told me not to turn on a light," Maggie whispered as a pair of pinchers appeared from behind the rock.

CHAPTER 25

The thing was small, no bigger than a housecat. But it wasn't the size that terrified Maggie. The thing looked more like a scorpion than anything else Maggie could think of, and its shining black armor forced bile up into her throat as she pushed away the memory of the monsters that had destroyed the Academy.

"What the hell are those things?" Maggie said as more of the scorpions crept out into the light.

"They live here," Tammond said. "And they don't like visitors."

"Then why the hell are we here?" Maggie grabbed Tammond's arm, dragging him toward the exit just visible in the darkness on the far wall. But their path had already been blocked by more of the creatures.

"Get rid of them," Maggie said. "I don't care what you wanted to do down here. We're leaving."

"I can't get rid of them." Tammond sounded afraid.

Maggie followed his gaze. He wasn't looking down at the floor where the creatures were growing in number, but rather three feet above them where Maggie couldn't see anything at all.

"What are you seeing?" Maggie asked.

Tammond answered with a scream as bright streaks of white light flew from his palms, striking some invisible thing that shrieked. He leapt in front of Maggie, sending another spell at something she couldn't see.

But the black creatures were moving closer.

Drawing the heat from her fear, Maggie let her magic flow. Flames poured from her hands, covering the floor in a sea of fire.

The creatures scuttled away from the flames. Some weren't fast enough, and with *hisses* and *pops*, the fire consumed them.

"Maggie, get down!" Tammond screamed, covering Maggie's head.

A sickening *crunch* sounded as Tammond flung his arm through the air, striking something that left blood dripping from his hand.

"Tammond!" But she didn't have time to see how badly he was hurt. The black creatures had surged forward again. With a shout that shook the air, Maggie slammed her foot onto the ground. The stone rippled like waves in the sea, throwing some of the creatures back.

Something sharp dug into the top of Maggie's head, and she swung her arm up. It connected with something hard, and rubbery wings flapped against her hand as the thing escaped her grip.

"Tammond, duck! *Primionis!*" Maggie screamed, praying the spell would work. The shield blossomed above Maggie's head, forming a shimmering dome around her and Tammond. She pressed her palm through the shield and closed her eyes, letting all the magic she could feel funnel into her.

Eyes shut tight, she let lightning and fire pour out into the cave.

Howls rent the air, but still Maggie didn't look. Soon the only sounds were the whooshing of the fire and the crackling of the lightning. Trembling, Maggie opened her eyes and lowered her arm. The cave's walls were scorched. The things that had been attacking them were gone.

"Maggie, are you all right?" Tammond took her by the shoulders, examining her.

Maggie touched the top of her head where blood coated her hair.

"I'll live," Maggie said, "but this is a really shitty way to train people. Sending monsters after them? I mean, what if we had been eaten alive? Wouldn't have been much good fighting against Jax now would we?"

"You weren't supposed to light the room." Tammond laid his palm on Maggie's head. Heat trickled down her scalp. "You weren't meant to jump right to the end."

"Still, fighting scorpion monsters and invisible things—not really my idea of advancing the learning curve."

Tammond took his hand from Maggie's head, and she felt where the cut had been. Her hair was still sticky with blood, but the cut had healed.

"Thanks," Maggie murmured.

"They don't usually attack like that, not with such force. They belong in the shadows and are creatures of darkness. They appear to everyone, but never in the same way. They'll fight us, but I've never heard of them attacking in such numbers."

"So what?" Maggie sat on the ground, hoping Tammond wouldn't notice her legs shaking. "The shadows just really hate me because I'm not from Malina, because I'm not a Wanderer?" She clenched her fists, digging her nails into her palms as tears welled in her eyes. "As if watching my mom die wasn't bad enough, I had to get attacked just for good measure?"

"We cannot learn to fight from the light or from the good things we know." Tammond knelt beside her. "Peace begets peace, and it is how we hope to live. But when fighting must come, we can't expect to learn to survive it staying only in the sun."

"Is that why I was lucky enough to jump ahead? Because I'm not made of peace and light? Because I know exactly what it is to fight, and hurt, and hate? Because I've seen death, and the shadows can smell it on me?"

"Maggie," Tammond whispered her name. In the dark cave, it didn't sound like a name at all. But like a prayer, rising up to the sun far above the darkness. A wish for something away from shadows and pain.

He kissed her gently, as though afraid she might push him away again. His mouth was warm on hers. He was alive, so very alive. With the burned rocks surrounding them, and unknown horrors ahead, he was there. Pulse racing in time with hers.

Maggie moved in closer so her body pressed against his, forgetting where she ended and he began. It didn't matter. Nothing mattered as long as he was holding her. If he held her tightly enough, nothing horrible would come for them. They would never have to go back up to the lake and everything that waited above.

Tammond's hands ran up her sides as his mouth moved to her throat, making her gasp with pleasure. The lights in the room faded away. But Tammond was there, holding her.

CHAPTER 26

*T*he floor was hard and cold. Maggie lay curled up, her head on Tammond's shoulder, listening to the steady beat of his heart. She wanted to stay there forever. Just the two of them in the darkness. But a forever of peace was meant only for the dead.

"How much longer until dawn?" Maggie finally asked, her voice echoing through the dark.

"Not much longer." Tammond kissed Maggie's forehead.

"Then we should go. I don't even know if I've finished my training."

"I don't think the training was ever going to work for you." Tammond shifted to sit up. "Not the way it's supposed to. The Wanderers found this place to teach other Wanderers. You aren't one of us."

Maggie froze for a moment. "Is that a good thing or a bad thing?"

Tammond leaned down, his lips finding Maggie's. "A very good thing. As Bertrand said—we know everything we know. You know different things. I think you proved you can use your magic here. There's nothing more the dark place can teach you. You did here in hours what most take years to find."

"I did spend years training in a dark place." Maggie pushed herself to her feet. "It just wasn't here."

"I only hope it's enough to keep you safe." Tammond's hand found hers in the dark as though it was the most natural thing that had ever happened.

Maggie smiled, letting him lead her blindly forward.

She didn't speak or ask how long it would take to make it to the blue cavern. She was listening too hard for the *click* of legs scuttling or *whoosh* wings flapping. But the only sound was the soft thudding of their feet as they climbed upward.

In only a few minutes, lights shone dimly in the distance. But it was a different cavern than the one they had been in before. This cave was barely wider than the passage they had been traveling. Green lights sparkled on the walls. Maggie tensed, waiting for the lights to crawl out of the rock and draw her back into the Siren's Realm, away from the battle to come. But she wasn't ready to leave yet.

"Why is it different?" Maggie whispered, leaning in close to Tammond. "We didn't go down this way."

"The way into the darkness can never be the same as the way back out."

"Right," Maggie said, not sure she understood. But it didn't matter as long as he took her back to the surface. The darkness that had felt mysterious and magical now seemed threatening and suffocating.

Her shoulders were tense, ready to fight more monsters from the dark, ready to hear her mother's screams again.

"I think I know why Bertrand couldn't come down here," Maggie said as the tunnel tipped steeply upward. "He wouldn't just have burned the shadows. He would have knocked the whole mountain down."

The children's voices echoed through the tunnel, and Maggie

broke into a run, dragging Tammond behind her. Torchlight gleamed in the distance, a small figure silhouetted against the flickering glow.

"Mina, don't!" a voice shouted, but the little shadow was already running down the tunnel toward Maggie.

"Maggie, Tammond!" Mina called as she ran. They had been far enough away that by the time Mina reached them, she was puffing. "I waited up for you all night!" Mina panted proudly. "It was a very long night, too. Though I suppose it will always look like night while we have to wait down here."

"You should have slept, Mina." Maggie didn't argue as Mina took her hand and dragged her up the tunnel.

"But I was worried about you," Mina said. "I wanted to be sure that if you needed help, someone would be able to hear you scream. But I didn't hear anything at all. Was it easy down there? Did you not get to do your training? I've heard stories about the tunnels, and it should have been awful."

"It was pretty bad," Maggie said, "but we survived, and that's what matters."

Mina stopped in her tracks, turning to face Maggie. "You are very brave."

Maggie blushed at Mina's wide eyed admiration.

"Thanks." Maggie took the lead, pulling Tammond and Mina behind her, knowing the shadows were no worse than what waited out on the lake.

The rest of the children huddled around the opening to the tunnel, peering into the dark.

"I told you not to go down there." An older boy grabbed Mina by the shoulders as soon as she was in reach. Apparently he hadn't been brave enough to venture into the tunnel to fetch her.

"I was going to Maggie and Tammond," Mina whined, wriggling away from the boy. "They can keep me safe."

"Don't ever say that," Maggie said, feeling the eyes of the children upon her. "When scary things are coming, you have to take care of yourself. Don't trust other people to protect you from the shadows. They might be willing to try, but at the end of it, you have to take care of you." Maggie's voice rang around the cavern.

A tiny boy behind her sniffed as tears crept down his cheeks.

Tammond looked at her, his brow wrinkled. "Maggie."

"I'm sorry, but it's true," Maggie said, her voice much gentler this time. "We're going to fight to keep all of you safe." She looked around at the frightened faces of the children. "Trust that. Trust that we will do everything we can to make sure none of the Enlightened come anywhere near you. But you can't go running at something dangerous with blind faith that it'll all work out okay, or that someone else will take care of you."

"B-but then what do we d-do?" the crying little boy asked.

"You take care of yourselves." Maggie knelt so she was at eye level with him. "Set up guards so you'll know if anyone is coming. They have to watch all the time."

"We do have guards," one of the older boys said indignantly.

"Good." Venom slipped into Maggie's voice. "Then teach the young ones to stand guard with you. Have a plan for if Jax comes through the dark. Know what you're going to do if we lose this battle."

More of the children were crying now, but it didn't matter. Better to have them afraid than dead.

"You can't count on the Wanderers rowing back in to take you from the dark place. You have to be ready to fight for yourselves." Maggie strode toward the boat waiting at the end of the rocky shore. She didn't look back to see if Tammond was following her. She didn't want to see the faces of the children staring at her with fear in their eyes.

"Get in." Tammond stepped into the tiny boat.

Maggie's hands shook as she gripped the sides of the boat while Tammond rowed them into the darkness. The Wanderers had penned the children into a cage they couldn't escape from. And there was nothing she could do about it.

"Why did you scare them like that?" Tammond asked as their boat was swallowed by the shadows.

"Because leaving them in a cave and hoping for the best is better?" Maggie said. "You think a couple of older kids and one old lady who can barely walk are going to be able to fend off Jax if he comes for them? They need a plan of their own, to be able to fight for themselves."

"They are too young to fight."

"Do you really think Jax is going to care?"

Tammond said nothing for a moment. The only sounds were his paddle dipping into the water and Maggie's angry breathing.

"He won't," Tammond finally admitted. "Jax will kill all of them if he finds his way into the dark place. But the jungle is no safer. The mountains are no safer. There is no safe place in Malina for the children of Wanderers. If he finds his way into the dark place, there will be nothing they can do."

"They can fight!"

"They'll lose."

"But at least they'll die fighting." Maggie's voice cracked. "It may not seem like a big difference to you. But if Jax comes, it'll be better for those kids to die fighting than hiding in the dark. Believe me, I know."

Tammond didn't say anything more as their boat emerged from the cave into the cool morning light.

The village was waiting as it had been the night before, tied up tight, ready to move at a moment's notice. A man stood watching the entrance to the dark place, and as soon as he spotted Maggie and Tammond, he gave a warbling whistle.

Abeyla appeared next to him before they reached the dock, and Bertrand was there a moment later.

Abeyla looked down at her son. "Are you all right?" Her voice sounded tired as though she had spent a sleepless night just like Tammond and Maggie.

"We're fine," Tammond said. "Maggie did very well. She moved much more quickly than I expected her to."

Abeyla turned an eye to Maggie as she climbed up onto the dock. "More quickly?"

"I made the room light up, and there were creepy black scorpions, so I burned them all." Maggie looked to Bertrand. "You were right, though. Shield spell works just the same as home."

"Do you think she is prepared to fight?" Abeyla asked Tammond.

Maggie resisted the urge to say she was right there and could speak for her own damn ability to fight.

"I—" Tammond began before looking at Maggie. "She is able to use magic, she is fearless, and she has seen many dark things before."

Abeyla nodded and gave a high-pitched whistle. "Then it is time for us to go to the safe place."

People emerged from their houses and moved to the docks, lowering boats into the water. Each person's face looked tired and drawn. But it wasn't the normal sleepy feeling of early morning. There was a dark resignation and fatigue that permeated the air. A heavy cloud of dread had settled over the village. They knew something terrible was coming. All that was left was to face it.

CHAPTER 27

*T*ammond jumped back down into the little boat that had carried them out of the dark place, ready to row with the whistle from the front of the village.

"What were you going to say?" Maggie knelt at the edge of the dock, speaking quietly so no one rushing by would hear.

"You know darkness." Tammond's eyes filled with pain. "You know how to work in it better than some who have studied the shadows for years."

"How is that a problem?" Maggie asked. "I'm good at magic here, I can fight, and I'm not scared. Those all sound like really good qualifications to me. I'm not going to be in the way or be a danger to the Wanderers. I can help, and you need all the help you can get."

"I don't think you'll be a danger to the Wanderers." Tammond's voice was dark and low. "I'm worried about you. You know so well the pain that is coming, I'm afraid you'll greet it as an old friend."

The whistle sounded from the front of the boat, and, as one, all the rowers pulled forward, moving the village away from the caves.

"I'm not…I…" But Maggie didn't know what to say.

"Come, Miss Trent," Bertrand said, laying a gentle hand on her shoulder.

Maggie stood and followed him toward the Fireside, grateful for the reason to not have to explain herself to Tammond.

"Don't be mad at the boy," Bertrand said as they entered the Fireside. The room was abandoned. It seemed vast in its emptiness. The sound of the ropes squeaking against the wood carried throughout the space with no voices to cover the noise.

"I'm not mad at him." Maggie sat at a table, grateful for the bread and fruit some kind person had left behind.

"He's worried about you." Bertrand sat opposite her, tenting his fingers under his chin. "A strange and beautiful girl fell into his life. A girl who is more dangerous than any he's ever known, and brave enough to use that danger. It's not his fault he's afraid."

"Is it my fault for coming here?" Maggie dug her fists into her eyes, wishing she could sleep for even five minutes.

"Miss Trent, one of the many things I have learned on my journeys is that blame is rarely significant. There are too many accidents, too many unforeseen consequences. I doubt even the Siren herself knows every possible outcome for all the choices she makes. You meant no harm. In fact, we are trying to help, and our help has been gratefully accepted. Beyond that, it is the fault of no person we can blame, including ourselves."

"I just…"

"Weren't expecting to care so much for the locals?" Bertrand finished for her. "Ah, Miss Trent. We adventure for knowledge and magic. We fight to help a just cause. But it's the people who pull us along when things become dark."

"Right," Maggie said, not sure if she really understood Bertrand and not knowing if she wanted to.

They fell into silence as the village rowed slowly forward. The sun crept up in the sky until it poured in over the high walls of the Fireside. Maggie tipped her head back and let the sun warm her face, trying not to wonder how long it would be until Mina felt the sun on her skin again.

The morning light glowed through Maggie's closed eyes. She could be anywhere. The Siren's Realm. Home. The sun always felt the same.

Then the light was gone. The warmth disappeared. Maggie opened her eyes, ready to fight whatever was blocking out the sun. She didn't wait for Bertrand's murmur of, "What have we here?" before running outside to look.

An overhang, larger than the village itself, jutted out over the lake. The thick stone clung to the side of a cliff with no cracks in its surface, no sign that it might crumble and squash them all.

"Well, that is one way to block an attack." Bertrand squinted at the rock above.

The overhang was made of the same kind of rock as the surrounding cliffs, but there was something about its perfection that made it seem like it didn't belong over the Broken Lake.

The whistle came, and the rowers stopped, digging their paddles into the water so the village came to a shuddering halt.

Maggie stepped onto the dock, facing away from the cliffs. The water beyond the shadow of the rock sparkled in the sun. In the distance, a low bank rose up to the base of the mountains. Cliffs surrounded them on either side, cradling them from behind and stretching out toward the mountains. There was no way to approach the village but from dead ahead. Jax wouldn't be able to catch them unawares.

"They really like penning themselves in," Maggie said softly to Bertrand as he stood next to her, gazing at the distant mountains.

"Like rabbits hiding in a den," Bertrand said. "The principle works as long as the fox can't dig deep enough to reach them."

"And is willing to give up if he fails." Maggie ran her fingers through her hair, picking out flecks of dried blood, trying to push past her fatigue to put her thoughts in order. "They need to have people on the outside who can help if they get penned in. Who can attack from behind and surprise Jax."

"Miss Trent." Bertrand turned to Maggie with a smile. "I think we might have just found how we can best be useful."

"We're going to go play hidey hole and then jump off a cliff into the battle and save the day?"

"I think that is the basic principle." Bertrand walked quickly away toward the front of the village, Maggie following close behind.

The Wanderers stored their boats, but the movements were different this time. It wasn't the same practiced motion Maggie had seen before. Some of the Wanderers knelt at the edges of the docks, pressing their hands into the water, eyes shut tight. Others gazed silently at the face of the rock. Instead of the village unfolding and the bridges being raised, sharply carved bamboo spikes were inserted on the edges of the docks, pointing out menacingly over the water.

Abeyla stood on top of one of the houses, surveying the progress of those working beneath her. Bertrand walked straight into the house and climbed the ladder inside. Maggie was a step behind, and soon they were standing on the roof.

The Wanderers worked on the decks below. The gentle hum of magic touched Maggie's skin as spells radiated from every direction.

Maggie wanted to ask what all the protections were, but Bertrand had already begun speaking.

"But of course if you don't agree, Abeyla, we are willing to serve you in whatever way we can."

Abeyla looked between Bertrand and Maggie. Deep creases and shadows marred her face. She looked older than she had just a few days ago when Maggie had first met her.

"I am not a warrior." Abeyla sounded weary. "I am not a general or a fighter. I am a teacher who has managed to keep her people alive and fed. The Wanderers have never been soldiers. Jax Cayde—"

"Cannot be allowed to win," Bertrand said. "I was never a soldier, either, but our weakness can be an advantage. Let Jax's men advance. And we will be waiting for them."

"Do it," Abeyla said. "Take three with you and go where you think it best. Do not attack until there is no other choice. Once Jax knows where you are, he will come for you, and then we shall have no one left on the outside."

Bertrand nodded and started down the ladder.

"Make sure Tammond is one of the men you take." Abeyla's gaze stayed out toward the sparkling water. "And be careful."

"We will."

Half an hour later, they were in a boat skirting the edge of the cliff.

Tammond stared back at the village as the rower propelled them forward.

"She'll be okay," Maggie said. "Abeyla can take care of herself."

"Better than the rest of us can," Tammond said. "She will stand at the front of the battle and face Jax herself. And now she's sent me away so I can't stand in her place."

Maggie slipped her hand into Tammond's, grateful when he squeezed it tight instead of pushing her away.

The boat gave a dull *thump* as it knocked into the rocks. They had stopped beyond the steep cliffs. Here the rocks were broken, and boulders had piled up, giving them a way to climb. Bertrand was the first out of the boat, quickly scaling the rocks to make way for the next.

Selna, a woman with dark hair and deep brown eyes, followed him. Then Giles, a young man with broad shoulders who looked as though he could row the whole village himself. Tammond took Maggie's hand, helping her balance as she climbed out of the boat.

"Lamil," Tammond turned to the older man who had rowed

them past the cliffs. "You go with them. I'll row the boat back to the village."

Lamil smiled sadly and shook his head. "Abeyla has given orders. You are to go with Bertrand. I am to stay behind."

"But you're a good fighter," Tammond said, standing resolute in the boat. "You fought Jax when he set fire to the lake. You should be on the cliffs. You'll be able to see what Jax is doing. You'll know better when to strike."

"Abeyla has given her orders," Lamil repeated. "Abeyla is our leader, and you will follow her commands."

"It is my place to protect her," Tammond said, desperation creeping into his voice.

"Tammond," Maggie said, "we aren't going to the cliffs because we aren't going to fight. We *will* fight. We only need to wait until the time is right."

"But if Jax attacks Abeyla, how will I help her from the top of a cliff?" Tammond rounded on her.

"You won't," Bertrand said. "It will be up to those near her to fight by her side. But we will play our part. We will fight. And I promise you, our chances of death in glorious battle are just as great as those who stay behind."

"And we have the worse job," Maggie said. "We have to be strong enough to watch and wait for the right time." Sickness twisted Maggie's stomach, knowing how terrible that wait would be.

CHAPTER 28

The rocks dug into her scabbed palms as they climbed the mountain. The ridgeline, which had sloped gently down to the lake, became steeper the closer they got to the over-hang. Boulders were replaced by smaller rocks that slid under their feet with every step, and for the last twenty minutes of the climb, they had needed to use their hands to steady and pull themselves up.

Sweat dripped down Maggie's back by the time she managed to drag herself, panting, up onto the top of the mountain. She rolled onto her back, catching her breath and staring up at the bright blue sky. Everything was peaceful and calm. Not a storm cloud in sight. No hint that danger would find them by dawn.

"It really is beautiful here," Maggie said as Tammond crawled up next to her.

"It is." Tammond rubbed the dirt from his hands onto his pants. "I'm told it's one of the most beautiful places in all of Malina."

"Perhaps when this is all over, you will be sent into Malina as a Wanderer and will be able to see which parts of Malina are most beautiful for yourself." Bertrand was already on his feet, standing thirty feet away, staring over the edge of the overhang.

The cliff was one solid piece of stone without a crack or imperfection, just as they had seen from below. Forty feet behind was a stand of trees whose roots had penetrated the rock, finding a way to survive on top of the mountain. Maggie tried not to think of how deep into the rock the roots might reach as she stood and joined Bertrand, walking carefully toward the edge.

There was no sign of the village below. No hint they were even standing on an overhang. From the top, it looked like a normal cliff leading down toward the water. Maggie's head spun from the height, and she stumbled back.

Tammond wrapped an arm around her waist.

"Careful," he murmured as he, too, looked down toward the village. "We won't be able to see what's happening below, only Jax's approach."

"And you're sure he'll come from the front?" Maggie asked, already knowing the answer as she surveyed the land. The only way to attack the village was from dead ahead.

"We know where he'll come from," Selna said. "We just don't know what he'll bring with him."

"Right." Maggie lowered herself carefully to sit at the edge of the cliff, her feet dangling over the water more than two hundred feet below. "So, we sit here and wait for something to happen."

Tammond sat beside Maggie, pressing his right palm forward. The air in front of them shimmered and thickened, blurring the lake for a moment before the world came back into focus.

"They won't be able to see us then?" Bertrand knelt and poked the air in front of the cliff, which seemed to bow at his touch.

Tammond shook his head.

"We should start watches," Selna said. "They aren't supposed to be here until morning."

"And you trust that?" Giles asked, his hands on his hips and his eyes narrowed.

"Not even a bit," Selna said, "but when they do come, we'll need to be as rested as possible. I'll take first watch. You all go sleep."

"Two at a time." Bertrand settled himself on the cliff. "I'll watch with you."

"Thanks," Maggie said, grateful for Tammond taking her hands as she stood up, her head swimming from fatigue and the height of the cliff.

Tammond led her to a patch of shade under a tree not far from the ledge. Maggie wished for a bed, but shade and hard rocks would have to do.

"I can take first watch, Selna," Giles said, still looking threatening.

"Rest, Giles," Selna said. "When the battle begins, I won't let you miss it."

Giles paused for a moment, looking as though he wanted to argue, before walking twenty feet away and lying down in the sun.

"Selna won't sleep," Tammond said as he stretched out on the rocks next to Maggie. "Not with Mina in the dark place."

"Is Mina her daughter?"

Tammond nodded.

Maggie had known the big brown eyes looked familiar. "What about Giles?"

Giles lay on the ground, facing the open water. Maggie had no doubt he was watching Jax's path.

"His brother was one of the Wanderers who were sent back out into Malina," Tammond whispered so softly Maggie had to move her face right next to his in order to hear. "His brother was one of the ones who didn't make it back to the Broken Lake. We know Jax took some of them. Tortured them for information. But we don't know if Giles's brother was with them. We don't even know if he's alive or dead. Just gone."

Maggie moved her head onto Tammond's shoulder, reveling in its warmth even in the midday heat.

"His brother might still be out there," Maggie whispered. "He could be a prisoner. He might have wandered so far he forgot to come home. He could have a wife and kids and be a farmer."

"I don't know which would make it worse for Giles." Tammond kissed Maggie's forehead. "Having Jax hurt someone he loved, or having the person he cared for forget to come home."

"Well, when we take Jax down, maybe we can get Giles some answers." Maggie closed her eyes, instantly falling into sleep.

"How was I lucky enough to find someone so brave?" Tammond's words followed her into the darkness.

~

"I see them," Bertrand's voice was sharp and firm, all hints of playful adventure gone.

Maggie was blinking and sitting up before Selna rushed over to her and Tammond. "It's time."

The sun hung low in the sky, coloring the horizon a bright, dazzling red.

"This isn't sunrise." Maggie crept toward the edge of the cliff.

"He's come early." Bertrand's face was dark. He looked older, harder, like a person Maggie had never met before. The adventurer was gone, replaced by a warrior with no fear of blood.

"We thought he would." Tammond crouched at the edge of the cliff, peering out into the distance.

"I'm not surprised by it," Bertrand said, "but it does make me dislike him even more."

Maggie knelt beside Tammond, trying to make her tired eyes focus on what the others were seeing. In the fading light, she glimpsed something near the shore on the far side of the lake. From this distance it looked like an animal swimming quickly out into the water. But trees were moving through the lake, too. A vast stand of trees.

"There are hundreds of them," Selna whispered.

Maggie rubbed her eyes with the heels of her hands before looking back out over the water. The trees that had been moving weren't trees at all, but groups of men standing on rafts that rowed across the lake. And the animal who had swum farthest was a man, standing on a raft only a few feet wide. There was no one on that raft rowing it forward. No sign at all of how the craft moved. But the man glided over the water, floating swiftly toward the village.

"Jax," Maggie said, not needing anyone to tell her she was right.

He had left his men far behind, struggling to catch him as they rowed.

When he was near enough for Maggie to make out his jet-black hair and pale skin, Jax spoke.

"Wanderers," his voice boomed, shaking the cliff under Maggie's feet.

She wanted to run from the edge before it came tumbling down, but something in Jax's voice made her stay.

"Too long have I allowed you to be a stain on the greatness of Malina. Too long have I let you spread fairy stories and lies. I will not permit the blight you have created to spread any further."

A shout rose from the village beneath, but unlike Jax's words, these were muddled.

But Jax seemed to have heard and smiled before he responded. "Would waiting until morning change your fate? My men are trained soldiers, and we outnumber you. You are not fighters. How long did you really expect to survive hiding in your hole?"

"Jax Cayde," Abeyla's voice carried up from the water as she appeared beyond the edge of the overhang. She stood on the front of a boat as Lamil rowed her steadily forward. "You think that's what we've been doing on the Broken Lake all these years? Surviving? We've been thriving, Jax. While you built your walls and trained your armies, we had families. We learned. We built a home. Who has spent their time better, Jax?"

"You've built homes." Jax smiled. "Had children. I gave you the opportunity to allow your children to survive. You denied my offer."

"That evil little—" Selna leaned forward as though readying herself to leap over the edge of the cliff to attack Jax herself.

Bertrand grabbed her arm and pulled her back. "Abeyla is running out of time."

Maggie looked back at the lake. The men on the rafts were catching up to Jax. In a few more minutes, they would be at his side.

"I never trusted your offer, Jax," Abeyla said, a hint of sadness touching her ringing voice. "Such a pity you turned against the Wanderers' calling. You would have been a wonderful teacher."

"I am more than a teacher. I am a master!" Jax spread his arms wide and the water rose up to meet them.

For a moment, he looked like an eagle with unbelievably large wings before the water began to churn. A wave raced forward, striking Abeyla and Lamil's boat, but Abeyla stood calmly on the bow as the boat lurched with the wave.

Tammond leaned in close to Maggie, staring down at his mother.

"A master, Jax Cayde?" Abeyla asked.

Tammond tensed, and Maggie took his hand.

"That is not the way. There is no master of magic." Abeyla stood on the very edge of the boat, balanced perfectly on the thin rail.

"If you truly believe that, then I have much to teach you before I allow your departure from this world." Jax threw his arms forward, and again the water surged toward Abeyla and

Lamil. But Abeyla was flying through the air, soaring above the water.

With a guttural cry, white-hot light flew from Abeyla's palms. For a moment, Maggie thought she had missed. The lightning hadn't struck Jax. Instead, it had hit the raft that held him above the water. Instantly, the raft gave a terrible *crack*. Jax swayed for a moment, but stayed upright as the raft caught fire.

Abeyla landed on the water not fifteen feet in front of Jax. Maggie expected her to sink, but Abeyla landed catlike on top of one of Jax's waves, which had frozen in place.

"Fire does not fear fire." Jax waved a hand, and the smoke from the fire disappeared. Flames still lapped at his feet, but his view of Abeyla was unobscured. "I am the one who burned the Broken Lake. Are you so anxious for me to do it again?"

The flames from Jax's raft melted down over the sides. The fire didn't extinguish or even falter as it touched the water. The blaze grew, absorbing the blue of the water and spreading quickly with dancing sapphire flames.

"Jax Cayde," Abeyla said calmly as the fire surged toward her. "You never think that anyone else can learn. You've never seen how magic can grow and evolve if you only let it."

Holding her hands below her mouth as though blowing sand into the wind, Abeyla let out a great breath. The fire in its path flickered as it was pushed back, its blue light fading. But in a moment the fire had grown brighter, flames leaping a foot above the lake.

"It's gone wrong." Maggie's mind raced, trying to find a way to save the village from burning.

"Wait," Tammond whispered.

The flames weren't racing toward Abeyla anymore. They had cascaded in the other direction, toward Jax and his men who were now right behind him.

The men shouted in fear as the fire streaked toward them. A few leapt from their rafts, but in a second the flames had engulfed the water around the boats, giving the men no way out.

A handful of the men seemed to be prepared, working magic Maggie could barely see. Shields shimmered around a few of the rafts. One lifted itself out of the lake, hovering out of reach of the flames, while another was now surrounded in a cocoon of water.

But other boats burned. The men on them screaming in fear and pain as the flames surrounded them. Maggie's throat tightened as the smoke scented with burning flesh reached the cliff, but she squinted through the haze to see what Jax was doing.

He wasn't helping his men, hadn't raised a finger to save any of the Enlightened who cried for his aid. He stood, staring at Abeyla.

"You've grown hard in these years," Jax said. "You aren't as squeamish as you once were."

"I will do anything to protect my people." Abeyla's words barely cut over the rush of water as a wave twelve feet high soared toward her.

Maggie bit her lips, tasting blood in her mouth as she fought not to scream.

But a spell leapt forward from behind Abeyla. Lamil had joined the fray. A bright purple streak of what seemed like airborne lava flew toward Jax, touching a point above his head and spreading over him, trapping him in its grip. Abeyla emerged from the water, dripping but apparently unhurt.

Two of the rafts had made their way out of the flames and, with a shout, the Enlightened began casting spells toward Abeyla. It was too much, far too much. There were too many for Abeyla to fight on her own. But spells soared from under the overhang as well. The Wanderers had joined the fight.

One of the rafts was hit, and two of the men were tossed overboard. The water around them hardened, leaving the men screaming as their fellows passed over them on their own raft, crushing them to death.

A flock of creatures that looked like water given life flew toward the Enlightened, scratching their eyes and faces, distracting them from casting more spells.

With a scream from Lamil, the water under one of the rafts sloshed into a spin, churning and twisting, sucking the raft under the water. One of the men knelt down on the raft, placing his hand on the deck.

For a split second, the raft rose from the grip of the funnel, but a shattering sound like a thousand glasses breaking shook the air, and the raft fell back into the vortex, disappearing under the water as Jax emerged from his shining purple cage, his eyes glowing with fury.

Before Maggie could take a breath, Jax was raining down spells upon the Wanderers. The remaining Enlightened had rallied by his side and were now pushing forward, toward Abeyla.

Spells flew from the village, too, the flashes of light and terrible smoke so thick, it was impossible to tell what was happening below. It was as though they were looking down on a lightning cloud, knowing there was destruction underneath but without any way to tell what the chaos was.

"We have to get down there," Tammond said, starting for the ridge that led down to the water. "We can't help from up here."

"And what good will you do down there?" Bertrand blocked his path. "We are to stay here. We are the last measure at the end. And listen to them fighting." Shouts echoed up from below, guttural war cries that seemed impossible on the Broken Lake. "They are still pushing back. It is not yet our time."

"They've lost men," Tammond said, shoving Bertrand aside. "We can come at them from behind."

"How?" Bertrand asked, following Tammond. Maggie stood and chased after them. "You have no boat. How will you fight?"

"How will you know if all our people are dying if you can't see?" A mad fury shone in Tammond's eyes. "I won't wait up here blind until it's too late to save anyone. I am going below the smoke so I can see."

He went to the edge of the cliff and began climbing down.

Bertrand looked to Maggie. "Abeyla wanted us to stay here. To wait until the time is right."

"Abeyla wanted her son to be kept alive," Maggie said.

"Follow if you must, Miss Trent," Bertrand said, "but know I will not be there to save you."

"I can save myself, thanks." Maggie walked past him as Tammond disappeared down the ridge.

"What I meant, Miss Trent," Bertrand said, "is do not go looking for the darkness. It seems to like you, and it might not let you go this time. And Miss Trent, I would hate to lose you so soon."

Maggie nodded, a knot tightening in her throat. "Don't you go looking for darkness either. Just because you're old friends doesn't mean he'll let you live."

Not waiting for Bertrand's reply, Maggie followed Tammond down the mountain.

CHAPTER 29

*G*oing down took much less time than climbing up. In a few minutes they were forty feet above the water, beneath the thick blanket of smoke and able to see the battle below. The time the battle had been out of view had made all the difference. The Enlightened had surged forward, moving past Abeyla and Jax, who fought each other head on now, throwing spells with such force the air crackled with the might of their magic.

The fire had disappeared from the surface of the lake. Magic from spells that had missed their marks remained in the water, dancing as vibrant, shimmering lights across the black. It should have been beautiful. But bodies lay in the lake, dark markers that marred the bright magic.

Maggie wouldn't let herself count the bodies or study their clothes to see if they were Enlightened or Wanderer. Nothing could be done to change the fate of the dead.

A horrible *crack* echoed under the overhang as a spell struck the village, splitting it in half. The docks shook, and Wanderers were tossed into the air, some hitting the water, others hitting the hard, wooden dock. Maggie didn't have time to see how many of the Wanderers struggled to their feet.

With a cry of pain, Abeyla fell backward from her tower of water made solid and disappeared into the lake.

For a moment, everything froze, then Jax gave a triumphant laugh.

Maggie clapped her hand over Tammond's mouth before he could shout.

"Stay quiet," Maggie said. "We have to stay quiet or we can't help." Tammond reached to pull her hand away, but she clung on. "I know she's your mom and you want to help her, but we have to be smart. She wants you to be smart."

Jax drifted toward the village. In a minute, he would catch up to the Enlightened, and what chance would the Wanderers have without Abeyla?

Abeyla dead.

Maggie shook the thought from her mind.

"Do you trust me?" She took Tammond by the shoulders, forcing him to look into her eyes.

"I do."

"Then we're going to swim." She took Tammond's hand and pulled him to the very edge of the ridge, hoping she could jump out far enough to clear the rocks. "On three. One, two—"

Her last word was swallowed by a *crack* that blocked all other sound. But she was already jumping, flying farther out over the water than her legs could have carried her without magic. As she fell into the water, she watched the edge of the overhang shatter and plummet toward the lake far below.

The shockwave found her in the water, striking her in the chest and forcing the precious air from her lungs. She clawed her way to the surface, holding tight to Tammond's hand.

She found the air, gasping for breath as Tammond emerged beside her. The rock had been cleaved off in one giant piece, forming a wall between the village and the Enlightened, crushing the attackers who had been underneath. But there were still sounds of fighting within the village. And on this side of the lake were Jax and Lamil.

Lamil stood tall on what was left of his boat, chunks of wood barely stable enough to balance on. He bled from a gash on his chest, gasping as he took shuddering breaths. And nearby, floating facedown in the water, was Abeyla, her gray hair drifting around her head like a shining crown.

"No," Tammond said.

"Get Abeyla," Maggie said. "Get her to shore. I'll go after Jax."

"Maggie, no," Tammond said. "I won't lose you, too."

"Don't worry about me. I have to help Lamil." Maggie kissed him, hoping it wouldn't be the last time. "Meet you in the village."

She turned back toward Jax in time to see a shadow fall from high up on the cliff. A jacket caught in the wind, making it look for a moment as though Bertrand had wings before he disappeared on the far side of the rock barrier.

Two other shadows followed before Maggie took a breath and dove deep under water.

There was no current in the lake. No more shaking from the fallen rock. Lights streaked overhead, making the water in front of her flicker in the darkness. But swimming forward was easy. In seconds she lost sight of Tammond. But she pushed herself as far as she could before coming up to take a breath. She was close to Jax now. He was still distracted by Lamil. If she could only reach—

A hand closed tight around Maggie's ankle, dragging her down into the lake.

The scream that flew from her throat was muffled by the water. But it didn't matter. Her air was gone. She twisted to see who was pulling her deeper still into the lake. It was one of the Enlightened, his face shining with victory as Maggie struggled. She lunged toward him before kicking hard. She felt her boot hit his face, but still the man didn't loosen his grip.

Her lungs were already screaming. Rage boiled in her. She needed to get away, needed to stop Jax. But her fury held power. Without thought for hurting herself, Maggie let her burning anger go, felt it fly in a white-hot sheet from her body, boiling the water around her.

The man let go of her ankle, and Maggie kicked toward the surface. The burning water didn't hurt her as she swam through it. Her own rage held no power to harm her.

Maggie's head broke through the surface of the water, and she gulped in smoky air. She blinked away the spots in her eyes, desperate to see what was happening around her. Screams came from the village, but the water near her was silent. Lamil knelt in his boat, his right arm hanging limp and useless at his side.

Jax moved toward him, laughing in a mirthless way, not seeming to care that his men still fought in the village.

Maggie swam as silently and quickly as she could toward Jax.

"You could have joined me, Lamil," Jax cooed. "You would have stood by my side, and the Enlightened would have been stronger for it. But then—" Jax looked toward the overhang "—I guess my Enlightened have grown strong enough without you."

"I never would have joined you, Jax," Lamil coughed. "I've never had it in me. I'm not a traitor."

With a scream, Jax raised his hand, ready to strike.

Maggie dove beneath Jax's shattered raft, flipped over in the water, and kicked the wood with every bit of strength she had left. The wood splintered as the impact sent her deep down into the water. Twisting as quickly as she could, she swam back up.

Jax had fallen into the water. She had seen it. Seen him sink for a moment. But by the time she neared the surface, he was already gone.

Maggie kept her head underwater, scanning the lake for a sign of Jax. But there was no shadow. Bodies and splintered bits of wood floated around her, but nothing moved. With no choice left, Maggie surfaced as quietly as she could, taking in a calm breath and looking around.

Jax was there, right in front of her. She forgot to swim for a moment and sank back down below the surface of the water. She could see him now even with the water clouding her vision. Hovering two feet over the lake, Jax stood on a dark cloud that crackled with light. The cloud drew water from the lake, growing larger every moment as Jax again advanced on the village.

Maggie slipped her head into the open air, pressing her hands to the surface of the lake. She shut her eyes tight, hoping against hope her magic would work.

A scream of pain came from nearby, but Maggie didn't dare look.

With more strength than she knew she had, she forced her magic out into the water, forming a solid sheet of ice that reached in every direction. She shivered as the water around her grew cold. The ice expanded, gaining ground every second, crackling and splintering as it surged toward Maggie. Soon the ice would close around her neck. She wouldn't be able to climb to the surface. Letting go of her magic, Maggie punched the ice, not caring as she felt it tear her skin. Before the ice had time to reform, she pushed herself onto its surface.

The spell had done what she'd hoped. The storm Jax rode couldn't pull any more water from the lake. He was slowing down, but not enough. He would still be able to make it to the fallen rock and then to the village beyond.

Jax raised his hands. Maggie could see magic between them, crackling with such force it bent the air. The village wouldn't survive that spell. It would be gone. Everyone gone. The children left in the dark place.

With a guttural scream, Maggie charged toward Jax, all thoughts of magic gone, her only hope to stop his spell. Jax turned to face her, surprise flickering in his eyes for only a moment before his mouth twisted into a hateful smile.

He swept his hand through the air as though choosing a piece of magic to kill her with, but with a scream, Maggie launched herself at him, grabbing him around the middle and tackling him onto the ice.

Pain shot through her arms as they met the ice, but she held on, pushing Jax into the frozen surface. He screamed as the ice pinned down his arms and legs before growing to surround him. Maggie leapt away as the ice engulfed his body in thick, glassy layers, leaving only his face in the open air.

His screams of rage and pain shook Maggie's bones.

He would break out of her spell. He had already broken free of a magical prison once before.

She didn't know a spell to stop him, didn't know how to bind him.

A *clunk* sounded on the ice nearby as Lamil pulled himself out of the shattered boat and ran limping toward Jax. Something silver shimmered in his hand, and the thing grew with every step, becoming as tall as he was with sharp tips on either end.

Before Maggie had time to think, Lamil drove the end of his shimmering staff through the ice, directly into Jax's heart.

A horrible scream rent the night. Blood filled the ice, coloring it red, and Jax's face became a death mask of his anger.

"He's—" Maggie began, searching for the words in the fog of her mind. "He's dead?"

"He is." Lamil lowered himself onto the ice, setting his staff down beside him and clutching his bad arm.

Jax was dead. The night should have gone silent. There was nothing left to fight for. The Master of the Enlighted was gone. But shouts and cries still came from the village.

"Will you be all right?" Maggie asked. She paused only long enough to see Lamil's tired nod before running toward the village.

CHAPTER 30

 he sheet of ice she had created reached all the way to
the fallen rock. Maggie sprinted toward the village,
grateful for her sturdy boots as she leapt onto the stone without
stopping.

The ice hadn't gone past the stone barrier. The water on the
other side was still liquid, reflecting the fires that burned in the
village. Half of the village had sunk and was nearly out of sight. A
corner of it had caught on the rocks in the shallow water and
clung hopelessly on. The other half of the village was still floating
and shrouded in haze from the smoke trapped under what was
left of the overhang.

People were shouting and fighting on the nearest dock, but
others had fled to the few clusters of rock by the cliff wall. The
shadows of the fighters danced in the firelight.

Bertrand was there, fighting two of the Enlightened, his face
calm as the air around him pulsated, sending daggers of broken
wood at the men. Selna fought, too. She had her attacker on the
run and backed up almost to the edge of the dock. Maggie
watched as the man toppled into the lake, and Selna hardened the

water around him, leaving him to drown. There was another person fighting, lightning blazing from both hands.

Maggie took a deep breath and shouted as loud as she could, "Jax Cayde is dead! The Master of the Enlightened has fallen."

One of the men fighting Bertrand faltered, and wood struck him through the arms, pinning him to the deck with a howl of pain. But the other fought on.

"There are none of your people left alive on the lake." Maggie's voice was louder this time, echoing off the rocks, drowning out the fighters. "The Enlightened have lost the battle. Leave now!"

The other Enlightened Bertrand had been fighting turned and sent a streak of bright red light toward Maggie. She dove to the side, out of the path of the spell. A shout carried across the water as the Enlightened fell.

There were only two left fighting, both of them moving so quickly they hadn't even paused. It wasn't until a bright white spell flew close to his face that Maggie recognized Tammond.

Maggie dove into the water, quickly swam the hundred feet to the village, and climbed onto the dock.

Tammond had the Enlightened backed against a house, but the man wasn't giving up. Screaming, he threw spell after spell at Tammond, who had formed a barrier around himself and pushed his way forward as the spells slammed into his shimmering shield.

Maggie wanted to shout for Tammond to back away so she could help, but she was afraid to distract him for even a moment. But Tammond's shield was faltering. The Enlightened's magic wasn't sliding harmlessly away anymore.

Tammond shouted in pain as one of the spells struck him.

"No!" Maggie screamed, charging forward, but Bertrand was closer.

With a wave of Bertrand's hand, the slats of the house behind the man reached out and grabbed him like a dozen angry arms before the house burst into flames.

Maggie barely heard the screams of the Enlightened as she ran toward Tammond. He fell to the deck, gasping but alive. Blood covered his hands and dripped down his face. A gash on his right side showed the bones beneath.

"Tammond." Maggie pressed her hands to Tammond's side, trying to stop the freely flowing blood. "He needs help! Please someone help!"

"Maggie," Tammond said, her name trembling in his voice. "Maggie."

"You're okay," Maggie whispered. "We won, you're going to be okay."

"Abeyla is gone," Tammond said. "I couldn't save her."

"But she saved you."

Hands moved Maggie's away from the wound as someone began healing Tammond.

"Abeyla wanted you to survive, and you did. She won. Jax is gone, and we're still here."

A dull light emanated from Tammond's side, and he gasped as his skin knit back together.

"The village was destroyed," Tammond said. "Our home is gone."

"You'll rebuild." Maggie held Tammond's hand.

Bertrand knelt by her side now, helping to lay Lamil down. The old man's eyes were half closed, but he was still breathing.

"First, we'll go get the kids," Maggie said, trying with everything she had to keep pain and fear from touching her voice, "then you'll find a new place to build. And none of you will have to be afraid of Jax Cayde ever again."

Tammond's eyes drifted slowly closed. Maggie looked to the woman who had been healing him.

"Let him sleep," the woman said, her voice weak with fatigue. "The village will still be broken when he wakes."

Maggie lay Tammond's hand gently down on the deck. There were still others moaning in pain, and fire still raged through part of the village. Pushing herself to her feet, Maggie started toward the place where the village had cracked in half, but Bertrand laid a hand on her shoulder.

"The Wanderers will put out the fire," Bertrand said, sounding tired for the first time. "We've done enough."

Maggie looked out toward the lake. Shadows danced on the fallen rock, cast by the dimming light of the fires, and beyond the lake was calm and still. The moon and the stars shone down as though nothing had happened.

"There are bodies out there," Maggie said, not feeling afraid of them or even sick at the death that surrounded them. Too much had happened in the last few hours for her to be able to feel much of anything. "We should collect them."

"We should collect the living first," Selna said. Her brown hair had been burned away in patches, and newly healed cuts marked her neck and chest. "As soon as the sun rises, we should go collect the children."

"Mina will be so happy to see you." Maggie nodded. That small movement made her dizzy. "I'll go with you."

"You'll sleep first," Bertrand said.

"Where am I supposed to sleep when the village is shattered and on fire?" Maggie asked as Bertrand took her by the elbow and led her to the far edge of what was left of the village. Most of the Fireside was still standing. Only one wall of books had crumbled into the water. There were injured lined up along one side. Most were already asleep.

"Dawn is in a few hours," Bertrand said. "Rest until then. Once it's light enough, we'll collect the children."

"I shouldn't be sleeping while others are working," Maggie said as Selna guided her to a bare bit of floor. "I should be up working with you."

"Maggie," Selna said, "you fought Jax. You helped us survive.

You went into the water alone. You're allowed to be tired. And you"—she turned to Bertrand—"you rest as well. When the others can't work anymore, then you'll be awake to continue."

The crackling of the fire had stopped. The patients were no longer screaming. The quiet of the village seemed haunting and unnatural. A faint murmur whispered over the sounds of mourning for those who had been lost.

They carried Tammond in and laid him with the other wounded. Maggie walked over, stumbling on the rough wooden floor. They had cleaned the blood from his skin. He looked as though he were ill, like he was coming through a bad fever, not like he had been through a battle.

Maggie lay on the floor beside him. Not touching him, just listening to his even breathing. Counting each inhale and exhale as another moment they had outlived Jax Cayde. Before she made it to fifty, she was asleep.

CHAPTER 31

*M*aggie woke with a gasp. Someone had touched her foot. Images of Jax rising out of the water flooded her mind, but before she let her magic loose, her gaze found Selna crouching at her feet, pressing a finger over her lips.

"The sun is rising," Selna mouthed.

Maggie nodded. Gray light peered in through the now open wall of the Fireside. She crawled out from beside Tammond. He didn't move as she crept away.

"I'll be right back," Maggie whispered, though she knew he couldn't hear.

Guards had been stationed on top of the fallen rock. They scanned the lake as the sun turned the sky a pale red.

"What are they looking for?" Maggie whispered to Selna.

"Others who might attack." Selna led Maggie into one of five boats that were manned and ready to be rowed toward the children. "Word from the watchers if any of them survived Jax. Just because Jax is dead doesn't mean there are no more dangers in the world."

Maggie nodded silently. She climbed down into the boat and

was grateful when Selna passed her a paddle. Bertrand nodded to her from the boat ahead of them as they joined the line rowing out toward the fallen rock.

Each of the boats stopped and had to be carried one at a time up over the stone before being lowered back down on the lake side.

"Can't we move the rock?" Maggie asked, the boat digging into her hands as they carried it.

"Down is much simpler than up," Selna said. "It wouldn't be safe, and it would take more magic than we can give."

They lowered the wooden boat back down on the other side with a gentle splash.

"But then you'll have to rebuild everything," Maggie said. "You won't be able to salvage any..." Maggie's words faded away as she looked out over the lake.

The ice had melted, leaving broken wood and bodies behind. The bodies of the Enlightened drifted across the surface. Carrion birds circled overhead, ready for their morning feast. A boat was already out in the water, collecting the Wanderers who had fallen.

"What are you going to do with the bodies?" Maggie asked, slipping as she stepped back into the boat. The *thud* of her misstep carried out over the water, making the birds cry even louder.

"The Wanderers shall be sent below," Selna said. "The others will be moved out of sight and left for the animals. It would be wrong for us to deny them fresh meat."

Maggie nodded and paddled forward, trying not to wonder where the Enlightened bodies would be left.

Paddling made her arms burn and her hands ache. But there was something comforting in the movement. Feeling the sting and soreness of the night before made it feel more real. She had fought Jax. There had been a great battle. Abeyla was dead, but her son had survived. The Wanderers had survived, and she, Maggie Trent, had helped to make sure of that.

The back of Maggie's throat hardened as she swallowed the tears that threatened to creep up into her eyes.

Before the sun had risen over the highest mountain, they reached the dark place. Maggie paddled into the blackness, closing her eyes and letting her magic lead her. The walls held the same energy she did. She recognized their power, as they recognized hers. Shouts carried from the darkness as the first boat reached the torchlight.

"It's okay. They aren't attacking!"

Maggie recognized the voice of one of the older boys.

"It's our people!"

"Mama!" a voice shrieked. "Mama!"

"Mina!" Selna shouted from the back of the boat.

Maggie opened her eyes as the torchlight came into view.

"Mina, I'm coming!"

Maggie could hear the tears in Selna's voice. Mina jumped up and down the rocky shore, waving her arms wildly over her head. As soon as she saw Selna, Mina dove into the water, swimming for her mother as only a child raised on the water could. In seconds, she had reached the boat, and Selna scooped her out of the water, cradling the sopping wet child to her chest.

"Mama!" Mina said. "We were so brave. I stood guard and everything."

"I'm proud of you, Mina." Selna pushed the hair away from her daughter's face. "I love you, little fish."

"Mama, can we go home now? I'm very tired, and I can go sleep in my bed."

"Our home was lost in the battle." Selna kissed her daughter on the forehead. "But we will build a new home, and I promise I will find you a safe place to sleep."

Mina stared solemnly at her mother for a moment. "Were people lost with the house?"

"Yes, Mina."

Maggie turned away, her heart breaking at the grief on Selna's face. Some of these children wouldn't have parents or beds to call their own anymore.

"Mama," Mina whispered so softly Maggie could barely hear, "I'm glad I didn't lose you."

CHAPTER 32

*T*he rippling of water from Selna's paddle told Maggie to row forward. Their boat hit the shore with a grinding bump. The last few children climbed onboard, their faces anxious and afraid.

"Selna," the last boy to climb into their boat said, "have you seen my parents? Do you know if..." The boy's words drifted away as though he were afraid saying them might make them more real.

"I don't know," Selna said. "I didn't see them."

The boy nodded as they rowed back out into the darkness.

The way back to the village seemed longer than the way to the dark place. It might have been that Maggie's arms were burning with fatigue or that anticipation stretched every moment.

Maggie held her breath as they started down the long, watery path to the village. More people were standing on the fallen rock now, waving their arms and shouting greetings to the children. The bodies had been taken out of the water, but two men labored by the side of the lake, building a long raft. And next to the raft floated a large boat whose contents were covered by blankets.

How many people could fit in that boat? How many graves would have to be dug?

"Maggie!" Tammond sat on top of the fallen rock. His face was pale and drawn, but he smiled in relief as he saw her. He struggled to his feet as her boat knocked against the side of the rock and, grimacing in pain, reached down to help her up. She took his hand, careful not to put any weight on it as she stepped out of the boat.

"You're awake," Maggie tried to say, but Tammond was kissing her.

"I thought you'd left," he murmured, keeping his forehead pressed to hers.

"I went with Selna to get the kids back."

Tammond kissed her again. "I know. It's just that, with the battle over, I thought you would disappear."

"I wouldn't leave without saying goodbye," Maggie said.

Fear flickered through Tammond's eyes.

"We just had to get them home." Maggie stepped away to look at the children. Most were in the arms of their parents. But for some, there was no one left to wait for them.

"What's going to happen to the orphans?" Maggie's heart dropped as the older boy who had asked after his parents sat on the rock, tears streaming down his cheeks.

"They'll stay with us," Tammond said, lacing his fingers through Maggie's. "Other families in the village will take them in. This is their home. They will not be sent away."

Maggie looked back at the remnants of the village. It looked worse in the daylight. If everyone crowded together, there might be enough buildings left to have some sort of a roof over everyone's heads.

"Lamil wants to begin rebuilding in the morning," Tammond said. "A new home on the Broken Lake."

"Is Lamil in charge now?" Maggie asked.

"He is." Tammond's eyes shone with unshed tears. "Lamil was

the one chosen by Abeyla to be the next leader of the Wanderers. And Lamil has chosen me as his second."

More boats paddled from the village to the rock. It seemed like every person who could move was coming toward the lake.

"Now that Jax is gone, the Enlightened will be weakened," Tammond said. "This is the time for the Wanderers to go back into the world. And Lamil"—Tammond paused, taking Maggie's other hand—"Lamil wants me to lead the others out into Malina while he stays here and protects the Wanderers' home."

"Wow," Maggie breathed. "Wow. Isn't that fast? To be sending people out there or making decisions. I mean, the battle just ended."

"The Wanderers have waited twenty-seven years on the Broken Lake. Abeyla"—Tammond's voice faltered—"my mother wouldn't have wanted us to wait a moment longer. Life is much too short to let grief stop you from moving forward."

Maggie nodded, unsure of what to say.

More men had rowed to the raft. It was finished now. All the knots tied tightly. One by one, the men gently lifted the bodies of the fallen Wanderers onto the raft, laying them out in one long line. Maggie's breath caught in her chest as they lifted out Giles right before Abeyla.

Tammond shuddered and stepped in front of Maggie, turning away from gruesome raft.

"I've never seen Malina," Tammond said, his words coming out in a rush, "but I've heard stories about it and seen a hundred maps. There are mountains and a great sea that stretches out to the east. There are a hundred villages. Places neither of us has ever seen before. Along the northern sea, there is a place where the trees are thicker around than the Fireside. Come with me, Maggie, and we'll find the great trees together."

Maggie froze. Her heart couldn't remember how to beat, and forming words was a foreign thing she might never manage again. Finally, instinct kicked in, sucking air into her lungs. "Go with you?"

"We'll teach magic to those who need us, and we'll see the world." Tammond leaned in and kissed her gently. "With you at my side, Maggie Trent, what couldn't we accomplish?"

"I—" Maggie looked into Tammond's bright blue eyes. He had just lost his mother and his home, but he was still filled with so much hope.

"Miss Trent," Bertrand said.

Maggie spun to face him, her face flushing.

"I believe it is time to return to the Siren's Realm."

"Return?" Maggie repeated.

"The battle is won, the children are safely home, the funeral will commence shortly, and what comes next is rebuilding. Rebuilding is for those who will stay for much longer than we are able."

"But we could help," Maggie said as Tammond's grip on her hand tightened. "We could help them teach, help them build a new village. You said you wanted adventure. Aren't there more adventures to be had here?"

Bertrand took a long look around the lake and the mountains. "There most definitely are, Miss Trent. If you wished to explore all the adventures this world has to offer, I would understand. But if you stayed that long, I fear you would never return to the Siren's Realm, and what adventures would you be missing then?"

"Maggie," Tammond said, "please don't go. Stay with me."

Maggie heard her decision in Tammond's plea before she knew she had made it.

"Actually, I have to go." Pain crept into Maggie's chest as she kissed Tammond on the cheek. "You'll travel. You'll see all of Malina, and it will be wonderful."

"But…" Tammond's face crumpled as Maggie stepped away.

"Malina is your home." Maggie pushed the words past the lump in her throat. "But it isn't mine."

"Maggie," Tammond whispered.

"I'm sorry, Tammond," Maggie said softly as she followed Bertrand off the rock and into a waiting boat.

Maggie didn't allow herself one last look at Tammond before she and Bertrand rowed away. She could never come back to visit, not even if she wanted to. The Siren's time didn't work that way.

The last of the bodies had been laid out on the raft. A thick net with stones tied to the edges was being laid over them.

"We should stay for the funeral," Maggie said.

"It is better to leave quickly, and I never stay for the funerals, Miss Trent," Bertrand said. Only the hint of sadness in Bertrand's voice kept Maggie from shouting at him. "And if we want to leave before nightfall, we'll have to paddle rather quickly."

Maggie took deep, shuddering breaths as she pulled the boat forward, not brave enough to look back at the Wanderers standing on the fallen rock. Not wanting to see Tammond's face as she left him forever. She willed herself not to think about Abeyla or what they would do to the raft. She paddled with all her strength, keeping her eyes forward on the Broken Lake.

"I just left behind a guy whose mom just died," Maggie said an hour later. "Is there some special sort of punishment for that?"

"Or course," Bertrand said from the back of the boat. "It's called *remorse*."

"So I should have stayed?"

"Are you in love with him?"

"No." The word sounded hollow even to Maggie's own ears. "I don't know if I'm sure what that would feel like. Maybe I'm not capable of loving anyone."

"You were raised in a cage, Miss Trent. Perhaps you should give yourself a larger taste of freedom before deciding what you're capable of."

"So, I'm not heartless and irredeemable?"

"Not at all, Miss Trent. I was hoping you'd follow me into this world, because I knew you were too great to live only one adventure. And while I would hold no ill will if you had fallen in love and chosen to stay here, I am very grateful you will be with me the next time an unknown enemy attacks."

"So we're going to do this again?" Maggie's heart lifted at the thought.

"Of course, Miss Trent." Bertrand laughed. "I am always looking toward the next adventure."

The sun kissed the tops of the mountains when Bertrand finally told Maggie to stop paddling. She stared up at the silhouette of the summit where she and Bertrand had spent that first cold night.

They sat quietly for a moment before Maggie spoke. "So how do we get home? And please don't say climb back up that mountain."

"I believe," Bertrand said, "and I have been wrong on occasion, we swim down."

"Swim down? But we fell from up." Maggie leaned over the edge of the boat and stared down into the water. There was no glimmer of green or hint of magic.

"Into and out of the Siren's Realm are not like walking through a door, Miss Trent. In and out are not the same thing."

"Swim down, it is." Maggie stood up in the boat. Without hesitating, she took a deep breath and dove down deep into the water, not waiting for Bertrand.

The way into the darkness can never be the same as the way back out.

The cool water pressed in around her, blocking out the sounds from above. With a few strokes, the light dimmed. The pressure made her ears throb, but she kept swimming down. She waited for her breath to run out or for her arms to get too tired to move. But the water seemed thinner.

She pulled against it so easily, it felt as though she were flying. And even as the world turned to black, she stroked forward again and again, moving so quickly the water became nothing. And all at once, light surrounded her, flashing such a bright green she gasped, filling her lungs with crisp air.

Maggie crumpled to the ground, panting and blinking. The green light faded, leaving only the dull blue of twilight.

She rolled onto her back, staring up at the sky. She was in the center of the circle of bright white trees. A dull *thump* warned her Bertrand had landed next to her before she'd turned her head to look. He was on his feet, looking completely calm without a hair out of place.

"Well done, Miss Trent." Bertrand smiled, giving her a little bow. "I must say for your first time, you did much better than I thought you would."

"Thanks." Maggie got to her feet without waiting for a hand from Bertrand. The pain in her arms from rowing had vanished. So had the cuts on her hands and arms from battle. "It's like it never happened." Disappointment crept into Maggie's chest. "It looks like we never left the Siren's Realm at all."

"That is one of the gifts of the Siren—she likes us to enter her realm healthy." Bertrand led her out of the circle of trees, past the large dead one, the slit in its trunk completely hidden in the falling shadows.

"But then what was the point?" Maggie clenched her fists as her heart started to race. "If we're just the same as when we left, then why did we go through all that?"

"Well, we did help to save the Wanderers from a massacre. We had our adventure, and don't forget, Miss Trent, we returned with a great deal of magic."

Maggie stopped on the spot, tentatively feeling for the magic inside her. It was dampened again, trapped deep within, but it was stronger than it had been since she had fallen into the Siren's Realm. Stronger perhaps than it had been in her life before the Siren's Realm.

Bertrand beamed at her. "There you are, Miss Trent, you

saved lives and received your reward. Now the only question is, how will you use it?"

Maggie smiled, her thoughts flying to the rock by the sea. "I know how to start."

"Well then, Miss Trent," Bertrand said, striding toward the edge of the woods, "all that is left is to enjoy our bounty and decide which adventure shall befall us next."

Dive into Maggie and Bertrand's next adventure in The Girl Locked With Gold. *Order your copy now.*

DISCOVER THE STEAMPUNK WORLD OF
HISTEM IN...

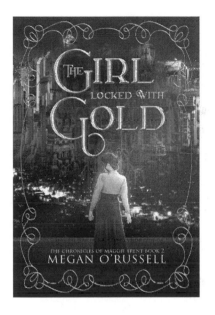

Read on for a sneak peek of *The Girl Locked With Gold.*

CHAPTER 1

The weight of the smoke seared her throat as it pressed down into her lungs.

"Ber—" her hacking cough cut off his name. "Bertrand!"

The roar of the flames swallowed her shout.

The world is on fire, and I'll burn with it.

A scream carried down from high above, the voice too shrill to be Bertrand's.

"Hello?" Maggie stumbled toward the sound.

The dense smoke hid the form of whatever landscape burned around her, but the flames danced higher in the direction of the scream, reaching far above Maggie's head with no sign of something she might climb to reach the terrified person.

"I'm coming!" Maggie gagged on a burst of sour smoke. Something in the haze burned her eyes, blurring her vision.

Sparks whirled around her as she swayed, retching black that tore painfully from her throat.

"Bertrand." Her lips formed his name as she fell to her knees.

The heat of the ground burned through her pants, searing her flesh.

"*Primurgo.*" The spell took the last bit of air she had. The shield shimmered to life around her, blocking the waves of smoke, but not the terrible heat of the flames.

Her palms blistered as she pushed herself to her feet, squinting through the smoke.

No figure stumbled toward her. Not Bertrand or even a poor victim of the devastation in this unknown land.

"Bertrand!" Maggie shouted, coughing up more of the black goo. "Bertrand, we have to go!"

A *crack* rent the air, and the ground shook a moment later. Shield or not, they were running out of time.

"Bertrand Wayland, if you've led me to my death—"

"I have not led you to your death, Miss Trent." Bertrand tore out of the darkness, embers licking the tails of his black coat. "Nor have I ever assured your safety."

"Where the hell have you been?" Maggie dropped her shield, and Bertrand grabbed her wrist, dragging her straight toward a tower of fire.

"*Hell* seems a fairly accurate assessment, Miss Trent." Bertrand ducked as a wall of embers collapsed in front of them. Not pausing, he veered around the flames. "It took you so long to arrive, I didn't know if I would be able to wait for you much longer."

"Thanks for not abandoning me." Maggie leaped over a crack in the ground, her toes landing an inch from Bertrand's heels.

"Of course. Now, if you would." With two giant strides, Bertrand plunged into a black pit that consumed the center of the path.

Flat, scorched walls leading to darkness far below were the only details Maggie managed to see before overwhelming nothing consumed her.

The void squeezed every inch of her being. Her lungs couldn't have expanded to pull in air even if any had been present for her to breathe. A whirling sense like rushing through a vast river tingled her toes, but there was no way to know how fast she moved in the nothing, if she was even moving at all.

As questions she would never get to ask trickled through her mind, a green light flashed into being around her, and pain shot through her knees.

"Ow." Maggie flopped to the side, not caring who might see her lying on the street. "Ow, ow, ow."

"Are you all right, Miss. Trent?" Bertrand hovered over her, silhouetted by the sun.

Maggie took a deep breath, testing her lungs as she rubbed her fingers over her unburnt palms. "No smoke inhalation or third degree burns, so I'd say the Siren worked her magic again."

"Then why are you lying on the ground?" Bertrand said.

Maggie shielded her eyes so she could properly see the furrowed lines on Bertrand's brow. His hair was perfectly slicked back in its customary low ponytail. His white shirt and coat tails showed no signs of burns. Even his buckled shoes hadn't been scratched by their brush with fire.

"I'm on the ground because I, unlike perfect you, am not used to jumping back into the Siren's Realm from a land of fiery doom."

"As long as the Siren hasn't decided not to heal all wounds upon entering her realm, I suppose we're all right." Bertrand offered Maggie his hand, helping her to her feet as a gray-speckled centaur rounded the corner.

"How's it going?" Maggie waved, letting an overly-bright smile fill her face.

"As the Siren wills it be done." The centaur nodded and trotted past them without waiting for further conversation.

"Have a nice day." Maggie brushed the dust from the street off her clothes. "So, how long until you find another stich for us to slip through?"

"Find another stitch?" Bertrand strode down the narrow street, not looking back to see if Maggie followed.

Allowing herself the luxury of rolling her eyes, Maggie trotted after him. "Maybe this time you could find a path out of the Siren's Realm that doesn't lead to Hell."

"The most interesting thing about fire, Miss Trent, is how very temporary it is." Bertrand cut down a wide road lined with tall tents. A gentle wind swayed the colorful fabrics. "Even the worst of blazes will burn out in time. We need only have patience while the flames run their course."

"Wait a second." Maggie dodged around a beautiful woman in red robes to match the tray of wine she carried. "Are you actually saying you want to go back there?"

"Of course, Miss Trent. There are a hundreds, perhaps thousands of tiny stitches joining the Siren's Realm to other worlds. Of all the stitches that exist, the Siren has only allowed us to find a tiny portion. She would not have left a stitch open for us to slip through were there not something interesting and wondrous on the other side. We should not deny ourselves an adventure simply because of a little poor timing."

"You know, that's what I think every time I almost burn to death. As smoke fills my lungs, making it impossible to breathe, *Wow, what a bit of poor timing.*"

"Sarcasm is rarely becoming, Miss Trent."

A wide square opened up in front of them, revealing a platinum fountain flowing in the middle of it all. A statue of a beautiful woman, her nakedness barely concealed by a thin strip of fabric, stood at the center of the pool.

A man had climbed up on the edge of the fountain, blocking the crowd from swimming in the sweet liquid. "The Siren's time is shifting away like sand. Her ways are beyond our ken, and times worse than storms are nipping at all of our heels."

"What?" Maggie grabbed Bertrand's sleeve to stop his momentum.

The people in the square were watching the man as he paced the rim of the fountain.

"For in light and peace, there must still come shadows, and it is only the will of the Siren that holds the darkness at bay."

"Let the Siren's will be done," a woman shouted, "and leave us in peace."

A cheer sounded behind the woman, then another.

"Those who do not read the wind shall be eaten by the storm!" the man warned as the crowd surged forward.

"Come along, Miss Trent." Bertrand cut out of the square and down a narrow alley lined with bright red tents.

"Shouldn't we help him?"

A roaring shout sounded from the square.

"Those people could really hurt him," Maggie said.

"A madman who's decided to speak on behalf of the Siren?" Bertrand said. "I don't think there is anything within our power to be done."

A wide lane opened up in front of them. Tables laden with goods from fine silks to fresh baked cakes were open for business. Maggie's stomach turned as a woman shook hands with a silk dealer. Her clothes shimmered for a moment as their colors twisted. Her plain green dress vanished, replaced by a red gown woven through with gold.

Maggie's hands tingled, remembering the feeling of magic zinging through her skin. The shock of it as it left her body in payment for goods, leaving a tiny hole that didn't refill. But if the woman hated the feel of it, her face showed no sign as she gleefully spun in her new gown.

"What do you think they'll do to him?" Maggie averted her eyes as a man paid for a diamond-accented pocket watch.

"I think what the crowd will do to him is the least of that man's concerns." Bertrand kept his voice low as they passed a woman tending a flowerbed filled with bright blue blooms in front or her matching blue tent. "He dares to speak for the Siren. It is never wise to make assumptions of one who provides all that is needed for survival."

"Because you've never tried to tell me how the Siren works?" Maggie whispered.

"I happen to have an uncanny understanding of the Siren and the wisdom to know that sometimes speaking the truth is best done quietly."

The road beneath their feet changed from dirt to cobblestone as they reached the fortress. Weathered and stately houses rose up around them. A lone gondola paddled down the canal, the boatman humming a slow tune. Iron barred windows stared down at them from above, and heavy wooden doors protected against unwanted visitors.

Maggie shuddered at the tingling feeling of dozens of unseen people glaring at her for intruding in this exclusive and intentionally private section of the Siren's Realm.

"I don't think we need waste our time as we wait for the smoke to clear." Bertrand's voice bounced off the stone houses. "You really should work more on your swordplay and hand to hand combat, and this provides an excellent opportunity."

"Remember that time when I was going to live out my days in the Siren's Realm in peace?" Maggie said as Bertrand stopped at a thick wooden door, barely visible beneath the stone overhang of a house. "I was going to fish and live on the rocks by the sea. Enjoy my time not almost dying."

"Let time drift by with nothing to show for it but a bit more wear on your shoes?" Bertrand heaved the wooden door open. The *creak* of the door had become too familiar to startle Maggie. "You would be miserable. If not now, then in a few years."

"Fine." Maggie followed Bertrand into the stone entryway, shoving the wooden door shut behind her and fixing the lock with a dull *clunk*. "But can we both at least agree this morning was not the kind of adventure we want to repeat?"

"But why? Isn't any adventure one survives a worthy undertaking?" Bertrand opened the door at the far end of the tiny, windowless room and strode up the steps to the main house, leaving Maggie barely able to hear his words as she chased him. "We'll give it a few days. By then, the inferno should have died, and slipping into a world of embers should be safe enough. Perhaps we can even discover the source of the blaze."

Bertrand stopped in front of the wide fireplace, lifting a teacup off the mantle and breathing in the sweet steam.

"Unless, of course, you'd like to stay behind and focus on your booming career in the fish trade."

Maggie exhaled, forcing her teeth to unclench. "I'll come with you." She took the second cup from the stone mantle, letting the herbal fragrance melt her frustration. "But only because I don't want you to burn to death."

"How very kind." Bertrand raised his cup to her.

A painting hung above the fireplace. Shadows crept in on either side of the frame with only a dull ray on sunlight peering through at the center. Hints of texture played in the background, but not enough to decipher what exactly the painting was meant to depict.

"You really should get a new painting." Maggie sipped her tea. "Something a bit more cheerful."

"In time." Bertrand nodded. "But I'm still enamored of this one for now."

Maggie shook her head, not setting her cup down as Bertrand dragged all of the furniture to the bookcase that lined the far wall.

"Would you like to begin with swordplay or boxing?" Bertrand removed his jacket, carefully folding the dark material before draping it on the arm chair.

"Do I want to punch you or try and stab you?" Maggie downed the rest of her tea. "Decisions, decisions."

"Swordplay it is." Bertrand knocked three times on the wall. A panel no more than a foot wide slid aside, revealing two swords and two daggers nestled in red velvet.

"How much magic did the secret compartment cost you?" Maggie asked.

Bertrand grabbed one of the swords, tossing the blade to Maggie.

Maggie caught the hilt and wrapped her fingers around the soft leather.

"I would rather pay the magic to the Siren to keep the blades safe than consider the possibility of weapons ever drifting into the Siren's Realm."

Bertrand lifted the other sword, examining the gleaming blade before bowing to Maggie.

Maggie bowed back, mocking Bertrand, though she knew he wouldn't respond.

"Besides, Miss Trent. We venture out of the Siren's Realm for adventure and riches. What good is bringing more magic into this place if we don't spend it?"

"Touché." Maggie lifted her blade.

"The term is *en garde*." Bertrand lunged, his sword bouncing off Maggie's with a satisfying *ting.*

CHAPTER 2

"Ouch, ouch." Maggie's legs throbbed their fatigue as she scrambled up the rocks by the Endless Sea. "Ouch."

A fine layer of sand coated the rocks, blown up from the stretch of beach where the waves gently lapped at the toes of the residents who preferred to bask in the sun. But the red of evening had begun to take hold of the sky, clearing the beach and leaving Maggie in peace to climb the rocks to her home.

Cracks split the giant stones. Each gap as familiar as the streets she walked every day.

"Learn to fight, Miss Trent," Maggie mumbled as she slid down the edge of an outcropping that hovered over the sea. "It'll be useful, Miss Trent." Blood trickled from the cut on her shoulder. "I'm not just being an ass who wants to jab you with a sword, Miss Trent."

A giant fluke broke through the sparkling water.

"I could just refuse to go with him, Mort," Maggie called to the whale as he lazily rolled in the water. "Tell him I'd rather not jump back into the fiery death world and just wait for the next round."

A plume of water shot into the air.

"I could do it. I could sit this one out. Don't doubt me, Mort. I might prove you wrong."

Maggie turned her back on the Endless Sea and smiled despite the blood on her arm. A tiny stone house hid nestled on the rock outcropping. There were no seams between the walls and the rocks above and below. Only the thick wooden door and large window with heavy shutters hanging open showed the greatness of the Siren's magic hidden within.

At a touch from her hand, the door swung open. The lamps flickered on before she reached for them, lighting the tiny room with their warm glow. A bed rested in one corner, and a table with one chair in the other. The curving gap where the two rocks that formed the back wall met held her fishing net, a spare fishing net, and three books Bertrand had lent her.

"Home, sweet home."

~

*T*he morning sun hadn't warmed the Endless Sea, but Maggie welcomed the chill on her sore limbs. Catching the fish came easily. The Siren provided plentiful fish in the Endless Sea for anyone who had the will to catch them.

Fill the net, bring the fish to town, sell the fish, purchase supplies, go to Bertrand's, come back home.

Maggie sunk under the water, letting the gentle waves lift her hair and sway her limbs.

It had seemed like enough. Before she knew slipping out of the Siren's Realm into other worlds was possible, the routine had seemed like enough. Then having the magic to ask the Siren for her tiny stone house seemed like enough.

Enough is never enough.

Maggie kicked up to the surface, gasping for air.

Fish. That was the first step. Catch the fish, sell the fish…adventure.

Maggie pulled on her boots before her feet had properly dried. Her arms didn't ache as she pulled the net of fish up the rocks. She had done it too many times before.

"You were right, Mort," Maggie turned and shouted to the Endless Sea though the whale was nowhere in sight. "You always are, buddy."

The people on the lanes moved quickly in the mid-morning light, giving Maggie space to haul her net without having to worry about darting around dawdlers.

"Veils for the covering of faces," a woman shouted, her own face draped with a lilac veil. "Worth every drop of magic for a cloth this fine."

"No thanks," Maggie said before the woman took two steps toward her.

"But, my girl—"

Maggie dodged under the woman's arm, knocking her with the net of fish.

A splatter of seawater soaked the front of the woman's gown.

"Sorry." Maggie held one hand up, keeping the other tightly on her net. "I'm so sorry."

"You little, vagrant fish monger." The woman dropped her basket of veils, curling her hands into fists.

"Sorry!" Maggie ran down a narrow alley between two rows of tents.

"I will beat you with your fish, you insolent little Derelict!" The shriek followed Maggie as she wove through a group of towering trolls and out onto the market square.

Heart pounding, Maggie ducked into a sweets stall.

"Do not drip fish on my cakes." The old man who owned the stall wagged a flour-covered finger at her nose.

"No problem." Maggie smiled broadly. "Just looking for a snack. This one is great."

Without truly considering, Maggie lifted a purple circular pastry, tucking it in her mouth before offering her hand to the man for payment. As his flour-covered palm met her sea salt-covered skin, a tingle buzzed in her arm. A shock flew through her, leaving a tiny hole where her magic should be. The unpleasant feeling lasted only a moment before the man let go.

"Thanks," Maggie murmured through her mouthful of pastry.

The market square was filled with its usual array of shoppers and people watchers. Some moved stall to stall, inspecting the wares though they hardly changed from day to day. Others lounged in the sun, watching the people inspecting the wares that hardly changed from day to day. No one ran into the square looking for the girl who had hit someone with her net of fish, so Maggie headed to the fresh food stalls at the far corner of the square.

The sweet jelly filling of the purple pastry coated Maggie's throat. The taste was something between blueberry and pear, but not quite either. Or maybe both. Good food had never been an expectation at the Academy.

"Mathilda," Maggie called into the shadows behind the counter of her tent. "Mathilda, what sort of fruit is in this?"

Maggie held the pastry out as Mathilda appeared from the shadows, her white mobcap bouncing as she ran toward her.

"It's good, I'm just not sure—"

"Maggie, child, where under the Siren's sun have you been?" Mathilda threw her arms around Maggie, knocking the rest of the pastry to the ground.

"What?" Maggie said as Mathilda took her face in her hands.

"I thought you were dead!" Mathilda grabbed the net from Maggie, tossing the contents on the back table. "Terrible things sweeping through the Siren's Realm, and you decide to just not turn up for a while?"

"What terrible things?"

"I ought to kick you out of my stall and never buy from you again." Mathilda grabbed a knife, lopping the head off a fish.

"Mathilda, what are you talking about?" Maggie leapt aside as Mathilda gutted the fish so enthusiastically, slime spurted from the scales.

"Consistency is important in commerce, and if I can't count on you—"

"Mathilda!" Maggie grabbed Mathilda's hand that wielded the knife. "I don't know what you're talking about."

"You don't, do you?" Mathilda looked up to the ceiling of her tent. "Have you been hiding under a rock for the five days you've been gone?"

"Five days?" Maggie balled her hands into fists, tucking them behind her back to hide their shaking.

Five minutes. Maybe ten. That's all we were gone.

"Were you hiding on that rock you call home? Lost track of time?" Mathilda turned back to butchering the fish. "Perhaps it would be better if you lost yourself by the Endless Sea for a while longer."

"Why?"

"I wish I didn't have to be the one to tell you." Mathilda kept her eyes to her task as she spoke. "A sickness has come to the Siren's Realm."

"A sickness?" Maggie rolled the word around in her mouth, searching for a meaning that made sense. "People can't get sick in the Siren's Realm. She keeps all of us healthy."

"She also keeps the sun shining, but that doesn't keep her from bringing the storms."

"What kind of sickness?" Maggie looked out to the shoppers in the square. They were keeping a larger distance between themselves than usual. Diners sat one to a table, not clustered together in groups.

"First heard of it right after the last time I saw you. Man came running into the square, begging for help for his lover who'd taken ill. We all thought he'd gone mad." Mathilda shrugged. "Body was found in the Siren's fountain the next day. Black sores on her skin."

"Someone died? In the Siren's Realm?"

"Stone cold dead." Mathilda accented each word with a chop of her knife. "Folks had quite a time trying to figure out what to do with the body. People have started asking the Siren for protection, but there's no way to know if that's working until it doesn't."

"Have more people gotten sick?" Maggie's mind raced back to all the things she'd touched.

The veil seller, the baker's hand….

"Two more have been buried, but there could be others sick, or dead, and no one's found them."

"That's terrible."

"It is what it is when there's no one in charge to keep things running save the Siren, and she doesn't seem too fussed about it. That's why I thought you were dead. People falling ill, and you just disappearing." Mathilda wiped her forehead with the back of her hand. "Maybe it would be better if you had stayed holed up on your own."

"Is anybody fixing it?" Maggie asked, hating herself for sounding so childish. "I mean, aren't there any doctors in the Siren's Realm?"

"None have come forward." Mathilda wiped her hands before reaching for Maggie. "Do yourself a favor and lie low for a while. I can make do without the fish, and you should have enough magic stored up by now you can ask the Siren to provide for your belly."

"What about you?" Maggie took Mathilda's hand. Her skin itched as Mathilda paid her in magic, but the feeling stayed on her hand like a tight-fitting glove.

"I'll not abandon my shop." Mathilda shook her head. "I don't know if my soul could survive it. I nearly languished to nothing when I lived a life of leisure here, and I don't fancy drooping back into nothing again. I won't risk it. Work is the best way for me."

Maggie took hold of Mathilda's hand again. "Promise you'll be careful and take care of yourself?"

"As the Siren wills it." Mathilda smiled, but the wrinkles around her eyes didn't scrunch up as they should have.

Maggie nodded, her throat too tight to speak.

The weight of the net kept her from tucking her hands behind her back as she walked through the square, carefully avoiding touching anything. A chair pushed out too far into the walkway. A centaur who took up most of the lane.

Heart racing, her cheeks flushed as she cut between two tents with their flaps tied tightly shut.

"Don't panic, Maggie Trent, you are fine."

Her heart didn't slow as she wove deeper into the Textile Town. In a battle, she could defend herself. Even without magic, at least she could see the danger coming toward her and fight for her survival. But with illness…

It could already be on me. It could already be killing me.

"Meat fer sale!" a familiar voice barked in the distance. "Fresh roasted meat fer sale! Don't let yerself get weak with hunger! Good food'll keep the body strong."

"Gabriel!" Maggie shouted from the far end of the street, relief chipping away at her panic.

"I thought you'd still be alive." Gabriel smiled broadly at her, leaning on the side of his cart. "Some I'd think rotting if I didn't see 'em fer a few days when death's come knockin'. But I knew you'd turn up in time."

"I didn't even know anything was happening." Maggie resisted the urge to throw her arms around Gabriel's neck. "I stayed in by the sea for a few days. I only came back into town this morning."

"Probably better if you head back out by the sea." Gabriel handed Maggie a leg of fowl. "I'm not so worried about you gettin' sick, but when people start to panic, it's best to stay out of the way."

"But for how long?" Maggie took Gabriel's hand, still speaking even as he drew magic from her for payment. "A few people have gotten sick, but if whatever this is spreads, it could be a long time before it's over."

"Perhaps. But stayin' safe won't make it move faster or slower. Besides"—Gabriel glanced up and down the empty street—"I think you and I'll come out of this just fine. None of us want to go screamin' about it, but all of them who've fallen with the blackness, they've all had magic. Powerful amounts of it. Maybe they hoarded so much it rotted them from the inside out. But us who come in here with nothing but our boots, none of us has so much as sneezed."

"Is sneezing a symptom?" Maggie asked, a sudden tingle growing in her nose.

"No one knows. Don't think anyone's been found with it who's still able to speak to tell how it started. But us without magic, we'll be just fine. Keep our heads down, keep quiet, and we'll make it to the other side of the Siren's wrath sure as sunrise."

"You think the Siren's killing people because she's mad?" Maggie looked instinctively to the sky as though an angry face would appear to smite her.

"Read that law of the Siren again, girly. No one could wish this hurt on another. It's come from the Siren herself."

"Excuse me," a man with a pink cloth over his mouth spoke from ten feet away. "I'd like to purchase some meat."

"Get on with you. And keep tucked in someplace safe." Gabriel waved Maggie off before speaking to the man. "I've got meat fer you, but yer going to have to touch me to pay me."

Head down, Maggie walked up the lane. A few brave folks still walked through the Textile Town, but the pattern of their movement had a strangeness to it. As though each person were carefully considering who to pass nearest to, checking each face for signs of illness.

That woman looked like she might be ill, or perhaps she'd had too much wine. The young man was hunched over as though fatigue had sapped his will to stand upright.

But I'm hunching, too.

Maggie squared her shoulders, holding her head up high. She wanted to walk home. To curl up in her little stone house and wait for the Siren to end her purge. But if something horrible had found its way into the Siren's Realm, she couldn't just sit back and wait for death to pick people off at will.

"Bertrand Wayland," Maggie whispered to the air. "I want to find Bertrand Wayland."

Tingles flew through Maggie's chest as a little void formed. Closing her eyes, she turned slowly on the spot, tipping her face up to the sky. The sun warmed her skin, beaming its brightness through her eyelids.

How can anything be awful when the sun is shining so brightly?

"Has the blackness taken your mind, child?" a woman's voice snapped.

Maggie gritted her teeth, biting back her retort at being called *child.* "Just looking for someone."

Maggie headed down a wide street, ducking around a woman with a scrap of fabric tied over her face. Tents large enough to house several people sat safely behind long strips of grass. Voices carried through the canvas, but the path was empty.

In the square ahead, groups of people crept past, staring at something Maggie couldn't see as though unable to look away. Maggie jogged forward, letting her net flop at her side. The Siren's fountain came into view, though Maggie had no idea how the warren of paths had led her there.

The fountain sparkled in the sunlight, but the clusters of people all held back, watching one man who stood on the ledge of the fountain, staring down into the sweet waters. The man turned his face to the side.

Maggie yelped at the awful profile. A long black beak had taken the place of his face, and black gloves covered his hands.

"Bertrand Wayland, what the hell are you doing?"

Get your copy of The Girl Locked With Gold *to continue the journey.*

ESCAPE INTO ADVENTURE

Never miss a moment of the danger and magic.

The fantastical steampunk world of Histem awaits Maggie and Bertrand in *The Girl Locked With Gold*. Be the first to step through the stitch by downloading your **free copy** of *The Child Wound in Gold*, available exclusively to members of the Megan O'Russell Reader Group.

Visit meganorussell.com/rena to join the reader group and get your FREE story.

If you enjoyed *The Girl Without Magic*, please consider leaving a review to help other readers find Maggie's story.

As always, thanks for reading,

Megan O'Russell

ABOUT THE AUTHOR

 Megan O'Russell is the author of several Young Adult series that invite readers to escape into worlds of adventure. From *Girl of Glass*, which blends dystopian darkness with the heart-pounding danger of vampires, to *Ena of Ilbrea*, which draws readers into an epic world of magic and assassins.

With the *Girl of Glass* series, *The Tethering* series, *The Chronicles of Maggie Trent*, *The Tale of Bryant Adams*, the *Ena of Ilbrea* series, and several more projects planned for 2020, there are always exciting new books on the horizon. To be the first to hear about new releases, free short stories, and giveaways, sign up for Megan's newsletter by visiting the following:

https://www.meganorussell.com/book-signup.

Originally from Upstate New York, Megan is a professional musical theatre performer whose work has taken her across North America. Her chronic wanderlust has led her from Alaska to Thailand and many places in between. Wanting to travel has fostered Megan's love of books that allow her to visit countless new worlds from her favorite reading nook. Megan is also a lyricist and playwright. Information on her theatrical works can be found at RussellCompositions.com.

She would be thrilled to chat with you on Facebook or Twitter @MeganORussell, elated if you'd visit her website MeganORussell.com, and over the moon if you'd like the pictures of her adventures on Instagram @ORussellMegan.

Made in the USA
Lexington, KY
30 November 2019

57878971R00160